MOLTEN DEATH

MOLTEN DEATH

Leslie Karst

SEVERN
HOUSE

First world edition published in Great Britain and the USA in 2024
by Severn House, an imprint of Canongate Books Ltd,
14 High Street, Edinburgh EH1 1TE.

severnhouse.com

British Library Cataloguing-in-Publication Data
A CIP catalogue record for this title is available from the British Library.

ISBN-13: 978-1-4483-1216-0 (cased)
ISBN-13: 978-1-4483-1217-7 (e-book)

All Severn House titles are printed on acid-free paper.

Typeset by Palimpsest Book Production Ltd.,
Falkirk, Stirlingshire, Scotland.
Printed and bound in Great Britain by TJ Books,
Padstow, Cornwall.

Praise for *Molten Death*

"A gorgeous yet deadly setting, a tenacious amateur sleuth, and a real head-scratcher of a mystery. Will leave readers longing for their next trip to the Orchid Isle"
New York Times bestselling author Jenn McKinlay

"As mysterious as a Hilo rain, fragrant as lychee, melodious as Hawaiian Pidgin, and tasty as loco moco, Leslie Karst's *Molten Death* transports the reader to the best that the Big Island can offer. You won't want to leave!"
USA Today bestselling author Naomi Hirahara

"A suspenseful dive into the Hawai'i tourists don't see, introducing engaging protagonist Valerie Corbin and the fascinating, quirky island community she learns to love. And of course there is delicious food! A terrific debut to a series that will go on my must read list!"
New York Times bestselling author Deborah Crombie

"With its compelling characters and engaging look at the culture and customs of the Big Island of Hawai'i, *Molten Death* is a delightfully immersive whodunnit. Fans of well-plotted, suspenseful mysteries with a foodie element will eat this one up!"
New York Times bestselling author Kate Carlisle

"Leslie Karst's passion and personal connection to Hawai'i shine on every page. She's created a heroine you'll adore and a mystery that's both touching and twisty. I loved it!"
USA Today bestselling author Ellen Byron

"A clever premise sets this mystery apart, but it's the chill island vibes, local traditions, and captivating couple, Valerie and Kristen, that will keep readers coming back"
Anthony Award finalist Rob Osler

For Mom, Dad, and Robin, my fellow lava-hunting adventurers

A note about Hawaiian grammar and language: I have used the spelling and punctuation routinely employed currently in the Hawaiian Islands. The *'okina*, or glottal stop ['], as in the word 'Hawai'i,' is similar to the break between the syllables in 'uh-oh.' A macron (*kahakō* in Hawaiian) over a vowel [ā] makes it slightly longer than other vowels. Note also that an internal 'w' is sometimes pronounced as a 'v'; thus 'Hawai'i' is often pronounced 'Hah-*vai*-ee' by locals.

A glossary of Hawaiian and Pidgin English (the creole spoken by many Hawaiian locals) words and phrases is included at the end of the book.

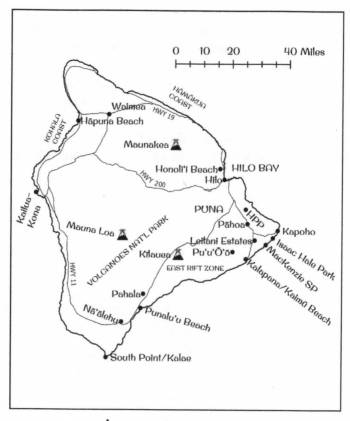

Hawai'i Island
May 2018

ONE

This was not what she'd imagined their Hawaiian vacation would be like.

Stretched out on a hibiscus-print couch, Valerie Corbin gazed wearily at the water streaming off the corrugated metal roof onto the shaggy lawn below and wondered when, if ever, it might stop raining. The temperature was plenty warm – she had on shorts and a tank top – but the air so damp that the pages of the *Big Island Revealed* guidebook she'd been flipping through felt wet to the touch. They'd now spent two days in Hilo and had yet to see the sun.

She was roused from her glum thoughts by the entrance of Kristen onto the lānai bearing a pair of drinks. 'Thanks, hon,' Valerie said. 'Just what the doctor ordered.' She accepted the proffered rum and soda and clinked glasses with her wife, who plopped down upon the wicker sofa beside her.

Being thoughtful house guests, the two had been holding off on cocktail hour pending the arrival home of their host, Isaac, a biology teacher at the local high school. But as soon as Kristen had heard him pull into the car port, she'd jumped up to make them all drinks.

Isaac joined Valerie and Kristen on the lānai, raised his gin and tonic in salute, and took a long drink. 'Ahhh . . . *Pau hana* – done with school till Monday!' He ran a hand through his dark hair, now wet and scraggly from a quick post-work shower, then sat forward and smiled. 'So. What'd you two end up doing on this rainy day while I was busy teaching kids about taxonomic ranks?'

'Nothing nearly as exciting as that,' said Valerie. 'We got up pretty late, and by the time we had our coffee and showered and stuff, it was after ten. We checked out the Tsunami Museum like you suggested, and the shops along the Bayfront.'

'And the farmers market,' Kristen added.

'Oh, yeah – I bought some mangos and a couple of *enormous*

avocados. I can't believe how huge they are here! After that, we came back and just hung out here the rest of the afternoon.'

Kristen fished the lime wedge out of her Mai Tai and squeezed its juice into the glass. 'We're starting to run out of rainy-day activities,' she said.

Isaac nodded. 'I hear ya. Hilo got plenty touristy stuff for outdoors, but when it pours down like dis, not so much.'

Valerie had observed since meeting him that although he could speak perfect Standard English when he chose, Isaac preferred to sprinkle it liberally with the local Pidgin.

'So it doesn't rain here every day of the year?' she asked with a smile, turning to watch a pair of brown-and-yellow mynah birds as they squawked and splashed around the small lake forming on the far side of the back yard.

'Well, not *every day*,' Isaac answered in a not terribly encouraging tone.

Valerie frowned as she took a sip of rum. 'No offense, but I gotta say the Big Island isn't exactly what I expected Hawai'i to be like. I know they call it "the Orchid Isle," but it seems like "the Rock-Covered Isle Where it Never Stops Raining" would be a far more appropriate name.'

'She was a bit taken aback by the landscape when we landed yesterday,' Kristen said. 'You know, the moonscape an' all?'

Isaac laughed. 'Yeah, dat happens all the time. The tourists comin' into Kona for the first time, they look out their window expecting to see some kind of tropical paradise, but instead of swaying coco palms and miles of white sand beaches like in da movies, they get hit by a barren expanse of black rock. Ha!' He took a sip of gin, then sank back into his chair. 'But you know what? The thing is, the whole island is pretty much just a collection of massive volcanoes, and those old lava flows you saw over dere Kona-side, they're part of what makes the Big Island so special. Once you've spent more time here, you'll understand.'

'Maybe.' Valerie wasn't convinced. In fact, ever since climbing down those steps onto the tarmac after their six-hour flight from Los Angeles, only to immediately start coughing at the acrid, sulfuric tang that hung in the air – 'vog,' Kristen had called it – she'd been starting to seriously doubt their choice of travel spot.

'But hey, I got good news,' Isaac continued. 'The storm's supposed to pass tonight, and tomorrow should be clear. Just in time for the weekend.'

'Awesome!' Kristen pumped her arm. 'You want to go check out the waves at Honoli'i?'

'I got *way* mo' bettah idea than surfing,' Isaac answered, his smile revealing a shiny gold tooth. 'A guy I know, he told me he was down at Kalapana yesterday and the flow is less than a mile from the road.' He leaned forward and almost whispered, 'Whad'ya say to goin' out to see – so close you can touch it – some *hot, flowing lava*?'

The crickets emanating from Kristen's cell phone woke them at a quarter to four. Valerie had protested this egregiously early start the night before, but Isaac insisted it was best to get down to the end of the road while it was still dark. That way they could spot the glowing lava flow from a distance and know which direction to head out.

Valerie, who'd tossed and turned much of the night, groaned and pulled the sheet up over her head, but then accepted the inevitable and sat up. Once assured she was truly awake, Kristen kissed her on the forehead, then left her to it in the converted basement guest studio and headed upstairs.

Staring out the window at the dark shape of the neighbor's coconut palm, Valerie tried to focus on the present – on the 'here and now,' as Kristen would say – rather than the memories that had intruded into her early-morning dreams.

They'd originally planned this two-and-a-half-week trip to the Big Island of Hawai'i as a joint celebration of Valerie's upcoming big sixtieth birthday and Kristen's recent retirement from her job as a journeyman carpenter.

Then had come the accident.

It was still hard for Valerie to think about. Or even remember clearly.

Five weeks earlier, she and her younger brother, Charlie, had been returning from a trip to the farmers market in Santa Monica to buy produce for the restaurant he co-owned – a trendy, French-style bistro in Venice Beach called Chez Charles. Valerie had been helping out a few days a week at the place for about a year, ever since retiring from her job as unit leader for a film and TV catering company. She'd fill in when an extra server was needed, and for the past several months, her brother had been teaching her how to tend the bistro's small bar.

But they didn't make it back to Chez Charles from the farmers market that day. And Charlie never made it out of the hospital.

As a result, the trip to Hawai'i had now become something much more than originally planned – an attempt to take Valerie's mind, at least briefly, off the horror of what had happened that day. And also to allow the two women to heal their twelve-year relationship, which had been suffering along with Valerie's emotional state ever since her brother's death. Prolonged silences during meals – Valerie brooding over what had happened, Kristen unwilling to interrupt her black thoughts. And when they did talk, it would often degenerate into bickering, the both of them strung tight as a high-voltage wire.

So maybe this vacation would be a chance to reboot – to remember what it was that had made them work so well as a couple for all those years leading up to the accident.

They'd decided on the Big Island as their destination, partly to check out a piece of property there that Valerie had been surprised to learn she'd inherited from Charlie. But it had been Kristen who'd suggested they stay in Hilo, as opposed to the more touristy Kailua-Kona on the leeward side of the island.

Several years before she and Valerie had met, she'd spent a few days in Hilo and had been enchanted by the town, which seemed stuck in some 1950s version of old Hawai'i. Plus, there was also the fact that Kristen's buddy, Isaac, who lived there, had offered to let them stay at his home. Kristen adored Isaac and had assured Valerie that he'd be a terrific host. And, she'd contended, wouldn't it be better to spend the time with a local who truly knew the island and its culture, rather than some antiseptic hotel?

Having now met Isaac, Valerie had to agree. Though she'd still need some convincing about Hilo.

By four fifteen, the three of them were on the road, heading south on Highway 11. Kristen promptly dozed off in the back seat, so Valerie and Isaac were left to their own conversation. 'This is the road to the volcano,' he told her. 'Or, rather, to Volcano

Village, and also Volcanoes National Park, where the active
volcano is.'

'There's a village on an active volcano?'

Isaac chuckled. 'I hate to tell you, but Hilo's in the path of a
volcano, too. A flow from Mauna Loa came within four miles
of town back in 1984.'

'Yikes!'

'You get used to it, living here.'

Valerie nodded, though she wasn't at all sure she could ever
get accustomed to living in the path of potential lava flows. And
having seen at the museum the day before the photographs of
the devastation caused to Hilo by a series of tsunamis decades
earlier, she'd decided that maybe their California earthquakes
weren't such a bad thing in comparison. It was astounding to
consider all the disasters that befell this tropical paradise.

Isaac turned off the highway onto a smaller road, following
the signs to a town called Pāhoa. 'Wait – I thought you said *that*
was the way to the volcano,' Valerie said, pointing backwards.

'We're not going up to the National Park. We're headed down
to the end of the road near Kaimū Beach, which is the closest
access to the flow right now. The lava's coming from a *puʻu* – a
vent – called Puʻu ʻŌʻō on Kīlauea volcano, which is up in the
Park. But it's flowing down the *pali* from there to an ocean entry
at Kalapana.'

'Uh . . . the *pali*?' This was way too many Hawaiian words
for her four thirty a.m. brain to absorb.

'Sorry. The hillside, cliff.'

'Oh.'

They drove on in silence, and in the dim dashboard lights,
Valerie studied the stylized dagger inked on Isaac's forearm. The
implied violence of the tattoo didn't jibe with his cherubic face
and boyish demeanor. But then again, she'd observed that many
of the Big Island locals she'd seen sported some kind of tattoo
or another.

After about a half hour they came to a sign that read: 'END
OF ROAD – ONE MILE.' Ignoring a series of notices reading,
'No Trespassing,' 'Restricted Access,' and 'Authorized Personnel
Only,' Isaac continued up what had now degenerated into a bumpy
gravel road.

This woke Kristen up. 'We there yet?'

'Almost.' Isaac negotiated a series of boulders and pits along the route and pulled up next to a dark-colored pickup truck. About fifty feet ahead, the road came to an abrupt end, having been engulfed by a thick ooze of hardened black rock.

Valerie climbed out of Isaac's Subaru and knelt to tighten the laces of her hiking boots. Straightening back up, her eyes took in the night sky, across which an astonishing number of stars were splashed – far more than she ever saw back home. 'Ohmygod, there's the Milky Way!'

'Told you it was worth getting up early,' Isaac said, shouldering his daypack. '*Hele* on, let's get moving. Pele awaits.'

Kristen switched on her flashlight and started forward.

'But don't try to rush,' Isaac added with a look backwards. 'It can be tricky walking over the lava.'

'Got it.' Locating Kristen and Isaac with the beam of her flashlight, Valerie followed them out across the rock.

Isaac was right – it took some getting used to, crossing a lava field in the dark. Valerie was glad he was leading the way, as he was able to pick out the easiest path over the uneven terrain. She was also glad she'd followed his advice to wear blue jeans rather than shorts, since it became clear after only a few steps that it would be easy to take a tumble and slash your knee on the sharp, glassy rock.

They'd been walking for less than ten minutes, Valerie – whose legs were considerably shorter than those of her two tall companions – consistently pulling up the rear, when Isaac called out, 'I see it!'

Catching up to the others, she turned off her flashlight and gazed out where Isaac was pointing. In the distance was a distinct red glow.

'Looks like it's still a ways from making an ocean entry,' he said. 'Too bad. But it's great the flow is so close to the road.'

As her eyes adjusted to the dark, Valerie realized there were numerous red patches forming a line stretching all the way up the hill. 'How far away is it?' she asked.

'Not too far. It's closer than it looks,' Isaac said. 'Gotta jam, so we can get there before sunrise.' As if on cue, a pink tinge

emerged on the horizon, stealing into the sky and giving defini-
tion to a line of puffy trade-wind clouds. They hurried on.

Just a few minutes later, they crested a small rise and there it
was: a shape-shifting mass of orange and red, creeping inch by
inch downhill. A couple of people were already at the flow, their
silhouettes drifting in and out of view as the steam and the smoke
from burning vegetation came between them.

'My, such a smell of sulfur!' Valerie exclaimed in a high-
pitched voice, fanning her hand dramatically in front of her face.

'Yeah,' Isaac said. 'You might wanna put on your bandanas
if it bothers you.'

'Oh, she's just quoting Glinda,' Kristen said with a laugh.

'Huh?' Isaac stopped and turned to look at her.

'You know, the Good Witch from *The Wizard of Oz*?'

'I don't remember that from the movie.'

'It's a throwaway line, so most people don't. It happens right
after the Wicked Witch disappears from Munchkin Land in a ball
of fire. But she got it wrong, in any case,' Kristen added, striding
toward the glowing lava. 'It's "*what* a smell of sulfur," not "such."'

With a shake of his head at the two women, Isaac walked on.

'Whatever . . .' Valerie murmured as she followed after Isaac
and Kristen. But when she stopped to look up, all irritation about
her wife's need to play the know-it-all flew from her brain.

It looked alive – like some slithering beast come up from the
depths to crawl slowly towards the sea. Orange fingers flowed
from the main body at all angles, taking on new forms and hues
as they made their way down the slope. A fine filigree of black
floated on the surface of the lava, where the viscous fluid quickly
cooled in the ocean air. But just underneath you could see the fiery
magma, its edges a searing yellow-white where the fingers stretched
till they burst, spilling forth their contents of molten rock.

'Wow.' Valerie stood there unmoving, unable to take her eyes
from the sight. Isaac, however, was busy rummaging through his
pack. He pulled out three small bananas and offered them around.

'Oh. Thanks.' Valerie managed to stop gawking long enough
to take one from him.

'It's sort of a tradition,' he said as they peeled their fruit. 'I
always eat a banana when I get to the flow, and then toss the
skin out and watch it burn.'

'It's not disrespectful?' Valerie asked. 'I mean, I read that folks sometimes leave bottles of gin as offerings for Pele, but banana peels?'

Isaac took a last bite and hurled the yellow skin onto a pool of lava that had broken out from the main flow. 'Everyone can use a little more potassium in their diet,' he replied. 'Even if you're a goddess.'

Valerie and Kristen followed suit. Valerie expected the peels to sink, but instead they simply sat there, floating on top of the red-black flow. After a few minutes, they finally caught fire and then were quickly gone.

'Well, I'm gonna head uphill a bit and get some shots back this way before that amazing backdrop disappears,' Isaac said, peering down to check the settings on his Nikon camera in the dim light. Valerie turned around and saw what he meant. A crescent moon hung low in the now-purple sky, with a single planet burning brightly above. She could just make out the thin line of the ocean, edged in the foreground by jagged black rock.

Kristen pulled her phone from her pocket and tagged along after Isaac, but Valerie stayed put. She wanted to simply sit down and watch the show. It was mesmerizing, the way the lava beast spread its limbs in its nonstop march downhill, and how it continually morphed into crazy shapes: a heart slowly breaking in two; a woman's face with long, streaming hair; a winged dragon. The flow came nearer and she felt the force of its heat – as if the doors to a massive oven had opened wide. Standing back up to step back, she wandered down-flow, watching a small finger dribble into a crevice and quickly fill it in. Tiny ferns had sprung up in a few of the cracks nearby – resilient little plants, doomed though they were.

Looking out toward the sea, Valerie saw that the sun was now above the horizon. The low-lying clouds had turned orange and gray, and the sky was a pale blue. She faced back uphill but could see no sign of Kristen or Isaac.

Nice. To be alone, with only the sound of the wind and the crackle of rock being blanketed by the newest land on the planet. She continued on, skirting the edge of the flow. Now that the sun was up, she could tell that there were two different types of the cooled lava rock: a twisty, ropey-looking kind and a more pillowy, smooth variety. And she could see that while the older flows were a dull gray, the brand-new rock was a shiny black, sparkling in the sunlight.

Her eye was caught by a color that didn't belong – a flash of fluorescent green – at the very edge of the flow. Curious, she walked over and saw that it was a shoe. No, more like a workman's boot, with bright-green laces. *Now, how could someone leave their boots here?* she wondered. *You'd never be able to hike back over the lava field without your shoes on.*

And then she got that queasy feeling you experience when there's a disconnect between what you expect to see and what's actually there. For the shoe had not been left behind, after all: it was still on a foot.

But that was all that was visible, because the rest of the body had been covered over by hot lava.

TWO

Valerie froze as a burst of adrenaline coursed through her body like an electric shock. She blinked several times, unable to wrap her mind around the confusing scene before her, then let out the breath she hadn't even realized she'd been holding.

No. It couldn't be . . .

But then she caught a glimpse of what looked to be the cuff of some tan khakis – though it was hard to be sure, since the material was ablaze and engulfed in black smoke – before the flow started to creep up over the top of the leather boot.

Yes. It was.

Letting out a cry akin to that of a wounded animal, Valerie glanced frantically about her, but could spot no one else in the area.

'Help!' she called out. 'Anyone there?' The words were carried off by the wind and met with silence.

What to do? No way could she get close enough to try to pull the body out; even at a distance, the heat was overpowering. *A photo – I need to at least get a picture of it!*

Reaching into her jeans pocket, she pulled out her cell phone and thumbed the home button to unlock the device. But by the time she'd flicked on the camera and zoomed in on the area where the boot had been, she could see nothing but a slight rise in the flow, with a wisp of smoke above.

Valerie stared at the advancing lava, trying to come to grips with what she'd just witnessed. It was as if she could have imagined the whole thing. Except, she realized with a twist in her stomach, for the aroma that hung in the air, faintly reminiscent of a barbecue.

And then a vision of her brother, trapped in his pale-blue Prius, made her drop to the ground. Panting, she closed her eyes tight as the image of his terror-struck face swam before her.

The guilt still seared into her soul every single day. For although she'd been able to extricate herself in time from the passenger seat of the burning car, Charlie had not been so lucky.

No. It wasn't my fault. There was nothing I could have done to save him.

Taking several deep breaths, she forced to the back of her mind the image of her baby brother surrounded by fire and black smoke. Then, after yanking off the sweatshirt tied about her waist and dumping it on the ground to mark where she'd been, Valerie pushed herself to her feet and took off running uphill.

Kristen came into view almost immediately. She was talking to two people, gesturing towards the flow.

'Kristen!' Valerie screamed, and sprinted towards her. 'Ohmygod, you won't believe—'

She was caught by her wife as she stumbled and nearly fell to the ground. 'What the hell?'

'I just saw a body!'

'You *what*?'

'In the lava. A body.' Finding herself unable to put together a complete sentence, Valerie pointed feebly in the direction she'd just come from. 'Down there.'

'Yeah, right.' Kristen glanced over at the man and woman next to her. 'Funny.' But the smile forming on her lips froze once she looked back. 'Jesus, you're shaking, girl.'

Valerie took a few deep breaths to try to regain her composure. 'I'm not kidding – there's a freakin' dead body down there! I just saw it covered over with hot lava!'

'Ohmygod,' was all Kristen could muster.

Valerie grabbed her by the shirtsleeve and tugged. 'C'mon, I'll show you.'

The three followed her downslope. It took a few minutes to locate her blue sweatshirt, since its color blended in with the black lava rock, and once back at the spot, Valerie had a hard time telling where, exactly, the body had been. In the few minutes she'd been gone, the landscape had completely changed. *Which was the rise where it had been?*

'Uh . . . over there.' She pointed toward an area that had already cooled and turned a shiny black. 'I think. Or maybe there. It's hard to tell now; it all looks the same.'

Valerie glanced back at the others, but they were looking at her, not the lava. 'You don't believe me.'

'No, no, it's not that.' Kristen was frowning. 'It's just kind of . . . hard to take in, is all.'

'Um, maybe we should be going . . . ' the woman said with a glance at her companion, and turned to head back upslope.

'No, wait – you can't leave!' The urgency in Valerie's voice stopped her. 'I mean, you might have seen something. How long have you been here, out at the flow?'

'They only just arrived a couple of minutes before you came charging up the hill,' Kristen said.

'You didn't see any other people? Maybe on their way out? 'Cause there were some others here – you saw them, Kristen – before we got here. And I don't see them here now. Maybe you got a look at them?'

The man and woman exchanged glances. 'You two are the only people we've seen,' the man said. 'Wait – here's someone else.'

Valerie looked up to see Isaac approaching, his big boots crunching on the newly cooled lava rock. 'Dude, I got *uku* killah photos! Wait'll you see— What?' He stopped and looked from Valerie to Kristen, and then at the other two. 'You all look so serious.'

'Val says she just saw a body being covered up by the lava,' Kristen said.

'What? No wayz!'

'Over there,' said Valerie. 'It was someone's foot, with a leather boot on it. And bright-green laces.'

'Chee, you give me da chicken skin, girl.' Isaac shot Kristen a quizzical look before turning back to Valerie. 'But uh . . . fo' real? I mean, you sure it wasn't just that that you saw – you know, an old boot?'

'No.' Valerie shook her head. 'I saw part of the leg, too. It was burning, and there was a smell . . .' She trailed off and then swallowed, attempting to stifle the shakes threatening to overtake her.

Kristen placed her hand on Valerie's arm. 'That sounds awful.'

'It was,' Valerie murmured.

The five of them stood there in silence, staring out at the

steaming black lava field. After a bit, Kristen cleared her throat. 'Look, maybe we should head back home. I mean, there's nothing more we can do here now, right? Even if . . .'

'Even if I'm not completely crazy?' Valerie shook off the hand and took a step away from Kristen. How could they not appreciate the gravity of what had just occurred? But then she nodded her head in resignation. Kristen was right. There wasn't anything they could do here. The body was gone, no doubt forever.

'Fine,' she said. 'Let's go.' She leaned down to pick up her sweatshirt and knotted it about her waist. 'But we've got to stop at the police station on the way and tell them what I saw.'

'Sure.' Isaac nodded. 'No worries.'

The couple took the opportunity to excuse themselves and hurried uphill, out of sight.

Valerie gave the lava beast one last look, visualizing the terrible prize now hidden within its fiery gorge. Then, with a shake of the head to try to clear the grisly image from her brain, she turned to follow Kristen and Isaac back across the barren black rock.

She knew they didn't believe her. Not Kristen, or Isaac, or the couple at the flow, and definitely not the police. Sure, they were sympathetic, all right, trying to empathize with how horrible it must have been for her to see something like that. And the officer on duty at the station – a burly fellow with a buzz cut and concerned smile – was a good listener. Valerie told him how she'd seen the boot and the leg, and about the people they'd seen from afar. And she mentioned the truck, which had been gone when they got back to the end of the road. The only other car there besides Isaac's was a cherry-red Mustang convertible – obviously the rental used by the couple they'd met.

The policeman dutifully took down her statement, frowning and clucking at all the appropriate places, but it seemed clear to Valerie that he thought she was a bit of a nut case. It didn't help any that neither Kristen nor Isaac could corroborate her statement about the body in the lava. And when she showed the cop the photo she'd taken, he squinted at the screen a while before saying, 'Uh, sorry, but I can't see anything that looks at all like a boot.'

She took the phone back and studied it herself. He was right. There was nothing in the photo to prove what she'd seen.

And then when they got back to the house, as Valerie was coming upstairs after changing into a pair of shorts, she heard Isaac and Kristen talking in hushed voices. She paused in the dark stairwell to listen.

'She's been through a lot lately,' Kristen was saying. 'You know, with her brother being killed in that car crash, and then the head injury she suffered in the collision, as well. The doctor says her concussion wasn't severe, but I know she hasn't been sleeping well ever since it happened, and sometimes when I come into the room, I can tell she's been sitting there replaying it all in her head. She and Charlie were super tight, and the whole thing truly traumatized her – seeing her brother die like that and being unable to save him? It's gotta have profoundly affected her.'

'But to imagine you see a body in the lava? I dunno. She nevah seem to me to be so *pupule* – you know, crazy.' Isaac, at least, appeared to be sticking up for her sanity.

'Oh, I'm sure she did see *something*. But I bet you're right; I bet it was just an old shoe that someone threw out for a lark, like we did with the banana peels. But given her current state . . . Well, let's just say that after what happened with her brother – and the whole thing was truly awful and horrifying, I can assure you – it wouldn't be all that surprising for her to still be on edge, especially around something so similar to the car fire, like hot lava. And maybe even a little bit prone to imagining bodies where they aren't, you know?'

Isaac made no answer. At the sound of the coffee grinder firing up, Valerie emerged from the stairwell into the kitchen. The simultaneous entrance of Isaac's girlfriend Sachiko through the other door saved her from having to decide whether or not to admit to her eavesdropping.

'I stopped by the store for some poke,' Sachiko announced cheerily, setting a white paper bag on the kitchen table. 'I thought maybe you lava-seekers would have worked up an appetite.'

'Auw right!' Isaac bent over to plant a kiss on her cheek. 'Thanks, babe.' He pulled the container from the bag, removed the lid and set it on the table.

Valerie peered inside: glistening chunks of bright red ahi flecked with green onions, atop a mound of steamed white rice. 'Looks great,' she said. 'But at nine thirty in the morning?'

'You bet. Breakfast, local style.' Isaac picked the container back up and, using a pair of chopsticks, helped himself to a large serving. 'Here, try.'

Valerie accepted the morsel of raw fish offered, chewing thoughtfully. 'Ginger and toasted sesame oil?'

'Correct,' Sachiko said. 'And they have it in a bunch of other flavors, too: garlic, shoyu, spicy mayo—'

'Oooh, I love the spicy kind,' Kristen interjected, grabbing bowls and chopsticks for the rest of them and heading out the door. 'C'mon, let's sit outside.'

'You should taste my mom's,' Sachiko continued. 'It's the best.' Pouring herself some coffee, she went to the fridge and added a healthy glug of milk to her cup. 'She makes it with *wakame* and *limu* – kinds of seaweed.'

Valerie helped herself to some poke and then took a seat next to Kristen on the couch out on the lānai.

'So how was the lava?' Sachiko asked once they were all settled.

No one spoke.

'What? You didn't see any?' Confused, she looked back and forth between Kristen and Isaac's faces, but both were studiously examining the fish and rice in their bowls.

Valerie broke the silence. 'Oh, we found the lava all right. And more . . . At least, on my part.' Doing her best to keep the emotion from her voice, she recounted what she'd seen.

Sachiko listened, eyebrows progressively raising and jaw falling, as Valerie told her story. 'Chee! How can you all sit here so calmly after *that*?'

'They think I imagined it.' Valerie jabbed her thumb in the direction of the still-silent Kristen and Isaac. 'Or that all I saw was an old boot. So even though they're trying to humor me—'

'It's not that I don't believe you.' Kristen's voice had an edge of hurt in it, as if it were she being wronged. 'It's just that, well . . . you've got to admit that it is pretty damn bizarre.'

Valerie nodded. It was indeed very bizarre. *But I know what I saw. Or do I?* Was it possible she had in fact imagined it – that it was merely an old boot? *No.* There had also been the burning cloth and black smoke. And that *smell*. That alone was enough to prove it had been real. It was far too grotesque to possibly invent. But how to convince them of that?

'Well, since the cops know, I guess you've done all you can.' Sachiko reached over and squeezed Valerie's shoulder, giving her a sympathetic smile. 'It's probably best to just try to get your mind off it now.'

Easier said than done. Nevertheless, Valerie was grateful when Sachiko turned the conversation to the plan for the rest of the day.

'How 'bout we go surfing?' Kristen suggested. 'You'd like going to the beach, wouldn't you, Val? It is our first sunny day, after all.'

'Sure. That sounds good.' The idea of flaking out with her copy of *The Descendants* while the others hit the waves – perhaps even dozing off in the sun for a while – was indeed appealing.

'I dunno,' Isaac said with a mischievous grin. 'I hear da action gon' be plenty big today. You sure you're up for it?'

'As I recall, last time we surfed together, you were the one who had to stop early because of a cramp. If it was in fact a cramp, and not some temporary paralysis brought on by the size of the waves.'

'Ho!' Isaac leaned back in his chair with a laugh. 'Watch it, cuz, or you gonna be sleeping in the street.'

Valerie and Sachiko listened with amusement as Isaac and Kristen traded jibes, acting like a pair of adolescent, mismatched fraternal twins – one blond and fair, the other dark-haired and tanned. After a moment, Sachiko asked, 'Isn't that how you two met – surfing?'

Isaac nodded as he took a swallow of coffee. 'Uh-huh. It was when I was in California last year – you know, when we took our school kids to L.A. for the science fair? So on our day off, I decided to rent a board and go check out the famous Malibu waves, an' I end up meeting dis one' – he jabbed a thumb in Kristen's direction – 'out in the water. We talked story a while, an' den went out for a beer afterwards.'

'I took pity on him,' Kristen said with a laugh, 'since it was obvious he was in need of some serious surfing lessons.'

Isaac snorted and went on. 'Anyway, once I was back in Hilo, we kept in touch, sharing surfing posts on Insta an' stuff. And then when I found out they were thinking of coming to Hawai'i for a vacation, I suggested they stay in da studio downstairs. I thought it'd be fun to get to hang out again together in person. But mostly,' he added with a grin, 'I wanted the chance to show Kristen some *real* surf action – way mo' bettah than those wimpy SoCal waves she's used to.'

Kristen slapped her knees, then stood. 'Right, brah. So what d'ya say we stop talking the talk and go walk the walk?'

THREE

'You have any vinegar?' Valerie asked the next morning. Shutting a cabinet door on boxes of cereal and bags of rice and pasta, she tried the one next to it.

'Up here.' Isaac nodded at the cupboard above the Mr Coffee machine he was busy filling with water. 'Why? You planning on making us a vinaigrette for breakfast?'

'It's for Kristen's sunburn.'

Isaac finished pouring and stepped back to allow her to peer into the cabinet. 'You use vinegar?' he asked.

'Yeah, I learned the trick from my mom. It really works – not to make the sunburn go away or heal any faster, but to stop the stinging. Of course, it's a lot better if you put it on right away, but she didn't tell me about her burn till this morning. You should try it sometime. Though one does end up smelling a bit like an Easter egg.'

'Me? No wayz. Just take a look at this skin. I never get a burn.'

'Right.' Kristen came into the kitchen, a short-sleeved cotton shirt decorated with orange hibiscus and yellow pineapples hanging loosely from her tall frame. 'Like I believe that.'

Valerie continued poking around the shelf but, being almost a foot shorter than Isaac, she was having a hard time seeing into the back of the cabinet. All she could find was a bottle of balsamic vinegar. 'Is there any plain?' she said holding it up. 'I imagine this would be kind of sticky to rub on your body.'

'Yeah, I'm sure there is. Sachiko uses it a lot when she cooks.' Shoving aside bottles of soy sauce, ketchup, and chili paste, Isaac reached deep into the cabinet and came up with a gallon container of white vinegar. 'Not sure if this will be enough, though,' he said with grin. 'You look like one *hulihuli* chicken been on da spit way too long.'

'Ha ha, very funny.' Kristen gingerly lifted her shirt and

allowed Valerie to pat a vinegar-laden paper towel over her scarlet shoulders and back.

'I told ya you should-a worn a T-shirt. Dis tropical sun can be harsh on you *haoles*.'

Valerie had had the same thought when Kristen headed out to the waves the previous day without anything protecting her fair skin. She always wore a wetsuit back home in the cold California ocean, and her pale, Scandinavian complexion wasn't used to the intense Hawaiian rays. But since Kristen had merely waved off Isaac's advice, Valerie decided to hold her tongue. They'd been quarreling plenty since Charlie's death; best to pick her fights judiciously.

As she gazed at Kristen's poor red skin this morning, however, she wished she'd pushed the matter.

Oh, well. Nothing to do for it now except use Mom's tried and true remedy. She capped the vinegar jug and handed it back to Isaac. 'Thanks.'

Helping herself to a plump papaya from the wooden bowl on the counter, Valerie grabbed a knife and sliced into its orange-red flesh. 'So where's Sachiko this morning?' she asked, cutting rough chunks into a bowl of yogurt and releasing sticky juice all over her hands in the process.

'Down at da restaurant,' Isaac replied. 'They started doing Sunday brunch a few months ago, which sucks – at least as far as our weekends together go – since she also works Saturday nights.'

Sachiko managed the front of the house at The Speckled Gecko, whose eclectic menu – including an array of Asian, Hawaiian, and Caribbean dishes – Valerie and Kristen had perused the other day as they walked along the Bayfront.

'And now it looks like she may have to start working Sunday nights, too,' he added, 'since one of the servers just quit.' Isaac grimaced, then shook his head. 'But I'm not gonna tink about dat right now.' Pouring himself a cup of coffee, he plopped down at the red Formica kitchen table and pulled the sports page from the Sunday paper.

Valerie and Kristen carried their breakfasts over to join him, and the three turned the pages of the newspaper as they ate.

'Huh, there's an article here about the decline of test scores at a bunch of Big Island schools,' Valerie said.

Isaac responded with a wave of the hand. 'Yeah, I know. But dat's another thing I'm not goin' tink about on a Sunday.' With an impatient shake of his shaggy hair, he went back to the golf story he'd been reading.

The other articles on the front page concerned a blast of some sort at a new geothermal plant down in Puna, and a group of hula dancers who were visiting Hilo from Oʻahu. 'What's a . . . *hālau*?' Valerie asked, trying to wrap her tongue around the Hawaiian vowels.

'Hah-*lauw*,' Isaac repeated, but putting his emphasis on the second syllable. 'It's what you call a hula school – a troupe, I guess, is how you'd translate it.' He set down the sports page. 'You know, you really should see some hula while you're here.'

'I dunno . . .' Valerie said. The idea of going to some touristy *lūʻau* and seeing a bunch of schmaltzy dancing girls in fake grass skirts didn't hold much appeal for her.

'No, really, Val,' Kristen chimed in. 'I know what you're thinking, but he's right – you should see it.' She folded up the comics she'd been so engrossed in and got up to take her cereal bowl to the sink. 'The first time I came to Hawaiʻi with my parents when I was a teenager, they dragged me to a performance, and I thought it'd be really corny, too. But it was fantastic!'

'Uh-huh.'

'I especially liked the men,' she added.

This was an unexpected statement, and Valerie waited for the inevitable 'not!' But it didn't come.

Instead, Isaac jumped up out of his chair. 'Da hula *kahiko* da kine!' he exclaimed. 'That's the ancient style. Check it out.' Placing hands on hips, he began to dance. Valerie watched, amazed, as he moved, bare feet stamping vigorously in time to a throaty chant, his upper body as calm and graceful as a wisp of bamboo sighing in the breeze.

With a laugh, he collapsed into his chair, fanning himself and panting. 'Oof! I am *so* outa shape!'

'Wow. That was . . . terrific!' She wasn't sure what to say. It was surprising, seeing this sensitive side to the burly, blustering, always-joking Isaac.

'Yeah . . . I used to dance with a *hālau* here in Hilo, long time back. And I can tell you, it ain't fo' no sissies.'

'Well, dang. I guess maybe I *should* see some hula.'

They went back to reading. Turning to the last page of the front section, Valerie scanned over the daily police report. She did this whenever she traveled, finding it intriguing to see what sorts of crimes were committed in different locales around the world. 'Seems to be all contempt, failure to appear, and domestic abuse again,' she observed, though neither Kristen nor Isaac appeared to be listening. 'The same as the last few days.' She was about to fold up the newspaper when she saw a notice at the very bottom of the page.

'Whoa! Listen to this, you guys: "Daniel Kehinu of Puna, age forty-three, has been reported missing since Friday morning. He was last seen when he left his home at seven thirty a.m."' She looked at Kristen. 'This could be my guy – the one I saw in the lava!'

'Ho, you know how many Puna types go missing every week?' Isaac shoved back his chair to go get more coffee. 'Da guy, he prob'ly somewheres sleeping off too much vodka or meth or sometin' else. You always be reading stories like dat in da paper.' The subject was bringing out the Pidgin in his speech big-time. 'I should know,' he added, refilling his cup, '''cause small kid time I wen' live down dere, and I been 'round plenty guys like dat.'

Chuckling to himself, he sat back down. But when he saw Valerie's sullen expression, he stopped his laughing. 'Sorry,' he said. 'I didn't mean to make fun.' He picked up his coffee and took a sip, eyeing her. 'You really saw that body, yah?'

She looked back at him, then nodded.

Isaac pursed his lips and frowned, continuing to hold her gaze. 'Okay,' he said after a bit, 'dis what we gonna do today. Go *holoholo* – take a ride – down Puna and Pāhoa town. Do some poking around, see what we come up with. Like I said before, I grew up down there and know lots of people. And you should see it anyway – both of you. Puna's a special-kine place.' He set his cup back down. 'If you want to, that is.'

'I do!' Valerie turned to Kristen, who had kept silent during this entire exchange.

She shrugged her shoulders. 'Puna, it is.'

* * *

It turned out Isaac was a pretty good tour guide. He drove them down near to where they'd been the previous morning for their lava adventure and then turned the car back towards Hilo, taking a route he called 'the Red Road' – though it wasn't the least bit red.

'It used to be paved with asphalt made from red lava rock,' he explained, 'so everyone still calls it dat. The Red Road's my favorite road on the island.'

Valerie could see why; it reminded her of a scene from an old movie – *South Pacific* or, better yet, *Blue Hawaii*. The winding lane hugged the rugged coastline, passing through groves of palm and wispy ironwood trees, then dipping down into sections of mangrove swamp bordered by pink and white impatiens. Every once in a while, they'd take a turn and there would be the ocean, high surf pounding against the jagged lava rock just a few feet from the car.

Isaac turned right at a sign marked 'MacKenzie State Park' and pulled over next to a picnic pavilion. 'You gotta see dis,' he said. 'It's amazing.' Climbing out of the car, they walked over a thick, spongy carpet of ironwood needles down to a series of high cliffs overlooking the sea. Valerie gasped when she gazed down at the water. It was so blue – a deep, super-saturated aqua – that it didn't seem real.

'Jus' wait,' Isaac said, and nodded toward a surge approaching the black rock face they were perched upon. A few seconds later the wave hit the cliff with a booming crash, hurtling a tower of foamy white water at least a hundred feet into the air. Valerie jumped back in surprise, but they all stayed dry save for a fine mist carried over by the sea breeze.

On the way back to the car, Valerie pointed to a flag someone had erected by the picnic pavilion. It had green, yellow, and red horizontal stripes, with a design she didn't recognize in the center. 'What's that flag?' she asked.

'Da Hawaiian sovereignty movement,' Isaac said.

'Huh. I didn't know they had their own flag.'

'Yah, an' they also fly da state flag upside-down to show support for the movement. You see um on lots of trucks 'round da island.'

'Is that a flower in the middle?'

He laughed. 'They're crossed paddles, and a *kāhili*, a – whadya call it in English? You know, dat feathered pole thing the Hawaiian royalty used back when.'

After a couple more stops – swimming at a warm pond fed by one of the local geothermal springs and snorkeling at the Kapoho tide pools – they headed back up to Pāhoa Town, along the third side of the triangle their jaunt would describe.

'*Kau kau* time,' Isaac announced with a gesture towards his mouth, and turned into a restaurant driveway. 'Orchid Drive-In' was painted in large pink letters on what looked to originally have been an old Arby's sign.

'And some investigation, right?' Valerie said in a low voice as they followed a pair of women across the parking lot and through the door.

'That's why I chose this place. Plenty guys I know like to hang out here.' Isaac led the way to the counter, above which hung a board displaying the menu items. There was a long line, which was good since it gave Valerie lots of time to decide what to order.

'What should I get?' Kristen asked. 'I'm starved.'

'Gotta try da loco moco. It's da best there is.'

'Oof. I dunno if I'm *that* hungry.'

'What's loco moco?' Valerie asked, prompting one of the women they'd followed in from the parking lot, who were ahead of them in line, to turn around and stare.

Isaac laughed. 'You'll see; that's what I'm gonna have. They also got *'ono* burgers, and da plate lunches here, they broke da mout'!'

They studied the board, and Kristen quickly settled on the plate lunch with Korean fried chicken. Valerie, as ever, agonized over her choice, trying to decide between the ahi burger and a plain old cheeseburger. When they finally reached the counter, Kristen jabbed her in the ribs and she blurted out, 'An ahi burger – rare.'

'I don't think they do rare,' Isaac said as they got settled at a booth by the window. 'But it'll still be good.'

After a few minutes, the woman behind the counter called out their number and Isaac and Kristen stood to pick up their food. Valerie was staring out the window at two young men sitting in a car passing a joint back and forth, when the sound of plates being set down on the table brought her attention back inside.

Isaac immediately dug in to his loco moco. Valerie gaped at the mammoth meal, which consisted of three scoops of white rice topped by two hamburger patties slathered in brown gravy, and crowned by two sunny-side-up eggs.

Stabbing one of the yolks with his fork, Isaac smiled as the yellow liquid streamed out, mixing with the gravy and giving the dish the look of a Jackson Pollock canvas. 'Want some?' he asked.

Kristen shook her head. 'I've had it before.'

But Valerie did; she always liked to try new dishes. Partly because of working at her brother's bistro, but also because the love of food was pretty much in her genes. Her grandfather – who'd emigrated to Southern California from France as a young man – came from a fishing family that owned a restaurant in the old port of Marseilles, long before the area transformed into the upscale tourist spot it was now. And although neither *Grand-père* Jacques nor her father had followed in the Corbin family's restaurant footsteps, both her parents were devout foodies and had passed their culinary love down to their two children.

Isaac pushed his plate across the table and Valerie filled her fork with rice, burger, egg, and gravy. 'Oh, yum!' she said, wiping the dribble from her chin with a paper napkin. 'They go really well together. And that gravy is delicious!'

Isaac grinned. 'Told ya so. But you gotta be careful where you get it. It's not so good everywhere.'

She turned her attention to Kristen's plate lunch, which also came with scoops of rice, as well as macaroni salad and several pieces of fried chicken glistening with glaze.

'I know that look,' Kristen said, and handed Valerie the wing. 'Here. Don't say I never did nothin' for ya.'

She bit through the crunchy skin, flecked with black sesame seeds and red chili flakes, and savored the tender meat below. It was tangy and spicy, with a strong shot of ginger.

As Isaac had predicted, Valerie's ahi burger was overcooked, but it wasn't bad. It's hard to ruin freshly caught yellowfin tuna.

And the French fries were skinny and crisp, just as she liked
them. She was poking a fry into the pool of ketchup on her plate
when a man approached their table.

'Eh, Trev,' Isaac said. 'Howzit?'

'*Maika'i*, cuz.'

Isaac introduced the two women to the man – Trevor – and
invited him to sit at their table. 'You stay work da kine eh, da
car repair place here Pāhoa?' Isaac nodded toward the splotches
of black grease that threatened to obscure the original color of
Trevor's blue jeans.

'Yeah. Dey makin' me come in Sundays now. But dey no can
stop me go lunch, eh, brah?' He patted the early-onset paunch
filling out his similarly stained T-shirt.

'Not even,' Isaac replied, mouth full of loco moco.

'Right now, get one guy's motor all over da shop floor.' Trevor
laughed and took a gulp of his Coke. 'Get choke parts everywhere! Da buggah goin' nowhere wit' dat car until I pau.'

Kristen and Valerie exchanged glances as Trevor got up to
retrieve his food. Getting to hear Isaac go full-blown Pidgin with
his friend was fascinating.

After Trevor returned with his bowl of *saimin* – a tangle of
fat noodles swimming in broth with vegetables and slices of
hot-pink fish cake – Isaac led the conversation to the missing
man.

'I wen' hear about dat,' Trevor said. 'A Puna guy, yah?'

'Right. Da paper said his name Daniel Kehinu. You know
'um?'

Trevor noisily sucked a noodle up into his mouth before
answering. 'I tink maybe I used to know one guy wen' hang out
with him all da time – Kevin. He went high school wit' us,
remember?'

Aha. Valerie had been staring at Trevor's shirt, which bore the
same stylized knife as the tattoo on Isaac's arm, with the name
Pāhoa Daggers above. *It's their high school mascot.*

'Mmm.' Isaac nodded his head. 'I remember 'um, but we
nevah hang that much.'

'Dass 'cause you was spendin' all your time back den with
da books, instead of yo' friends.' Trevor chuckled and took
another bite of soup. 'Ya know,' he said after he'd swallowed, 'I

tink maybe dat guy – Daniel, da one missing – somebody wen' tell dis morning at da shop, he workin' for BigT couple months now.'

Now they were getting somewhere. 'BigT – what's that?' Valerie asked.

'Big Island Geothermal,' Isaac answered. 'We passed it on the way down to Kaimū this morning. It's the new geothermal plant – you know, where they generate electricity from hot water and steam produced by the volcanic activity underground?'

Valerie was struck by how he'd automatically switched from Pidgin back to Standard English – more so, even, than he usually did when talking with Kristen and her. Was it, she wondered, because he was addressing a *haole* in front of his friend? Or because of the scientific subject matter? He was, after all, a science teacher. Curious, in either case.

'Was that where the explosion was Friday night?' Valerie asked.

The other three turned to her, a 'huh?' expression on their faces.

'It was in the paper this morning – didn't you see it? There was some kind of blast at the new geothermal plant, they said.'

'If dey said da new one, must be BigT, den,' Isaac said with a glance at Trevor, reverting once more to Pidgin. 'Stay open only like five months, yah?'

'Yeah.' Trevor nodded in agreement. 'Da other place – PGV – it was dere long time already.'

'You think the explosion could have anything to do with that guy's disappearance?' Valerie looked from Trevor to Isaac. 'I mean, if he worked there an' all . . .'

They both just shrugged.

Behind Isaac, at the next table over, Valerie noticed a woman eyeing them. Saying something to the man she was with, she stood and walked towards their table. Her tight-fitting tank top showed off a lean, muscular frame and afforded full view of a tattoo of the Hawaiian Islands, the archipelago descending from her shoulder clear down to the elbow.

'Ho, long time, brah,' she said, slapping Trevor on the back.

Trevor looked up from his soup. 'Eh, Jordan, whassup?'

'Just got back from fishing the last two nights down Ka'ū side.

I caught me one big *ulua*.' Holding her hands wide apart, she demonstrated the size of the fish.

'Solid,' Trevor responded. He introduced the group to his friend and then asked her, 'You like grab some brews after I finish work?'

Jordan tucked an errant strand of her shoulder-length brown hair behind her ear. 'No can. I promised I'd make dinner for my grandparents tonight. Gotta go shopping and then head down there and cook.'

'What are you making?' Valerie asked.

'Kālua pork,' Jordan answered, seeming to notice her for the first time.

'Really? It has Kahlua in it – the coffee liqueur?' This prompted chuckles from everyone else at the table.

'She's new to the island,' Kristen said with a theatrical shrug. 'You gonna dig a pit and do the whole nine yards?'

'Naw – too much trouble. I just wrap it in ti leaves and then tin foil and slow cook it in the oven. But it's super *'ono*, for sure. And I make my own papaya chutney to go with the pig.'

'Yum!' Valerie licked her lips dramatically. 'What do you put in it?'

'It's pretty simple: ya just cut up the papayas in chunks and cook it with sugar, vinegar, ginger, and chili powder till it thickens up good.'

'Oh, man, that sounds awesome. Can I come?'

Jordan smiled at Valerie, holding her gaze for a moment as she scratched absently at O'ahu on her upper arm. 'Maybe next time,' she said with a wink, then turned back to Trevor. 'Anyway, I gotta finish eating and get down to the store, but I just wanted to say hey.' They exchanged fist-bumps. Returning to her table, Jordan sat down and said a few words to her friend, and they both laughed.

Trevor lifted his bowl and slurped down the rest of his *saimin*. 'Gotta jam. Da boss-man gon' snap if I no dere soon.' He scraped back his chair and stood.

'Before you go,' Valerie said, 'what about this guy's friend – Kevin, right?' Trevor nodded. 'You still in touch with him?'

'Las' time I seen 'um, he da bartender-guy down Raul's. But as' a while back, now.' Carrying his bowl to the bus tray, he flashed them the shaka sign with his pinkie and thumb. 'Latahz.'

'What's Raul's?' Valerie asked Isaac after Trevor had gone.

'It's a restaurant 'round the corner. Wanna check it out after we finish here?'

Did she ever.

FOUR

It started to pour right as the threesome emerged from the Orchid Drive-In. Since the weather had been sunny when they'd left the house, no one had thought to bring an umbrella. But most of the storefronts along the main drag had awnings, so they managed to stay fairly dry.

The coverings, along with the rustic, clapboard-sided buildings and raised wooden sidewalks, gave Pāhoa the feel of an Old West town. That is, if you ignored all the Rastafarian flags in the stores and the propensity of the townsfolk to sport tie-dyed clothing. 'Maui Wowie got nothin' on the *pakalolo* they grow around here,' Isaac commented when he saw Valerie eying the giant bamboo bhangs and cannabis leaf T-shirts in one of the shop windows.

Rounding the corner and dashing across the street, they dodged the muddy water starting to pool in the gutter and ducked into Raul's. From the neon Cuervo signs and Cinco de Mayo decorations on the walls for the upcoming holiday, Valerie shrewdly deduced that it was a Mexican joint. The tables were mostly empty, it being that slow time between lunch and dinner, but several people were seated at the bar.

They took the three empty stools at the end, and the man at the bar set down the glass he was drying and came toward them. 'Afternoon,' he said. 'What can I getcha?'

All three ordered bottles of Pacífico beer, and Valerie fiddled with a table tent advertising guacamole and chips for four and a half bucks (which seemed like a great deal – too bad she'd just eaten a huge lunch) while Isaac made small talk with the bartender. Mike, his name was, from Brooklyn. Which was obvious after he'd said about five words. The hard consonants and broad vowels seemed jarring after all the lilting Pidgin she'd been hearing of late.

Figuring Isaac wouldn't be any better than her at getting info out of a New Yorker, Valerie jumped into the conversation when

Mike mentioned that he'd been in Hawai'i for just a few months. 'So, how long have you worked here?' she asked.

'Only a couple of weeks, actually. I lucked out, 'cause one of the bartenders had just quit right when I was asking around about a job. And since I'd been a barkeep back home in Flatbush, well, right place right time, ya know?'

'Congrats.' Kristen raised her bottle in salute. 'She's been learning how to tend bar,' she said, jabbing a thumb towards Valerie.

'Oh, yeah? Cool,' he said, then stepped away to mix another round of Margaritas for the couple at the other end of the bar.

'So,' Isaac said once he came back over, 'is there a guy named Kevin who works here?'

'Yeah. You know him?'

'We were at Pāhoa High together. A friend just told me he was working here, so I thought I'd stop by and see him.'

'Sorry, man – Kevin's not here today. He's off till Tuesday.'

Isaac shrugged his shoulders. 'No worries. I can come by some other time. Any chance you know a guy named Daniel – a buddy of Kevin's?'

'Sure, I've met him a few times. He comes into the restaurant pretty regular-like, before his shift at the plant.'

'BigT, right?'

'Yeah, he's a night watchman there, so he'll hang out at the bar and have a couple cups of joe before heading off to work.'

''Cause he's the one I really wanted to see,' continued Isaac. 'When was the last time he was in here?'

'Daniel?' Mike walked back over to the dishwasher and picked up where he'd left off, drying highball glasses and stacking them on the shelf behind him. 'Seems like it's been a few days, but when exactly . . .? Here, maybe my boss can tell you. He knows him better than I do.'

An older man in a spattered chef's jacket had come out of the kitchen to help himself to some Coke from the bar's soda gun. 'Hey, Ramón,' Mike said. 'This guy was wondering when was the last time that guy Daniel – the one who hangs out with Kevin – was in the restaurant.'

Ramón drank down his Coke before responding. 'Why you so curious about him?'

It was Valerie's turn to jump back into the game. 'Well, he's a good friend of Kevin's, so when we read in the paper this morning that he'd gone missing—'

'Kevin's been reported missing?' Mike ceased his glass-drying and stared at Valerie.

'No,' Valerie answered, 'Daniel has.' Spying a pile of newspapers by the front door, she slid from her stool and rifled through it. 'Here, check it out.' She folded the paper to the back page and held it out.

'So, anyway,' Isaac continued as Mike and Ramón studied the missing-person notice, 'after seeing dat, you can imagine we got kinda concerned about the guy. And when we heard Kevin worked here, we thought we'd see if maybe we could ask him about Daniel.'

Mike tapped the newspaper with his forefinger and turned to his boss. 'Wait – wasn't Kevin really pissed off last week about something to do with Dan—'

At a sharp glance from Ramón, Mike shut his mouth and returned to his glass-drying.

'Sorry,' Ramón said, flashing a smile that didn't look all that sincere, 'but I really don't know anything about Daniel, or where he might be. But I'm sure, if he is in fact missing, the police will no doubt be looking into it.' He nodded toward their empty beer bottles. 'Can I get you another round?'

'No, thanks.' Isaac stood up. 'We bettah be heading back up to Hilo.'

'I gotta hit the bathroom before we go,' Valerie said. 'I'll meet you guys out front.'

The other woman at the bar had apparently also taken this moment to use the restroom, however, and she found the door locked. While she waited, Valerie perused the bulletin board in the dimly lit hallway. The ceiling lamp bulb had apparently burned out, but enough daylight filtered through the screen door leading out back to the parking lot to allow her to read the notices posted on the board – once she'd fished her reading glasses from the depths of her bag. There was the usual batch of neon-colored flyers advertising concerts – mostly reggae and country, by the looks of them – as well as hand-printed 'For Sale' and 'For Rent' signs.

Political-type posters and flyers had also been pinned up. One
was protesting the use of Hawaiian Home Lands property for a
new shopping center and called on people to contact their legis-
lators. Another advertised a bake sale, concert, and rally in
support of the Hawaiian sovereignty movement. A third caught
her eye and, ignoring the now-vacated ladies room, she bent to
read it:

Geothermal: One Was Bad Enough –
Where Will It Stop?
Say NO to BigT

Puna is the sacred land of the Goddess Pele. Its magma
chambers are her beating heart, its waters her lifeblood, its
steam and vapor her fiery breath. Geothermal development
of these elements injures her body, violates her spirit and
depletes her creative force.

We allowed ourselves to accede to the first geothermal
plant. Now there are two. Where will it end?

Protect Pele – Shut Down Big Island Geothermal!

Kā Pelehonuamea Keiki – Pele's Children
www.kapelekeiki.com

With a quick glance around to make sure no one was watching,
Valerie unpinned the flyer, folded it up, and tucked it into her
back pocket.

After their enormous late lunch, no one wanted any dinner that
night. Sachiko came over a little after seven, and she and Isaac
cozied down in front of the TV to stream a few episodes of *The
Walking Dead*. Kristen, pleading exhaustion, retired to the studio
downstairs.

Valerie considered joining Sachiko and Isaac, but decided to
forgo a night of zombies for some down time herself. Smiling
and waving at Kristen, who was at the small desk with earbuds
in, watching some courtroom drama, Valerie plumped up the
pillows on the sofa-bed and settled down with her laptop.

Time for some research. She pulled the pilfered flyer from her pocket and typed the web address printed at the bottom into the browser's address bar.

There it was – the Pele's Children website. Front and center on the homepage was more or less the same language as on their flyer: a diatribe against geothermal development on the Big Island. She skimmed the text. The site contained lots of unfamiliar Hawaiian words – phrases like 'geothermal cannot be *pono* because it takes from Madame Pele's life force' and 'Tūtū Pele is the *'aumakua* of present-day Hawaiians, and we must protect her and the *'āina* from geothermal development.' But it was easy enough to get the gist of their position.

She'd expected the site to be all just a political tract, so Valerie was surprised when she scrolled down to see the group appeared to have artistic and cultural elements as well. There was an item about an upcoming workshop on carving and applying dye to gourds – *ipu*, they were called – and crafting them into containers and musical instruments. The photos were beautiful, showing dried gourds decorated with intricate flowers, vines, turtles, and geometric shapes.

Below that was an announcement about an upcoming hula performance. The *hālau* (she allowed herself a self-satisfied smile, pleased to recognize at least this one Hawaiian word) would be dancing to, among other things, the ancient chant '*Ke ha'a lā Puna*,' the notice said, which recounted the story of the origins of hula on Hā'ena Beach in Puna.

Huh. Who knew hula had come from Puna? she thought, and continued reading:

> The chant is also a cautionary tale. For it tells of Pele's rage when she suspects her younger sister Hi'iaka of attempting to steal away her intended husband, and of the Goddess's revenge by turning Hi'iaka's best friend to stone and covering her sister's beloved 'oʻhi'a forests with lava.

> This hula is therefore a reminder to us of the power and wrath of Madame Pele, and the devastation by the Goddess that we risk should we continue to violate her body and spirit through geothermal development on the Big Island.

Whoa! Valerie stopped reading. That description was enough to give even a nonbeliever like herself some pause. Pele sounded like a goddess you really didn't want to be messing with. And her preferred form of punishment appeared to be covering things with lava and turning them to stone – exactly what happened to that body she'd seen down at the flow. *Could it have been a copycat murder? Was someone out there playing goddess?*

She went back to the announcement. The show was this coming Wednesday night at seven o'clock, at the Palace Theater in Hilo. A reception with the dancers and audience would follow.

Closing her laptop, Valerie leaned back on the pillows and stared up at the ceiling, listening to the patter of rain on the ti leaves outside the window.

She'd found the hula performance she wanted to see.

FIVE

'You guys should really head over to Hāpuna today,' Isaac said during breakfast the next morning. He was dressed in his school clothes, which meant his Hawaiian shirt was buttoned and tucked in, he'd swapped out his khaki shorts for a long-legged version, and instead of flip-flops – slippahs, the locals called them – he had on leather sandals.

'Good idea.' Kristen grabbed the box of Wheaties sitting in front of Isaac and dumped cereal into her bowl. 'Doesn't look like this rain is going to let up anytime soon. What d'ya say, hon?'

Valerie, who'd only been half listening, looked up from her yogurt and sliced banana. Once again, she'd awoken to a vision of her brother's death – only this time his body had been burning up in a pool of blood-red lava – and was having a hard time erasing the image from her mind. 'Uh . . . what's Hāpuna?' she asked.

'The best beach on the island,' Kristen answered. 'At least in my opinion.' Shaking the empty carton of milk sitting on the table, she stood up to fetch a fresh one from the fridge. 'It's got like a half-mile of white sand, beautiful blue water—'

'Not to mention da kine boogie-boarding,' Isaac added, 'which is what she's really interested in.' He swiveled in his chair to face Kristen. 'There's a couple of boogie boards out in the carport next to the surfboards you guys can use.'

'Cool. Thanks.' Kristen sat back down and set to work opening the new milk carton.

Valerie nodded toward the kitchen window, through which the fronds of the coco palm next door could be seen whipping about in the hard rain. 'You think it'll be nice over there today?'

'Oh, yeah, for sure. Da Kohala Coast, it gets less rain than anywhere else in the whole country – only a few inches a year.'

'Weird,' Valerie said. ''Cause I read that Hilo was the rainiest city in the US.'

'That would actually be Ketchikan, Alaska.' Kristen finally succeeded in peeling the two cardboard flaps apart, managing to squirt milk onto her arm and the table in the process. 'They have about ten inches more annual rainfall than Hilo,' she added, wiping up the milk with a paper napkin.

'Maybe,' said Isaac, his mouth full of toasted Hawaiian sweet bread topped with guava jelly. 'But we got way more bettah weather. Our rain is warm.'

Choosing to ignore the who's-the-rainiest question, Valerie pressed on with what she considered the more interesting issue. 'So the Big Island has both the driest *and* the wettest – or close to it, anyway – places in the country? That seems really bizarre.'

'Not when you factor in the two fourteen-thousand-foot mountains that lie between them. Here, check it out.' Kristen picked up her spoon.

Oh, boy, Valerie thought with an inward rolling of the eyes. *Lecture time.* But since she was in fact interested in what was to come, she refrained from making any snide remark.

'Okay, so here are Maunakea and Mauna Loa,' Kristen said, forming the cereal in her bowl into two cone-shaped mounds. 'The trade winds come in from the east, full of moisture they've been collecting during their long trip across the Pacific Ocean.' Waving her fingers and making a *whooshing* sound, she mimicked the wind blowing across the table from Isaac toward her bowl of Wheaties. 'And what happens when they arrive at the Big Island?' Neither Isaac nor Valerie answered, knowing they'd spoil her fun if they didn't let her finish. 'They run smack into those enormous volcanoes – which are higher than the trade winds – and all that moisture comes down as precipitation on the east side of the island, right onto little Hilo Town.'

Kristen picked up the carton of milk and drizzled white rain down the windward side of her cereal cones until it formed a pool at the bottom of the bowl. 'And the west side of the island? Well, look for yourself.' Swiveling the bowl around, she jabbed her spoon into the still-dry flakes on its leeward side. 'See? Being in the rain shadow of those massive mountains, it loses out and remains an arid desert.'

She could be pretty damn adorable sometimes, Valerie had to admit.

Kristen bowed her head in acknowledgement of Isaac and Valerie's applause, then proceeded to spoon a large spoonful of Maunakea's summit into her mouth.

'What are you clapping about?' Sachiko came into the kitchen rubbing her eyes and yawning, a blue-and-white cotton kimono-style robe knotted at her waist.

'Just Kristen giving us a meteorology tutorial. How'd you sleep, babe?'

'Too well. Why didn't you wake me up? I have to get to the restaurant.'

'But wait – it's Monday. Aren't you closed today?'

'Yeah, we are.' Sachiko poured a cup of coffee and joined the others at the table. 'But I promised to meet with the owner to figure out which of the applicants we're going to hire to replace that guy who just quit.' She squinted at the clock on the stove across the room. 'Damn, it's later than I thought. And I have to swing by my place on the way down there.' She stood back up. 'Better go get dressed.'

After she'd left the kitchen again, Kristen turned to Isaac. 'Did you talk to her yet?'

'Uh-huh,' Isaac said with a sigh. 'Last night. She said she wanted to think about it.'

'Think about what?' Valerie asked.

'About moving in with me.' Isaac carried his coffee mug and plate to the sink and rinsed them with water. 'She knows it would save a lot of money, and we spend most nights together anyway, but she's not sure she's ready to make that kind of commitment.' He made quote marks in the air around this last word. 'I do get that it would be a big deal – a real change in her life. And mine. So I no gonna pressure her too much. But . . .'

Letting out a sigh, he set the dishes in the drainer and dried his hands on the towel hanging on the oven. 'I guess I should get going to work, too. So you think you gonna head over Hāpuna side?'

Kristen turned to Valerie, her eyebrows forming a question.

'Sure, why not?' Valerie said.

'Kay, den. Have fun. *Latahz.*' Isaac grabbed his leather brief-case and darted out the side door into the rain, letting the screen bang shut behind him. This was followed by the slamming of a car door and the starting of an engine.

Valerie drank down the last of her coffee. 'I want to call that real estate agent before we go. You remember where I put her number?' Sifting through the pile of papers sitting on the counter by the toaster, she came up with the page she was looking for. 'Here it is – Sandy Spenser.'

Isaac had provided the name of a gal he knew who worked for a local realtor, so Valerie could figure out what to do with the property her brother had owned. The unimproved residential lot was in a place called Hawaiian Paradise Park, which wasn't too far from Hilo, Isaac had said. She was hoping to take a look at the place and find out what it was worth, so she could decide whether it would be best to hold on to the lot as an investment or simply unload it.

Valerie punched in the number and, getting voicemail, left a message explaining the situation and asking the woman for a call back. 'Okay,' she said, shoving the phone into her shorts pocket, 'lemme grab my bathing suit and stuff. I'll be ready in a jiff.'

Isaac had neglected to mention that the Kohala Coast can also be the windiest place on the island.

As the two women strolled from the parking lot down to the ocean, enjoying the warmth of the sun on their faces, Valerie was impressed by how few people were at Hāpuna. After all, it seemed the perfect day and the perfect beach. Not a cloud marred the sky, and the sea glistened in a combination of blues and greens she'd only ever seen in travel magazines. They laid out their towels on the broad swath of sparkling white sand and stripped down to their swim suits, relishing the fact that they had the place virtually to themselves.

Within five minutes, they learned why. The wind came up, and the two were instantly pelted by thousands of grains of sand stinging their unprotected skin. It was then that they realized there were in fact lots of folks there; they'd simply been wise enough to stake their claims on the grassy area near the showers, rather than out on the sand.

Once Valerie and Kristen joined the others on the lawn, it was lovely. The wind was still present, but now, instead of battering the pair with a constant sandstorm, it seemed more just a refreshing breeze, a welcome respite from the intense tropical rays.

Valerie put on her Dodgers cap and sunglasses, and Kristen rummaged around in their beach bag and pulled out the sun screen. 'Good idea,' Valerie said, eyeing her wife's still-pink back.

'So, old lady, what do you want to do for your big six-oh next week?' Kristen asked, generously applying the cream to her neck and shoulders. 'Maybe go out for a nice dinner somewhere?'

'Actually, I've been thinking it would be fun to do something outdoors for my birthday – if it's not raining, that is. Being able to hang out outside after the sun goes down is such a treat.' She took the proffered lotion and began spreading it on Kristen's back. 'You know, given how rare it is we get hot nights back home.'

'So true.'

Valerie did love where they lived in Mar Vista, a quiet neighborhood nestled between Venice Beach and the 405 freeway in West Los Angeles. But what she did not enjoy about the place was how chilly it could be, especially in the summertime, when the fog would roll in each time it was hot farther inland. Many people counted this as a blessing, but she'd always been envious of folks who could have evening barbecues without having to bundle up in hoodies and warm blankets.

'I was thinking maybe a picnic somewhere. With more of that delicious poke.'

'I've got an idea,' Kristen said. 'There's this place I remember going to last time I was here – Coconut Island. It's right in town, but you have to walk across a footbridge to get there. It's a great place to hang out and look back at the Bayfront and watch the sun set over the mountains. We could have a birthday picnic there.'

'Awesome. That sounds perfect.'

They stretched out on their towels, and Valerie considered what Kristen had said, calling her 'old lady.' Kristen was actually five years younger than Valerie, but as a result of her years working in the trades, she said she sometimes felt as if she had the joints of someone fifteen years older.

Valerie, however, didn't feel sixty. In fact, her body didn't feel much different than it had in her forties – other than an occasional stiffness in her hip and the recent need for reading glasses. And even though her once near-black hair had faded to salt-and-pepper (heavy on the salt), in her mind she was still that thirty-year-old girl who'd quit a well-paying job as an assistant to a TV mogul to run off to France for a year to discover her roots.

She was startled from her musings about how quickly all the years seemed to have passed, when Kristen sat up and said, 'Okay, I'm hot enough.' Pulling on a T-shirt, she grabbed Isaac's boogie board and trotted down to the water, where several teenagers were catching some pretty good rides.

Valerie wasn't much into boogie-boarding but was content to gaze out at the ocean, watching Kristen and the other beachgoers and generally spacing out. Above her were palm trees and a cerulean sky. The strains of an ukulele floated in the distance, along with laughter and the melodic rise and fall of Pidgin.

Ah . . . Now this *was what Hawai'i was supposed to be like.*

Three kids were building a sand castle down by the water's edge and screamed in delight when a wave rolled far enough in to fill their moat. Beyond them, several snorkelers were paddling about near the rocks at the south end of the beach. It looked like tough going, what with the white caps they were swimming through. Looking to the right – north – she spied a patch of clouds starting to form on the horizon. One appeared to be way larger than the others. Removing her sunglasses, she squinted, trying to see it better. Was that a mountain?

She asked Kristen about it when she returned, shaking water from her short blond hair like a shaggy dog. 'That's Maui,' Kristen said, pulling off her T-shirt and wringing it out. 'Haleakalā volcano.' She laid the shirt out carefully on the boogie board to dry and picked up her blue-and-white striped beach towel.

'I can't seem to get away from them.'

Kristen stopped drying her hair and looked at Valerie.

'Volcanoes,' she explained.

Kristen smiled. 'Well, given that you're standing on one anytime you're anywhere in the state of Hawai'i—'

'That's not what I mean. I can't seem to get away from them . . . here.' Valerie touched her head. 'In my brain.'

Kristen was about to say something in response but was

interrupted by the ringing of Valerie's cell. It was the real estate
agent calling back.

'Hi, Sandy. Tomorrow morning? That would be perfect. Yeah,
okay, thanks.' Valerie returned the phone to her bag. 'Nine thirty
tomorrow, I'm meeting her at her office and then I'll follow her
down there to take a look at the place.'

'Oh, good.' Kristen spread out her towel and stretched out on
her back.

Valerie laid down on her stomach facing Kristen. 'So were
you serious about us seeing a hula performance?' she asked.

'Yeah. It would be fun.'

''Cause there's one the day after tomorrow that I'm interested
in going to see.' She explained about the flyer she'd found and
the Pele's Children website, and how she thought they might be
connected somehow to the body she'd seen out on the lava flow.

Kristen sat up and hugged her knees. 'Okay, so here's the
thing.' She blew out a slow breath before going on. 'It's just that
I'm not so sure your worrying about that missing guy is real
healthy for you. I mean, after what you just went through, don't
you think maybe right now—'

'As if being made to feel like a delusional nutcase *is* good for
me? Jesus, Kristen. The way you looked at me out there when
I told you what I'd seen – and the way you're looking at me
right now, for that matter?'

'All I'm saying is maybe it would be better for you to just let
it go and instead try to relax a little while we're here. Which
was the whole point of the trip, after all.'

Valerie stared at her wife, then shook her head. 'Don't you
get it? I saw a *burning body* out there, for Chrissake! In the
process of being covered over with hot lava! Can you even
imagine how freaked out you would be?' Fighting to hold off
the tears she could feel coming, she bit her lip. 'And how much
worse it would be if no one believed that you'd even seen it?'

'Look.' Kristen reached out to touch her arm, but Valerie
yanked it away.

'No, *you* look. I know you think I imagined the whole thing,
that it's 'cause I'm still "traumatized" – yeah, I heard what you
said to Isaac – about what happened to Charlie. Isaac, at least,
has the good grace to act more sympathetic, though I'm sure

he's only humoring me. So it's clear the only way anyone is going to believe me is if I can somehow prove what I saw.'

'Oh, now there's a *great* idea.' Kristen said, throwing her hands up in the air. 'So you come to Hawai'i, a place you've never even been before and know next to nothing about, and now you're going to single-handedly solve the great mystery of some supposed body in the lava. Just terrific.' She stood up. 'Fine. Well, while you go about playing amateur detective, I'm going to try to actually enjoy some of our vacation.'

Picking up the boogie board once more and shoving it under her arm, Kristen stomped back off towards the beach. She didn't, Valerie observed, put on the T-shirt this time.

The drive back to Isaac's house from Hāpuna was no fun. Kristen was sullen, and Valerie pouted, and it began to pour as soon as they left Waimea, rendering the visibility down the Hāmākua Coast sketchy, at best.

Valerie knew she shouldn't have gone off on Kristen like that. She was well aware she'd only been trying to help, to protect Valerie from any more pain than she'd already experienced of late. But she couldn't help it. The potent emotions – anxiety, despondency, rage – they'd been coming upon her so suddenly these days. It was as if she'd been experiencing menopause all over again for the past five weeks, only this time with double the hormones.

But still, Valerie couldn't help fuming as they made their slow way down the winding road back to Hilo, *that doesn't excuse how incredibly patronizing her attempt to 'help' was.*

Then Sachiko didn't show up for dinner as she'd promised, which put Isaac in a foul mood as well. The conversation was minimal as they ate the stir-fried eggplant in black bean sauce that Valerie had prepared. Afterwards, while they were doing the dishes, Valerie brought up the hula performance on Wednesday night and asked Isaac if he and Sachiko were interested in going.

'Yeah, sounds good to me. But don't get a ticket for Sachiko. I'm not sure what her schedule is like dis week.' He smiled as he said it, but his sad eyes didn't match the rest of his face.

'So how about you?' Valerie asked Kristen. 'You never did answer the question this afternoon.'

Kristen switched off the burner under the wok drying on the stove. 'Sure, I guess so.' Tearing a paper towel from the roll on the counter, she dribbled canola oil into the wok. Valerie watched as she methodically rubbed the oil into the hot steel, but Kristen stared at the pan, refusing to meet her gaze.

'Ho, sistah,' Isaac said, and slapped Kristen on the back. 'Show a little enthusiasm. It'll be good fun time!'

'Right.' Kristen tossed the oily paper towel into the trash. 'Well, I'm going down to our room to check my email an' stuff. 'Night.' With a quick look Valerie's way and a barely perceptible shake of the head, she made her exit.

Isaac didn't ask what was going on between the two of them, and Valerie didn't volunteer any information. He wiped down the countertop with a sponge, dried his hands on the dish towel, and leaned against the fridge door. 'Wanna watch a movie? I was thinking of streaming the new James Bond.'

'No, thanks. I'm pretty beat. I guess I'll turn in, too.'

Kristen had changed into her sleepwear – an oversized T-shirt bearing a picture of the Hollywood sign – when Valerie got downstairs, and stood at the bed, carefully folding the clothes she'd worn that day. 'I'm sorry,' she said, smoothing out the neat squares and then sliding them into a dresser drawer. 'I shouldn't have said what I did at the beach. And I shouldn't have been so snippy during dinner.'

Valerie took a seat at the small desk and studied the painting on the opposite wall, a watercolor of a pair of black-and-white geese in front of a bush filled with bright red berries. *You shouldn't have* said *what you did*, she was thinking. *Not that you shouldn't have* thought *it to begin with.*

But she didn't want to go there right now. They'd had enough conflict for one day. Instead, she leaned over and gave Kristen a hug.

'Thanks, hon. And I know how weird this whole thing is. But I think for the sake of my sanity, maybe it's best if you just let me do what I think is right for me, okay?'

Kristen nodded in acknowledgement, but the frown that accompanied the assent signaled a definite mixed message.

Whatever.

Kristen climbed into bed with her laptop, and once she'd

inserted her earbuds and clicked the screen to life, Valerie turned to her own computer atop the desk. Locating the Palace Theater website, she used a credit card to buy tickets to the hula performance, requesting that they hold them at will-call.

Now all she had to do was figure out what the heck she'd ask if given the opportunity to meet any of the Pele's Children members at the theater.

SIX

Her brother's property was not what Valerie had envisioned. The name of the subdivision – Hawaiian Paradise Park – along with the fact that most everywhere she'd visited so far on the east side of the Big Island was lush and overgrown, had led her to assume that Charlie's place would be the same. But as she walked the parcel with Sandy Spenser the next morning, she wondered what could have prompted her brother to buy it. No tropical paradise this: a layer of compacted red-and-gray rock covered the one-acre lot, through which stunted 'ōhi'a trees were poking their slight forms, doing their best to compete with a host of scraggly bushes and weeds.

'Is there water?' she asked, guessing the answer.

'Everyone's on catchment around here,' the real estate agent replied. 'But there's enough rain that with a ten-thousand-gallon tank it's rare to have to buy any water. Unless you've got a papaya grove that needs watering, or something like that.'

'How about electricity and sewer?'

Sandy pointed at the power lines running along the road. 'Yes to the first. And you can get cell reception and landlines down here, too. But as for sewer, no; it's all septic.'

'Sounds like it could be expensive.' Kneeling down, Valerie scraped at the hard ground with her fingernails. 'Digging through this lava rock can't be easy.'

'Huh-uh.' Sandy shook her head in agreement. 'A friend of mine just spent six grand putting a tank in down here.'

'Ouch. And add to that the cost of clearing the lot, plans, permits, labor and materials. Could end up being quite a pricey endeavor for anyone who wanted to build.'

Even though she was still peeved at Kristen from yesterday, Valerie wished that she, along with her construction expertise, were here right now. But seeing the look in her wife's eyes that morning when Isaac had announced that the surf was up at Honoli'i, she hadn't had the heart to keep her from the waves.

So instead, she'd dropped Kristen off at the beach, telling her she'd need to find an Uber or Lyft back to the house when she was done.

But there was a silver lining. Perhaps she could do a little poking around regarding the missing man on her own today without having to worry about what Kristen would say.

Valerie brushed the lava dust off her hands and stood back up. 'So, you have any idea what the lot is worth?'

Hands on her hips, Sandy surveyed the land. 'I couldn't say for sure, obviously. But you're only a few blocks from the ocean here, so it'll go for more than some HPP lots would. I'm guessing . . . thirty, forty thousand? That's what the comps around here have been going for lately, but don't hold me to it.'

Valerie climbed onto a small patch of lava flow and contemplated the property. 'Any chance it might go up in value in the next few years?'

Sandy shrugged. 'It's possible. Prices have already raised a little since the bubble burst. And I think pretty much everyone agrees they've got to rise even more – though not necessarily to what they were before. But when? Who knows. Could be only a year or two, or maybe five.'

Valerie appreciated her honesty. 'Or ten,' she added.

'Yup. And of course it always depends on the location. Up in Waimea, things are looking pretty good – I've sold several properties there for my full asking price in just the last month. But down here in Puna, not so much. Places anywhere near the current lava flow, of course, aren't going to sell. But it's also getting harder in other areas. Here in HPP, for instance, so many people bought lots back in the eighties and nineties – a lot of them from the Mainland. I think half the buyers never even saw the land before their purchase. But the properties were cheap – five, ten grand for a whole acre – and they just assumed that, being in Hawai'i, they'd be able to turn them over for an enormous profit. Well, that didn't happen.'

'Yeah. That's around when my brother bought this place. And I'm pretty sure he never saw the lot. I can't imagine his buying this if he'd visited it first.'

And now he'll never see it. Valerie swallowed, conjuring the face of her cherubic and enthusiastic brother – the boy she'd play hide-and-seek with in their 1950s ranch-style home, who taught her to mix and then consume mud pies, and whom she protected from the neighborhood bully, kicking him with her pointy cowboy boots. If Charlie were with her now, he'd wave his hand and recount his grandiose plans for the beautiful home he was going to build and the fabulous kitchen it would have, where he and Valerie could prepare elaborate meals, relishing in their shared love of food and cooking.

Should she keep the property, as a memory of Charlie? *No*, she decided, gazing at a fat green gecko with red spots on its back as it stalked a slow-moving fly. *It would be too painful to come back here on any regular basis; this one time would be enough.*

'But at least HPP is doing better than Leilani Estates,' Sandy was saying. 'Those poor people who bought – especially on the southern edge of the subdivision – they're having a hell of a time selling these days. You know, ever since that new geothermal plant went in next door.'

This last comment startled Valerie from her reverie about her brother.

'I've got a client down there,' Sandy went on, 'whose house has been on the market for going on eight months now, and he has yet to get a realistic offer. It's only a half-mile from BigT, and I guess folks are spooked about buying near the plant.' She shook her head. 'Which is ridiculous, since it's perfectly safe.'

'What about that blast that happened there last week?' Valerie asked.

The real estate agent waved her hand dismissively. 'Just a good story for the newspaper. You know it wasn't anything serious.' She started back towards her car. 'So, you want to see some of the comps while you're down here?'

After they'd checked out three similar lots that had sold recently in the HPP subdivision, Sandy dropped Valerie back at Charlie's property before heading off for an appointment with another client down in Kapoho. Climbing into the rental car, Valerie rolled down all four windows to let the trade-wind breeze clear out the baking air within and realized her stomach was complaining. *Time for some of that four-and-a-half-buck guac and chips at Raul's*, she decided.

Not to mention a bit of investigation – assuming the missing man's buddy Kevin was indeed working today.

Cruising down Highway 130, she was almost to the Pāhoa turnoff when she spied a fruit stand on the side of the road. Someone had set up one of those pop-up canopies seen all over the island, and underneath sat a rickety table piled with papayas, bananas, and other local produce. But it was the hand-lettered sign that caught Valerie's eye: 'Avos 2 for $1.00.' With a quick glance in the rearview mirror, she hit the brakes and pulled over.

Valerie had a love of avocados that some might say bordered on the obsessive. There was something about their rich flavor and silky texture that she simply couldn't get enough of. And this was apparently her lucky day, for not only was she about to get a terrific deal on guacamole for lunch, but she could now stock up on a bag full of luscious avos for the coming days, as well.

A young woman seated in a folding chair looked up as she got out of the car. 'You like rainbow papaya?' she asked, holding one up for Valerie's inspection.

'No, thanks. But I am interested in your avocados. The sign says you have them for fifty cents each?'

'Uh-huh. Those there . . .' She pointed to a cardboard box containing small, knobbly, black specimens. 'The Mexican kine, they two for a dollah, yah? And we got these Greengold kine for one dollah each.'

This second box held slightly larger and greener avocados, but the woman shook her head and waved Valerie off when she went to reach for one. '*This* da kine you gotta try – you like way mo' bettah.' Selecting a large, bright green specimen from a box marked '$1.50,' she cut off a thick slice and held it out.

Right. Of course she wants to sell me the most expensive variety. But Valerie wasn't going to turn down a free taste, so she gladly accepted the sample.

'Ohmygod.' The words flew out involuntarily. It had a rich, buttery flavor and smooth, creamy texture she'd never before encountered in an avocado.

The woman nodded and smiled – one of those I-told-you-so grins. 'Dey the best kind. Sharwil, from here in Puna. How many you like?'

After helping her pick out four that were ready to eat and four that would need several more days, the woman took Valerie's twelve dollars and then added an extra one to the bag. 'This one don't have da stem, so I no can sell. You take fo' free.'

'What's wrong with the ones without stems?'

'Da pears, they no ripen evenly without da stem.'

'Pears?' she repeated.

'These, yah?' The woman tapped the paper bag, and Valerie remembered that they were called 'avocado pears' in some parts of the world. 'So,' she continued, wagging a finger in warning, 'you no buy unless they got da stem. Besides, someone probably wen' cock-a-roach 'em – stole them' – she translated at Valerie's blank look – 'if the stem gone, 'cause they pull 'em off da tree, real fast like, instead of cut 'em off like you supposed to do.' She shook her head in disgust. 'There's lots of that goin' on down Puna side these days.'

'Really? People steal avocados?'

'Dass right. It's a real problem down here. My dad just got some dogs, and our neighbor, he had so many pears stole from his trees, he wen' bought a gun last week.'

'Wow. That's terrible.' *So I'm not the only one who has an avocado addiction.* But at least she had hers under control.

Valerie thanked the woman for her help and – after placing the bag carefully in the back seat where it wouldn't get squashed – continued on down to Pāhoa. She was fantasizing about the avocado and grapefruit salad she'd make for dinner that night as she pulled up in front of Raul's.

The restaurant was busier this time. From the number of folks in tropical-print blouses and shirts – the 'business casual' of the Islands – the place was clearly popular with the local lunch-hour crowd. Spotting a seat at the bar, she slid onto the vacant stool.

The guy next to her was working on a trio of fish tacos that looked mighty tempting, but she already knew what she wanted. Valerie picked up the table tent sitting next to a Tapatío bottle stuffed with toothpicks. Drink specials were advertised on one side – Margaritas, Piña Coladas, Mai Tais. She flipped the card over and there it was – the guacamole and chips she'd seen before, still for four-fifty. *Good.*

While waiting for him to come take her order, she studied the bartender. It was obvious the man worked out; or perhaps he was a paddler, like the guys she'd seen skimming across Hilo Bay that morning in sleek outrigger canoes. He definitely had the triangular body shape associated with a rower or swimmer.

Right now, his oversized arms were occupied with mashing limes, sugar, and mint leaves for a pitcher of Mojitos. He added cracked ice and dark rum, then set the pitcher and four glasses on a bar tray. 'Thanks, Kev,' the waitress said as she retrieved the order.

Ah-ha. So that was Daniel's buddy. He turned to Valerie with a bartender smile. 'What can I get you?'

'I'll have the special here,' she said, pointing to the folded piece of cardstock. 'With a small green salad, and a bottle of Pacífico.'

With a nod, Kevin turned and grabbed the beer from the cooler, popped its cap and placed a lime wedge on the lip, and set it down in front of Valerie.

She squeezed the lime and shoved it down the neck, then raised the bottle in salute. 'Cheers.' As she sipped the ice-cold beer, she watched Kevin clear the fish taco guy's plates and wipe errant grains of Spanish rice off the bar with a damp towel. Glancing up, he caught her staring and smiled again.

'So, where you visiting from?' he asked.

'Is it that obvious?'

'No, I just . . . Well, I haven't seen you in here before, and . . .'

Valerie laughed at his discomfort. 'It's okay. You're right; I'm here on vacation. But I am staying with someone who knows you, I think: Isaac Pinhero?'

'Isaac? Sure, we went to school together. Haven't seen him in a long time, though. Last I heard, he left the island to go to college somewhere.'

'He's a biology teacher at Hilo High, now.'

'Nice. Tell him I said hey.'

'Will do.'

The waitress waved Kevin over, and he left to take her bar order and make a round of Margaritas. After a few minutes, he returned, bearing Valerie's salad and guac and chips.

'Can I get you anything else?'

'No, thanks; this should be plenty.' The servings were

generous – something she'd noticed at all the restaurants she'd been to on the Big Island – and the chips looked thick and crispy, clearly homemade.

Kevin filled a glass with soda water and drank from it as he leaned against the back counter. Glancing around, Valerie saw that the bar had mostly cleared and the few customers still left had already been served. A good time to get on with it.

'So, wasn't it a friend of yours – Daniel – who was reported missing the other day?'

Kevin turned around to face her, his bartender smile now gone. 'That's right.' He didn't say it, but she could hear the implied 'And what's it to you?' in his voice.

But she was not to be so easily dissuaded. 'Isaac mentioned the article in the paper,' she lied – convincingly, she hoped – 'and said he knew you. He seemed kind of concerned about Daniel. And I can only imagine you must be, too. I mean, if it were my good friend who'd gone missing . . .'

Kevin shook his head. 'I'm not worried about Daniel. This isn't the first time he's gone AWOL.' Walking to the dishwasher, he dumped out the rest of his soda and set the glass in the peg rack. 'I'm sure he just had another fight with his wife, is all, and split for a while to cool off.'

'They fight a lot, I gather?'

She was afraid Kevin would be annoyed by the nosy questioning, but he merely snorted in response.

Valerie had always thought it utterly unbelievable the way people in those old mystery novels could poke their nose into everybody's business and how the villagers would act as if it were the most natural thing in the world. *But maybe it's not so unrealistic*, she mused, observing Kevin's reaction. *Maybe people simply have a real need to talk, even if it's a stranger doing the asking.*

And luckily, one trait she possessed in spades was the gift of talking up strangers and putting them at ease. Not for nothing were all those years she'd spent schmoozing with harried stagehands, nervous directors, and self-absorbed actors as they passed through the caterer's tent, fortifying themselves with her sumptuous buffets.

Encouraged, she pressed on. 'I take that as a yes?' she asked Kevin.

A guy two seats down spoke up. 'Faith – she don't deserve that name, 'cause she sure don't got much faith in her husband.' The man slapped his hand on the bar with a short laugh, downed the last of his Longboard lager, and motioned for another. 'Maybe it's that new job she got – listening too much to da stuffs they been saying down at the Mission store.'

Kevin chuckled and replaced the man's empty with a new bottle and then left to wait on two new bar customers. Extracting her phone from her pocket, Valerie opened the Yellow Pages app and typed in 'mission store pahoa.' There it was, the True Hope Mission thrift store, just a few blocks away. She glanced at the time. *Yes*, she mused as she finished her lunch. There was definitely time for a quick used-clothes shopping spree – with some sleuthing thrown in for good measure – before heading back to Isaac's.

Better hit the ladies' room first, though, after that beer. Valerie got the check from Kevin, paid, and headed back down the hallway where she'd seen the Pele's Children flyer two days earlier. A door into the kitchen was propped open and she glanced inside. The owner they'd met before, Ramón, stood at the stove stirring a large pot and talking to another man constructing a mammoth burrito. Distracted by the kitchen activity, she failed to notice in the dim light that a cart had been left out in the hall and, turning toward the restroom, whanged her shin on the corner of its bottom shelf.

She swore, then started to shove it impatiently into the kitchen. Having worked at her brother's restaurant, Valerie knew damn well that the cart – loaded with boxes of produce – had no business being out in the hallway. Ramón heard the commotion and hurried over, apologizing.

As he took the cart from her, she noticed the top box was full of avocados. She had just enough time before he wheeled the cart through the door to see that quite a few were missing their stems.

SEVEN

Valerie could spend an entire afternoon browsing a thrift store. Wandering through the racks checking out patterns and colors, fingering fabrics, pulling out a jacket to examine its design – she found the process soothing, meditative. Though it could be frustrating as well, since the number of shirts and slacks that fit her tiny frame was limited. She tended to have better luck in places that had a special 'petite' section, where she had a chance of finding shoes in size five and pants whose legs didn't require rolling up into cuffs.

There was, of course, no such section at the True Hope Mission thrift store. If, however, she'd been in the market for a Metallica T-shirt or a hot-pink *mu'umu'u*, now that would have been a different story.

The only clerk in the shop when she arrived was an elderly Asian lady with snow-white hair. Definitely too old to be Daniel's wife. But she could still look around.

After a disappointing perusal of the myriad polyester women's blouses, she turned her sights to a rack of Hawaiian shirts. She was hoping to bring one back home to California – something retro, with tikis, or grass shacks or ukuleles, or, better yet, all three.

Pulling out a specimen with blue and yellow tropical fish, she observed that it would have fit someone three times her size. She was about to put it back when a high-pitched voice called out, 'Sorry it took so long, Darlene, but the line was really long!' A woman whose girth was rather wide proportionate to her height set a plastic bag down by the cash register with a thump. 'And they were out of the beef, so I got you chicken. Hope that's okay.'

Valerie sidled down the rack of shirts, closer to the register.

'Oh, that's fine, dear. Thank you for going out.' Darlene – the white-haired lady – pulled a large to-go container out of the bag, and Valerie was hit by the powerful tang of garlic. Carrying the

box to the back of the store, she sat upon a rickety chair next to
the dressing room, broke apart a pair of wooden chopsticks and
began to take dainty bites of what looked to be some sort of
stir-fry.

The other, younger, woman smiled at Valerie. 'Hi. Can I help
you find anything?'

She held up the shirt in her hand. 'I'm looking for a Hawaiian
shirt, but they all seem humongous. Do you have any that would
fit me?'

'Oh, you're in the double-XL section; the medium and small
aloha shirts are over there.'

Ah, so they call them 'aloha' shirts here. It made sense, once
you thought about it – like how they're not called 'French fries'
in France.

'Thanks,' Valerie said, and followed the woman to the other
side of the rack, where another thirty or so brightly colored shirts
hung. 'Are you by any chance Faith?'

'Yeah, I am. How'd you know?'

'I was just having lunch at Raul's, and the bartender, Kevin,
sent me down here when he heard I was looking for a Hawai— I
mean, aloha shirt.' Two fibs in less than an hour. Did Hercule
Poirot find it necessary to tell so many lies? She couldn't remember.

'Oh,' said Faith. 'That was nice of him.' The quick frown told
Valerie she knew who Kevin was, and also suggested surprise
that he would do such a thing. Which, of course, he hadn't.

Valerie extracted from the smalls a violet, orange, and yellow
shirt bedecked with cocktail glasses of assorted styles, and immediately replaced it. Too tacky, even for her.

'I'm actually staying in Hilo with a friend of Kevin's. He told
me about your husband going missing.' Funny, how by simply
repeating this same story she was starting to believe it herself.
'I'm sorry to hear that.'

Faith was gazing out the open front door into the street, twisting
a strand of light brown hair around her finger. The emerging
roots revealed her true color to be a much darker shade. She
merely shrugged by way of response, so Valerie went on.

'He's been missing, what, four days now?'

The shopkeeper ceased her hair-twisting and turned to face
Valerie. 'So, what, you one of his girlfriends?'

'No, I told you: I'm staying with a friend who knows—'

''Cause I heard he's been hanging out with some *haole* girl, looks kinda like you. Though you're a bit old to be his type, I'd say,' she added with a snort.

'Gee, thanks. But, no, really. I've never even met Daniel.'

'Then why do you care so much about him?'

'Look,' Valerie said. 'Here's the deal. I was down at the lava flow Saturday morning, and I saw something there.'

'Uh-huh.' The hair-twisting was back now.

'It was a foot, wearing a leather boot – the kind construction workers wear – and part of a leg . . . being covered over by hot lava.'

'No way!' Faith exclaimed, then glanced back at the white-haired woman. She was still eating her lunch, however, and didn't appear to be paying any attention to their conversation. 'You really saw that?'

Valerie nodded. 'I really did.'

'Wow. That must-a been . . . intense.'

'It was.' Recounting the details of what she'd seen was bringing back some of Valerie's previous anxiety, but at the same time it was a relief to finally find someone who actually believed her story. 'So anyway, the next morning, I found out about Daniel's being missing and got to wondering if maybe it could have been him I saw.'

'Yeah, right.' Faith waved her off, just like the real estate agent had done earlier in the day regarding the BigT explosion. 'I mean, c'mon, what are the chances? Lots of people go missing 'round here – every day, it seems like. And besides, I know damn well he's just off with his new girlfriend somewheres.'

'When's the last time you saw him?'

'Friday morning. He'd just gotten home from work and I was on my way here.'

'I bet he wears boots, since he works at the geothermal plant.'

'Yeah . . .'

'Did they have green laces?'

'Huh?' Faith's look would have been no different had she asked if he was wearing a giraffe suit.

''Cause the boot I saw in the lava, it had bright-green laces.'

Faith shook her head. 'I don't think he had no green laces,

but then again, I never really noticed what color they were. Could be, I guess.'

'Was he acting weird Friday morning when you saw him?'

'You sure got a lotta questions, don't ya?'

'It's just that I'm worried about him.'

'Yeah, well you probably the only one, 'cause *I'm* sure not.' This time, the clerk eating at the back of the store looked up at the sound of Faith's raised voice, and the younger woman went on more quietly, but with equal emotion, 'I don't give a damn anymore where he is, or who he's with. He can go to hell, for all I care.'

'But aren't you the one who reported him missing?'

'Sure I was, but that was only so the cops would find him and drag his sorry ass away from that *haole* girl. I am so sick of hearing about his fooling around, how he can't ever keep his pants zipped up.' She was gripping the clothes rack so hard her knuckles were turning white. 'And I'm not the only one feels that way. He got beat up good last week by one of the husbands.' Her laugh was sharp, like a terrier's bark. 'Dunno what the guy said to him, but I never seen Daniel so scared as after that.'

'Who was it beat him up?'

'Who knows? There's a lotta people would like to see the last of him.' Seeing another customer approach the register with an armful of clothes, she laughed again and left Valerie to go ring up the sale.

That night, Valerie, Kristen, and Isaac retired to the lānai for after-dinner drinks. It was just the three of them again: Sachiko still hadn't given Isaac an answer about moving in and appeared to be maintaining radio silence pending her decision.

'I stopped at a fruit stand today,' Valerie said as they settled into the cushions of Isaac's wicker furniture. 'That's where I bought those amazing avocados for the salad tonight. Sharwils, the woman said they were called. I've never seen them on the Mainland.'

Kristen swatted a mosquito that had landed on her forearm and flicked away its remains. 'Val's in avo heaven,' she said. 'We might just have to leave her here permanently.'

'Not such a bad idea.' Unbuttoning the top of her new shirt

from the True Hope Mission thrift store – no tikis, alas, but it did have cool petroglyph designs of sea turtles and outrigger canoes – Valerie began to fan herself with an *East Hawai'i Dining Guide*. 'Though it might take a while to get used to this humidity.'

Isaac smiled. 'Well, that salad was a great combo,' he said. 'I've never had avocados with grapefruit before. And what was in that dressing?'

'Let's see . . . yogurt, papaya, honey, apple cider vinegar, lime, oil . . .' Valerie ticked off the ingredients on her fingers. 'Oh, and a smidgen of cumin, too. Just throw it all in the blender for a few seconds till it's creamy.'

'Sounds easy enough. I'll have to make it for Sachiko sometime.'

Silence.

Valerie cleared her throat and reached for her gin and lime atop the bamboo table. 'So, speaking of avocados . . .' Ignoring Kristen's chortle, she took a sip and continued. 'The fruit-stand woman told me there's been a rash of avocado thefts down in Puna lately. "Cock-roaching," she called it.'

'Yah, that's the local slang,' Isaac said.

'It's good; I like it.' Having beheld the size of the actual insects in Isaac's kitchen, the euphemism struck Valerie as apt. She could well imagine one of the two-inch-long creatures making off with an entire loaf of bread. 'Anyway, she said her neighbor recently even went out and bought a gun to protect his trees.'

Isaac nodded vigorously. 'For *realz*, it's a big problem down Puna side these days. They're worth *uku* plenty those avocados. Especially this time of year, when there aren't so many varieties in season. So I'm not surprised about a guy getting a gun. I've heard more than one story of people taking the law into their own hands, since the police haven't been able to do much about the problem so far.'

'Huh.' Sipping her drink, Valerie listened to the coquí as they tuned up for their nightly performance. The locals despised these tiny frogs – recent stowaways from Puerto Rico that had multiplied beyond number in their newfound Hawaiian home – but she found their sound charming.

'A minor seventh,' Kristen had observed the first night they arrived, imitating the rising two-note song for which the frogs were named: 'Koh-*kee*. That's what they mostly seem to do. Though sometimes they manage to make it all the way up the octave.' The sometime guitarist for a garage band back home in LA, she had a good ear for this sort of thing.

With the coquí as their background music, the three sat quietly. A gentle rain began to fall, resulting in an immediate increase in the number and volume of the frogs' voices, the rhythmic pitter-pat on the metal roof adding a percussion section to their evening's concert.

'I think I might know who's been stealing those avocados,' Valerie said after a few minutes, but so softly that neither Kristen nor Isaac seemed to hear.

EIGHT

Hilo is perhaps best known outside of Hawai'i for its farmers market, which is written up in all the Big Island guidebooks and glossy tourist magazines. On its big days – Wednesdays and Saturdays – the colorful and vibrant outdoor market has over a hundred vendors hawking a variety of products wildly exotic to those visiting from the Mainland: pungent tropical fruits, eye-popping anthuriums and orchids, odd-shaped Asian vegetables, Kona coffee and Japanese teas, fresh-baked Portuguese sweet bread, pad Thai noodles and Peruvian tamales, Puna goat cheese, local jams and macadamia nut blossom honey. And with plenty of free samples to boot, it's something definitely not to be missed.

By the time Valerie and Kristen arrived there a little after eight the next morning, Wednesday, the market had been going for over two hours and the crush of people was intense. Dodging a mud puddle at the entrance to the tarp-covered area, they stopped at the first booth, which displayed a host of brightly colored fruits.

Valerie pointed to a pile of shaggy red balls reminiscent of the sea anemones they'd seen snorkeling down at the Kapoho tidepools. 'What are those?' she asked the moon-faced man behind the table.

'Rambutan,' he answered. 'Like lychee. Here, you try.' Selecting one from the pile, he ripped off half of its spiny red skin to expose a rounded white center and offered it to her.

She'd expected the spines to be sharp, but they were soft and pliable. Raising the fruit to her nose, Valerie inhaled its sweet and floral scent. She took a cautious nibble – a bit like a grape, but with more of that heady floral flavor so typical of tropical fruit.

'Huh, interesting. Tarter than I expected. And those – what are they?' She pointed to an oblong yellow-green fruit with protruding fins.

'I know that one,' Kristen said. 'It's star fruit.'

The vendor picked up a knife to cut into the waxy skin, and Valerie immediately discerned the reason for its name: the slice he handed her made a perfect five-point star.

'Oh, let's get some! It would be beautiful in a fruit salad. How much?'

'Three for a dollar,' the man said. 'You need a bag?'

'No, thanks, we've got our own.' She paid him and then chose three of the largest star fruit from the pile, placing them carefully into one of the canvas bags Isaac had loaned them. Thanking the man for his help and the samples, Valerie turned and followed Kristen down the crowded aisle to a stall towards the back of the market.

'Hallo!' called out a diminutive woman arranging a row of pineapples. She had a swath of ebony hair and her olive complexion set off a row of perfect white teeth. 'What you want today?'

Valerie held up a packet of flat green beans. 'How much for these?'

'Two dollah,' the woman answered in a nasal, high-pitched voice, and took the beans from Valerie. Grabbing two more packets, she dropped them all into a plastic bag. 'You take three fo' five dollah. I give you dis too,' she added, setting a bunch of overripe apple bananas on top of the green beans and holding the bag out to them.

Valerie glanced at Kristen and laughed. They had dubbed this woman 'the bossy lady' on their visit to the market the previous Friday, after being coerced by her into buying two heads of lettuce, four avocados, and a pineapple, when all they'd wanted was a couple of cucumbers.

'Isaac told me to be sure to get some tomatoes,' Kristen said over her shoulder, accepting the proffered beans and bananas. 'Three for five dollars for these, too?' She held up a baggie of plump cherry tomatoes.

'No,' the woman answered with an emphatic toss of her hair. 'Two dollah each.'

While Kristen settled up with the bossy lady, Valerie peered at the avocados stacked into a pyramid at her stall. 'They all have stems,' she commented as they headed around the corner past the tamale stand and back up the other aisle.

Kristen stopped in front of a table spilling over with papayas. A piece of cardboard with '6 x $2.00' scrawled on it lay atop the fruit. 'Here,' she said, handing Valerie the bag with produce in it. 'Whad'ya mean, "they all have stems"?'

She told Kristen what the fruit-stand lady had said the day before about stemless avocados probably being stolen, and how she'd seen a box of avocados like that at Raul's.

Kristen gave the man at the stall two dollar bills and opened their other canvas bag. Valerie watched as she carefully picked out papayas – some ripe, some still green for later in the week.

'So anyway,' she went on, 'I'm thinking maybe the avocado thefts down in Puna might be related to Daniel's disappearance.'

Kristen made no response and Valerie wondered if perhaps she hadn't heard. Completing her selection, she set down the heavy bag, narrowly missing a puddle, then turned to face Valerie. Her exasperated expression made clear she had.

'Okay, Val,' she started, but never got to finish the thought. Which was probably just as well.

'Eh! Howzit?'

Valerie turned at the voice. It took a moment, but then she realized it was the woman from the Orchid Drive-In – Trevor's friend, the one with the Hawai'i tattoo down her arm. though a pale-blue T-shirt was covering most of the northern islands today. *What was her name again?*

'Jordan,' she said, as if reading Valerie's thoughts. 'We met the other day, down in Pāhoa.'

'Oh, right,' said Kristen. 'Good to see you again. What brings you up here to Hilo?'

Jordan held up three bags bulging with produce.

'Okay, dumb question.'

'So how was the kālua pork the other night?' Valerie asked. 'And the papaya chutney?'

'We didn't end up eating till pretty late 'cause I got such a late start, but it was great. You should-a been there.'

'As I recall, I did request an invitation.'

Jordan laughed. 'Right. Well, we'll have to do that sometime. I also make a really *'ono kine* mahi mahi, cut into steaks and then fried with butter and 'bout a pound of ginger and garlic.'

'Oh, man, that sounds amazing. I wish someone would cook that for me.' They'd eaten breakfast just an hour ago, yet Valerie found herself salivating like a half-starved dog.

'So, what, you don't ever cook da fish for her?'

This was directed at Kristen, who laughed. 'I'm not that great in the kitchen. That runs in Valerie's family.'

'Oh, yeah?' Jordan looked back at Valerie, this time with more interest.

'Well, my brother owns . . .' She stopped, then cleared her throat. 'Owned a restaurant in Los Angeles, but he . . . well . . .'

Kristen came to her rescue. 'And Val's grandfather was from a restaurant family back in France – a seafood place. They've been fishermen and restaurant owners for generations.'

Now Valerie really had Jordan's attention. 'Oh, yeah? So, you into fishing, too?'

'Sure, kind of. I'm not an expert or anything, and I haven't done it in years, but I used to fish sometimes with my *grand-père* when he was still alive.'

Jordan set her bags down. 'Well, hey. I got an idea. I'm goin' down to Pohoiki tomorrow morning, gonna do some cliff fishing. You two maybe wanna ride down with me and check it out? See some of the real Hawai'i while you're here?'

'Oooh, that sounds fun,' Valerie said with a glance at her wife. 'I read about that in a book Isaac has – how the local style of fishing is totally different from the way they do it back home. It'd be cool to get to see it in person. What do you think, Kristen?'

'I dunno,' she said. 'I'm not that into fishing . . .'

'She's more of a surfer chick,' Valerie explained.

'Ho, there's awesome surfing down there, too, girl. Some of the best on the island.'

'You got room for my board?'

'No worry, beef curry – my car's plenty big.' Jordan slapped Kristen on the shoulder. 'Let's meet at the Orchid Drive-In at six. That too early for you?'

Kristen sighed, but said 'Fine.'

''Kay, den. See ya tomorrow.'

'Thanks, hon,' Valerie said to Kristen once Jordan was out of earshot. ''Cause you know I wouldn't have agreed to go unless you went along, too.'

'Well, it's good to hear you haven't completely lost track of your senses.' Kristen grinned as she picked up the bag of papayas. 'But you owe me one.'

After an early dinner at home that night – teriyaki chicken, sautéed green beans, sticky rice, and fruit salad – Valerie, Kristen, and Isaac drove downtown for the hula show. As Isaac had predicted, Sachiko had declined the invitation to join them, choosing to spend the evening by herself at her apartment. 'I guess she jus' gotta do her own thing,' was all he would say of her absence.

Although there was plenty of daylight when they left Isaac's house, it was dusk by the time they found a place to park along the Bayfront. Valerie had noticed that the sun set much faster in Hawai'i than in California. According to Isaac, this was because the sun's trajectory in the tropics is nearly perpendicular to the horizon. In other words, it goes straight down, rather than at an angle as it does in California, so sunsets happen a lot more quickly. As a result, when the three of them turned the corner and walked up Haili Street, it was already dark enough that the neon sign above the theater entrance was ablaze in green and orange.

Valerie got in line at the will-call window while Kristen and Isaac milled about with the others in the lobby waiting to go into the auditorium. A large woman in a purple and white *mu'umu'u* waved at Isaac and left her group to come over to give him a hug. They were still chatting when Valerie joined them with the tickets.

'This is Luana,' Isaac said. 'She was my *kumu hula* – my hula teacher – back when I still danced.'

'I was just telling Kristen that Isaac was one of my best students.' Luana shook Valerie's hand and then turned to slap Isaac on the arm. 'But I'm still angry with him for quitting when he did.'

'Ow! It's only because da teacher, she so *mean*!' Isaac made a show of rubbing his arm and then leaned over to plant a kiss on Luana's cheek, prompting a toothy smile from her.

'Are you the teacher for the group that's dancing tonight?' Valerie asked.

'Oh, no. My *hālau* isn't nearly as . . .' She paused, searching for the right word.

'Activist?' Valerie volunteered.

'Well, I was going to say something more like "political," but I guess that word works. We concentrate more just on the dancing aspect, though, of course, we do plenty of traditional hulas featuring stories about Pele and the other ancient gods.'

'Yeah, I read about Pele's Children online,' Valerie said. 'They seem pretty militant about the whole geothermal thing.' She was trying to keep her voice down, but given how loud it was in the lobby with so many people talking at once, she probably didn't need to worry. 'So what do you think – is it really all that bad? I mean, it seems to me anyway, using steam that's naturally generated by volcanic activity is actually a pretty green way to produce energy.'

'It's not about whether it's green or not to them,' Isaac jumped in. 'It's about what they perceive as disrespecting Pele, and the spiritual practices of the native Hawaiians. It's the same reason they're opposed to building that new Thirty Meter Telescope on top of Maunakea – because they see it as the desecration of one of their most sacred sites.'

'But you're a scientist,' interjected Kristen. 'You don't believe all that, do you?'

'No, I don't personally believe it. I'm just saying I get where they're coming from. Don't you, Luana?'

'I'm almost half Hawaiian,' she answered. 'So, yeah, of course I do. When you look at what's happened to Hawai'i since Captain Cook landed here – the decimation of the native people, and the ones that are left own hardly any of the land anymore. Not to mention the spread of Christianity, which pretty much wiped out the ancient religion – have you seen how many churches there are in Hilo alone?'

Valerie, who had commented on this very thing to Kristen, nodded.

'So I'm not at all surprised that some people feel it necessary to take a stand, draw a line in the black sand, so to speak. But . . .' She raised a forefinger for emphasis. 'That said, I also have to add that I personally think geothermal is a good thing. Did you know that King David Kalākaua – the "Merrie Monarch" that these same people revere as the savior of Hawaiian culture – was fascinated with the idea of geothermal energy? I read somewhere that he even visited Thomas Edison in New York to talk about it.'

'Wow, I didn't know that,' said Isaac.

'And he was right. Why shouldn't we be able to use the geothermal resources we have, right here on-island, to reduce our dependence on imported oil? Or, God forbid, something like fracking?'

'But isn't it dangerous?' Valerie asked. 'I read about an explosion at the new plant last week.'

'Well, I don't know anything about any recent explosion. But, yes, back in the eighties, when the first plant opened, there were problems – they let gases escape and there were some accidents, too. But the technology's changed since then. They used to use an open cycle for the process, but now it's a closed one and all the gases are pumped back into the earth. So it's way more safe now.'

'You seem to know a lot about it,' Kristen observed.

Luana laughed. 'Yeah, well, you're not the first people to ask me about geothermal. It's kind of a hot topic these days, and being a *kumu hula*, everyone just assumes I'm against it. So I thought I'd better do my homework and actually learn something about the subject.'

She looked up as a lithe young man in a red skirt-like garment dashed through the lobby with a wave in their direction. 'Aloha, Aunty!' he said as he passed by.

'Aloha, Keoni – I missed you Friday night!' she called out after him, and then leaned closer to Isaac, Kristen, and Valerie. 'He's one of the more political types in Pele's Children we were talking about before. He dances with my *hālau*, as well. Though he didn't manage to show up for our performance last week, the little brat.'

'He's sporting quite the shiner tonight,' Kristen observed. 'Did you see his eye?'

'Huh,' said Luana. 'I didn't. But maybe it's instant karma for his no-show.'

'Is he your nephew?' Valerie asked, prompting a laugh from Isaac.

'Aunty is a term of respect and endearment here,' he explained. 'She's *my* aunty, too,' he added, wrapping his arm around Luana's generous waist.

The crowd started to move into the auditorium.

'Oops – I'd better get back to my people.' Luana kissed Isaac on the cheek and turned to go. 'But we can talk more afterwards. Are you staying for the reception?'

'Free pog and cookies? You kiddin'?' Isaac stuck out his belly and patted it. 'Wouldn't miss it!'

NINE

'Pog?' Valerie asked as they found their seats.

'We had it on the airplane,' Kristen said. 'Remember that super-sweet juice? It stands for passion-orange-guava.'

'It's sort of like our national beverage,' added Isaac. 'But I gotta say I prefer it cut with some dark rum.'

After an opening act of an ukulele trio performing a mix of traditional Hawaiian and jazz-influenced songs, it was time for the main event. A man wearing a loincloth came out from behind the wings with a large gourd and sat down cross-legged on the wooden floor. Valerie recognized the instrument as one of the *ipu* drums she'd seen on the Pele's Children website.

He was followed by a woman in a floor-length skirt and billowy blouse. Sweeping her long blond hair out of the way, she stepped up to the microphone that had been set up stage left.

'Aloha, everyone, and welcome to this performance by *Hālau Kā Pelehonuamea Keiki* – Pele's Children. You are in for a real treat, as I can tell you these dancers are magnificent!'

Everyone applauded as a troupe of six men and six women walked out on stage, hands on hips, and formed two lines. The women wore strapless red-and-yellow knee-length dresses with dark-green ti-leaf skirts on top, and the men were clad in puffy red loincloths, their chests bare. Garlands of some sort of dark-green leaves were draped about the dancers' necks and heads, as well as tied to their wrists and ankles.

Valerie looked for Keoni and spotted him in the center of the back row, between two much heftier men.

'The first dance tonight is a traditional hula *kahiko* – in the ancient style – called *Aia Lā 'O Pele I Hawai'i*,' the announcer said, 'which means "Pele is in Hawai'i." Watch the dancers' movements, and you will see fiery explosions and then torrents of molten lava as they pour down the cliffs towards the sea, consuming all that is in Pele's path. But then, at the end of the dance, notice how gentle and calm the gestures become. For we must not forget that the result of this destructive force is the creation of new lands, and that Madame Pele is both destroyer and creator, personifying the eternal cycle of birth, death, and rebirth.'

With a nod to the seated percussionist, she left the stage, and the man began to chant in Hawaiian, his voice rising and falling in a sonorous baritone. After a few phrases, he commenced pounding the gourd on the floor and slapping it with his hand, establishing a rhythmic cadence. The *hālau* began to move as one, stepping with bare feet and swaying their hips in time to the chant and the beat of the *ipu* drum.

Valerie couldn't, of course, understand any of the words being chanted, but it was easy to tell what was going on. First, the men, wearing fearsome expressions, stamped their feet and shook their fists towards the sky, punctuating their movements with lusty shouts in unison. This was obviously the fountaining of the volcano – with some not too subtle sexual overtones thrown in for good measure. Watching their muscular bodies twist and gyrate, she had to admit that the volcano wasn't the only thing that was pretty hot. Kristen had been right, she thought with a smile.

Then it was the women's turn, their dance representing the river of hot lava as it coursed downhill. Valerie leaned forward, captivated by the flowing crimson-and-yellow cloth and the quick but fluid gestures. It was as if they had truly become the lava flow. And then, in a flash, she was back there, inhaling the acrid fumes as the molten rock crackled and hissed its way over the coastal plain. An image of a burning leather boot swam before her eyes. The heat was so intense . . .

'You okay?' Isaac touched her shoulder as the dance came to a close, and Valerie started. 'You looked like you were about to pass out,' he said over the applause.

Leaning back in her seat, she realized she was sweating like crazy and her hands and face were clammy. 'It's just that it's kinda warm in here, is all,' she said, wiping her palms on her pant-legs.

'Yeah, it can get awful hot and stuffy in dis old building. Here, wait a sec.' Isaac jumped up and, climbing over Kristen's legs, darted down the aisle and out into the lobby. He was back almost immediately and handed Valerie a fan – one of those round paper ones on a stick that you sometimes see prim ladies using in the courthouse or theater in old movies.

Laughing, she took it from him. 'Why, thank you kindly,' she said in her best Southern voice and began fanning herself in what she imagined to be a genteel manner. They all hushed as the next hula began, but though Valerie continued to smile, the disquiet that had settled over her remained.

The *hālau* performed several more dances before coming to the finale, the hula she'd read about on their website. By that time, Valerie had recovered enough to be able to sit up and pay close attention – to both the performers and the audience. She wanted to see if any had particularly strong reactions to what she knew was coming.

The woman with long blond hair walked back out on stage. 'This last chant,' she said, 'is *Ke ha'a lā Puna*, which tells how Pele's younger sister, Hi'iaka, is taught the hula by her best friend Hōpoe, and how they dance together on Hā'ena Beach in Puna.'

She then recounted the story Valerie had read online, of the vengeance the jealous Pele takes on her younger sister – whom she suspects of attempting to steal away Pele's betrothed – by covering Hi'iaka's cherished forest with lava and turning her beloved friend to stone. 'So let this hula be a lesson to us all,' the announcer concluded, 'for in the very same way, when we allow geothermal development in Puna, we are stealing from Pele her lifeblood and her fiery breath, and violating her spirit and creative force.'

She paused, her severe eyes surveying the now-still audience. 'And who knows,' she went on in a lowered voice, 'what wrath we risk unleashing if these geothermal people are not stopped. We must therefore take whatever steps necessary to prevent this desecration. Now.'

Steps such as taking on the role of Pele? Valerie wondered. *And turning someone to stone by placing their body in the path of an active lava flow?*

There was a smattering of applause, but most in attendance, she observed, did not seem to be in agreement with the sentiment expressed, and a fair number were shifting in their seats uncomfortably. Glancing around the theater, Valerie did catch two of the dancers – Keoni, she noted with interest, as well as one of the women – nodding sympathetically, and from a section at the very front of the audience came a few shouts of agreement. She couldn't see any of this group's faces, so she tried to commit to memory the fabric of their shirts and blouses. Perhaps she could talk to them, or at least eavesdrop on their conversation, after the show.

Notwithstanding this heavy-handed introduction, the dance itself was a perfect finale – showcasing the blend of grace and athleticism Valerie now realized was at the heart of the hula – and the audience showed its pleasure by jumping to their feet and yelling and clapping like mad when it was over. The announcer walked back out on stage, accompanied by the ukulele trio who had opened the show.

'Mahalo, everyone! Thank you so much! Now, because of your great enthusiasm, for an encore we're going to invite any of you who know *Ka Uluwehi O Ke Kai* – the Seaweed Dance – to come up and join us in a communal hula.'

'Ho, I know dat one!' Isaac jumped up once more, squeezed past Kristen, and joined the dozen or so others from the audience who had kicked off their slippahs and shoes and climbed on stage.

They were a diverse bunch – several hesitant children urged on by their parents; a scrawny hippie with a shaggy beard and white Nehru-collared shirt; a number of young local women with gleaming black hair; two tiny Japanese ladies who needed assistance with the stairs; and Isaac. With his khaki shorts, dagger tattoo peeking out from his rolled up sleeve, and wide smile exposing his gold tooth, he reminded Valerie of a mischievous schoolboy.

The trio began to strum their instruments and sing, the man on the biggest ukulele crooning high above the others in a soaring falsetto. Following the lead of the *hālau*, the dancers from the audience stepped back and forth in time to the music. An ocean of arms accompanied their steps, evoking a forest of kelp drifting to and fro in a gentle sea.

Valerie watched Isaac. He clearly knew the hula well and, rather than look to the other dancers for direction, gazed confidently out into the hall. Crouching, executing quick scissor moves with his knees and then turning, his hips and upper body remained fluid and smooth.

How strong you'd have to be to do that, she thought, a bit awestruck by the muscles she could see flexing in his calves. *And to keep the rest of your body so relaxed at the same time.* As she watched, Isaac caught her looking and winked. Then, with a grin, he spun around with the rest of the *hālau* to face the other direction.

'Told you there'd be pog!' Isaac strode to the long table that had been set up in the theater lobby, grabbed a fluorescent orange drink, and drained it in three successive gulps. 'Guess I worked up some kinda thirst dancing in those hot lights up there.'

Picking up one of the paper cups, Valerie took a sip and was surprised by the drink's flavor. The juice on the plane had tasted like fruit-infused sugar syrup, but the tartness of the guava in this one did a good job of cutting the sweet pineapple and orange. She found she actually kind of liked the stuff.

Kristen joined them with a plate of white-frosted cookies decorated with pink sprinkles. 'Want one?'

'No, thanks,' Valerie said, waving them off. 'I might go into sucrose-shock if I did.'

Isaac helped himself to a cookie, and while he and Kristen munched the sugary confections and washed them down with their pog, Valerie scanned the lobby for the fabrics she'd committed to memory during the performance. *There – over in the alcove by the women's room – wasn't that the madras shirt of one of the guys she'd seen applauding the announcer's diatribe?* He was talking to a young Japanese-looking man and a *haole* woman with frizzy hair and a tie-dyed tank top. They were standing, she noted with interest, apart from everyone else in the lobby.

'Be back in a sec,' Valerie said, and made her way over to the threesome. Situating herself on the opposite side of a wide pillar, she was hidden from view but could still hear what they were saying.

'. . . in our own backyards now,' one of the men was saying. 'I don't know what we're gonna do about the buggahs.'

'Next thing you know, they'll be all over the island,' said the woman.

Aha! Very interesting. She resisted the urge to peek around the pillar.

'We got to stop 'um now, before it's too late.' This was the other man.

'But how?' asked the woman. 'What, we gonna poison them all?' She let out a sarcastic snort.

Whoa. Valerie held her breath, hoping they wouldn't notice her listening. *Was Daniel poisoned and then dumped down at the lava flow?*

'I don't think that's necessary,' said the first man. 'There are other less drastic ways to do it.' A pause. She thought at first it was for dramatic effect, but then she heard him take a drink of pog. 'I heard about a citrus-based spray that kills fire ants, kind of like the stuff they use for the coquí. You can get it at . . .'

Damn. With a sigh, Valerie started to head back over to Isaac and Kristen, who had now been joined by Isaac's *kumu hula*, Luana, and another woman. Halfway there, though, she spied the young dancer with the black eye, who had emerged in street clothes – board shorts and a white T-shirt. *Keoni – that was the name Luana had called him.* He was near the concessions window, talking with several other guys who were fellow dancers, from their looks. Keoni laughed and turned in Valerie's direction, and she saw that his shirt had a flag on the front – the green- yellow- and red-striped Hawaiian sovereignty flag, which Isaac had pointed out to her that day he took them down to Puna.

Changing direction, she crossed the room and pretended to study the menu items chalked on a board next to their group. Since they were standing out in the open, she couldn't get too close without being obvious and had to settle for hearing just snippets of their conversation.

'. . . got you good,' a man in a tight black shirt was saying. This was followed by raucous laughter and one of the other guys pointing to his eye.

Keoni clearly didn't think it funny, however. '. . . da oddah guy,' she heard him say, '. . . not so good aftah.'

Valerie couldn't make out anything more for a while. The combination of Pidgin, the loud room, and the distance between them was just too much. Then, out of what had been sounding like pure gibberish, she heard Keoni say, quite clearly, 'TNT.' His friends laughed again.

More unintelligible words – the group had lowered their voices – and then in answer to something about 'Where?' she heard Keoni answer: 'Down da hot lava.'

A shiver flashed from her shoulders down to her gut. Why would he be talking about explosives? Try as she might, however, Valerie couldn't understand anything else, and when she saw one of them staring at her, she chickened out and made her way back to Kristen and Isaac.

'Where's Luana?' she asked. She was dying to tell her what Keoni had said.

Isaac jabbed a thumb in the direction of the street. 'She just left. Said she had to get home to a sick husband.'

'Speaking of getting home, we've got that early fishing date tomorrow.' Kristen reached across the table and grabbed the last cookie off the plate. 'So, perhaps we should be getting a move on, too?'

'Sure, I'm ready.' With one last look at Keoni and his pals, Valerie followed Kristen and Isaac outside into the balmy Hilo night.

TEN

Kristen headed straight for bed as soon as they got home, but when Valerie suggested a nightcap to Isaac, he readily agreed. 'Let's go sit out on the grass where we can see the night sky,' he said as they mixed their drinks. 'It's not so often we get a clear night like dis in Hilo.'

Taking deck chairs from the lānai, they set them up in their reclining position and leaned back to stargaze. The display wasn't as spectacular as it had been down at the lava flow – Hilo does have its fair share of light pollution – but Valerie was still easily able to make out the Milky Way, something she could never do back home in Los Angeles.

'You know the names of the constellations?' she asked. 'I've been looking for Orion – he's easy, because of his belt – but I don't see it up tonight.'

'Some of them, I do. I should really learn more, though, since I got Hawaiian blood in me. Those ancient Hawaiians, they *really* knew their stars – 'course, they had to, since that's how they navigated. It's amazing when you think about how they were able to travel thousands of miles, back and forth between Polynesia and Hawai'i, in these little canoes, using just their knowledge of astronomy and the ocean swells. Man . . .' Isaac shook his head and drank from his gin and tonic. 'I can't even imagine doing something like dat.'

They stared at the stars, not speaking. Valerie inhaled the spicy perfume of Isaac's pink plumeria tree, carried across the lawn by a gentle breeze. It hadn't rained all day, so the coquí were more subdued than normal, but there was still plenty of chirping coming from the plants surrounding Isaac's yard. The only other sounds were an occasional car and the sporadic barking of a neighbor's dog.

'What's that constellation there?' Valerie asked after a few minutes, pointing straight up. 'It looks kind of like a kite.'

'Au right, I actually know that one,' Isaac said. 'It's Boötes.'

'Booties? Like baby shoes?'

He laughed. 'No, it's Dutch or something, I dunno what it means. But definitely *not* a shoe. I can tell you about the Hawaiian name, though – *Hōkūʻiwa*. '*Hōkū* means star, and *iwa* is some kind of sea bird.'

'Way more pretty than "boo-tees." Which actually sounds kind of rude, when you think about it.' Valerie reached for her glass and took a sip. 'So, do kids here learn the Hawaiian names of stars and stuff in school?'

'Nah. At least I didn't. Sachiko's into astronomy, and she taught me what little I know.'

'Oh.' She took another drink. 'Hey, look – isn't that the Big Dipper?'

'Yah, *Nāhiku* – one of the other ones I know.'

'So, um, how's it going with Sachiko, anyway? If you don't mind talking about it, that is . . .'

'No, that's okay.' A pause. 'Not so great, really. I tried calling her after work but she didn't pick up, an' she still hasn't called me back, even though I left a long message. So, I don't know . . .'

'Maybe she forgot to charge her phone?'

'Maybe.' He picked up his glass and drained it. 'I'm gonna make another. You want one?'

'Sure.' While he went into the kitchen to get the drinks, Valerie settled back in her chair and stared up at the thousands of bright pinpricks piercing the inky sky. How decadent it felt to be outside at night in just a halter-top and shorts, the air heavy with earthy smells, the light breeze tickling her skin. This was clearly the climate that humans were meant to live in.

She started at the touch of a frosty glass laid against her bare shoulder. Isaac chuckled. Jingling the ice in her gin and lime, he handed it to her and then plopped down in his deck chair.

'So, it seems like you and Kristen are having some sort of relationship issue, too,' he said once he was resettled in his chair. 'You wanna talk about it?'

She took a long drink before answering. 'I doubt you need to hear anyone else's problems right about now.'

'No, really. I'm interested.' Isaac turned to face her, but it was too dark to make out his expression. 'Who knows, maybe I could learn something from what's going on with you two. After all, you've been married, what, five years now?'

'Well, we only got officially married three years ago – after it was legalized by the Supreme Court. But we've been together for twelve years.'

'Ho, long time! So you really could give me some advice, then.'

'Hah,' Valerie said with a snort. 'I'm not so sure about that.' She leaned forward and plucked at a blade of grass, but being a sort of Bermuda variety, the entire runner came up in her hands. Breaking it off at its roots, she tossed it aside. 'It's mostly 'cause of what happened to my brother, I guess. He's the one who introduced us, actually – when Kristen was working on a remodel at his restaurant.'

'Yeah, Kristen told me about him and about the car crash. That has to have been just awful.'

'It was. And is. Charlie and I had always been really close, and after I started working at his restaurant, we became even closer. Besides Kristen, he was the only one I could really talk to about stuff. And now, it's like there's this hole in my soul . . .' Valerie trailed off.

Isaac let the silence hang in the dark, starry night, and after a moment, Valerie took a sip from her glass and went on. 'It just happened all so fast. One minute he's there and the next, he's . . . gone. And I guess, I dunno, I can't help feeling . . .'

'Guilty? For being the one who survived?'

Valerie fingered another strand of grass. 'Yeah, I suppose. Even though I know it's not logical.'

'Emotions like that rarely are. But that doesn't mean they're any less real in your head.'

They sat for a moment, then Isaac said quietly, 'And I take it his death has affected your relationship with Kristen?'

'Yeah . . .' It came out more as an exhalation than an actual word. 'I mean, I get that this whole thing's been hard on her, too. And she's never been that great at expressing her emotions, so it can take a while for her to process stuff.' Valerie let out a short laugh. 'Not that I've been super great at opening up lately, either. I feel like some kind of protective wall just suddenly sprang up inside me after Charlie's death, and the only way I've been able to communicate my feelings is when I have some sort of crazy outburst, which is what happened the other day at Hāpuna Beach when we got into that argument.'

Picking up her glass, she fished out a piece of ice and crunched it. 'Anyway, as for Kristen, I know it's not fair to just assume she understands everything that's going on in my head. And she clearly realizes how much Charlie meant to me. His death has been hard on her, too. It's just that we need to talk about it more – really talk. But it's hard. Especially when she gets, you know . . .'

'You mean when she acts like a total know-it-all?' Isaac finished in a rather loud voice.

'Shhh!' Valerie cupped her hand over his mouth and giggled. 'Our room's right over there,' she said in a stage whisper. 'But I can't imagine *how* you could have possibly figured that out,' she added right as Isaac took a drink, which prompted a fit of laughing and coughing on his part.

'Yah, I seen her do that,' he said once his throat had settled down. 'Only like a hundred times. Did you know when we first met out dere in the water that day in Malibu, she actually tried to tell me – a guy who grew up surfing in Hawai'i – about how to read da waves?'

'Ha! I'm not surprised. I mean, I know she only tends to do it when she is in fact right – not that you *didn't* know how to read the waves that day,' Valerie added quickly, prompting another laugh from Isaac. 'But she can be so bossy about stuff sometimes. Like about my trying to learn more about that body I saw in the lava. She acts as if I'm crazy for wanting to figure it out, but if you were in my place, wouldn't you want to?'

''Course. Anyone would.'

'Anyone but Kristen, apparently.' Valerie drummed her fingers on the wooden arm of the deck chair. 'You know what the problem is, of course. We've got the perfect storm going on: her being annoyed by my wanting to figure out who that body was, and me being annoyed with her for being so controlling. It's kinda guaranteed to cause a conflict.'

'So, speaking of your investigation, did you discover anything else about this Daniel guy when you were down in Puna yesterday?'

'A little.' Valerie told him what she'd learned from Kevin and Faith, about Daniel being a known philanderer. 'But I'm not sure that alone would be enough for somebody to kill him and dump his body down at the lava flow.'

'Guys have been killed for a lot less,' Isaac said.

'You think they could be killed for stealing avocados?'

He chuckled. 'I know I said it's been a problem, but I doubt it's come to killing people over it. They're not *that* valuable, da pears.'

'But what if it was an accident – someone just meant to scare the thief off by firing a gun, but he gets hit by the shot and dies? And then the guy who owns the orchard freaks out and decides to get rid of the body.'

'I suppose . . .'

''Cause I did see those avocados without stems down at Raul's. Kevin and Daniel could have been in it together. You know, Daniel does the raiding of the orchards, and Kevin – since he works at the restaurant – acts as distributor? But then Daniel gets caught in the act, and is shot and killed.'

'Maybe.' Isaac did not seem convinced.

'Okay, I have another theory.' Valerie sat up and turned to face Isaac. 'You know how we talked earlier with Luana about all the people on the island who are against geothermal? And remember how Trevor said that Daniel was a night watchman at BigT?'

'Uh-huh . . .'

'So, check this out.' She recounted what she'd heard after the hula performance, about Keoni talking about explosives and hot lava. 'And this is the guy Luana said was one of the anti-geothermal activists, and she also said he'd missed their performance last Friday night. Well, that just happens to be the night of the explosion at BigT that was in the paper last Sunday, and – get this – also the day Daniel went missing. And then Keoni shows up tonight with a big ol' black eye.' She folded her arms in a '*voilà!*' manner.

'Huh . . .'

'So it all fits together perfectly! Keoni hates BigT with a passion and manages to get hold of some dynamite or TNT to blow it up. Where would you get something like that, I wonder?'

Isaac shrugged. 'Beats me.'

'Anyway, the problem is Daniel is there that night working and sees what Keoni does. They get in a fight, and Daniel ends up getting killed. Keoni freaks out and calls someone to come help him take the body down to the hot lava to dispose of it. That's why we saw two people there at the flow when we first got there. It's the perfect crime. Or it would have been, except that I ended up seeing the body before it was hidden for good.'

'Okay, so how do you prove it?'

Valerie sighed. 'Yeah, that's a problem.'

They sipped their drinks and listened to the coquí chirp.

'Do you know when Luana's group practices?' she asked after a bit.

'You thinking of confronting Keoni? 'Cause if you're right, I'm not sure that would be such a good idea.'

'Well, I figure I could at least tell Luana what he said and see what she thinks.'

Isaac considered for a moment before responding. 'Used to be Friday afternoons,' he said finally. 'At least, back when I danced with her. I could take you; it's a short day this Friday at da school.'

'Would you? Wow – thank you so much!'

'Minors.' Isaac waved his hand. 'It's no big deal.'

'No, really. That would be awesome. And it's not just your taking me there; it's the other stuff, too. You have no idea how nice it is to have someone I can talk to about all this, and who's so supportive like you are.'

'Must be all that aloha spirit I got,' he said with a grin.

ELEVEN

Valerie's sleep was even more fitful than usual that night. Visions of bomb blasts and dark groves of gnarled trees had invaded her dreams – images that refused to dissipate as morning approached, instead stubbornly persisting through each succeeding sleep cycle.

By five o'clock when Kristen shook her shoulder, she'd finally fallen into a deep slumber, and it took her a few moments to return to consciousness.

'Rise and shine, toots!' Kristen exclaimed in a voice far too cheery for the hour. 'No complaining, now. Remember, it was you who wanted to go on this fishing expedition.'

She was right, in more ways than one – though Valerie wasn't about to mention everything she planned to fish for today. In fact, the primary reason she'd been so eager to join Jordan was indeed for the purpose of a metaphorical fishing expedition: she was hoping to pump the local Puna gal for locals-only information that might help with her investigation.

Sitting up, Valerie put on a good face, determined to at least pretend she'd had more than four hours of shut-eye – about half what she generally required to resemble a normal human being.

There was no sign of Isaac in the dark house as they got ready to go. Trying to be as quiet as possible, Valerie set about brewing a pot of coffee – a definite necessity if she was going to succeed in her endeavor to appear at all normal today. But the grinding of the beans posed a problem in the noise department. She finally settled on wrapping the machine in a towel to muffle the racket and hoped Isaac was a heavy sleeper.

Coffee in hand, they headed down to Pāhoa. When they pulled up at the Orchid Drive-In parking lot, Jordan was already there, in a faded yellow Volvo station wagon with bondo-gray sides. She had on a knit cap and sweatshirt and was clutching a metal travel mug.

'What, you cold?' Valerie asked, gesturing toward her own shorts and flip-flops.

'Eh, it gets chilly this early in the morning 'round here.'

'You're just spoiled, is all.' She took her daypack from the back seat of the rental car and moved aside to let Kristen grab her own pack and Isaac's surfboard. 'If you had foggy summers like we do, you'd appreciate this weather more.'

At Jordan's direction, Kristen set the board next to a pile of fishing gear in the back of the Volvo, and they all climbed into her car – Valerie riding shotgun.

'Gotta make a quick stop on the way,' Jordan said as she turned right onto the highway. 'I forgot to bring something. But no worries, it's real close.'

After a couple of miles, she turned left at a sign for Leilani Estates, followed the road for a few blocks, took another left on to a smaller street and pulled into the driveway of a one-story bungalow-style home set back from the road.

'My grandparents live here, but I'm crashing with them for a while. Be right back.' Jordan ran inside the house and emerged a minute later. Climbing back into the car, she tossed a small cardboard box onto the back seat.

Kristen picked up the box. 'Thirty-gallon Hefty garbage bags? What, you anticipate generating a lot of trash today?'

'We use 'em for fishing. You'll see,' she added with a glance in Valerie's direction.

Jordan continued through the thickly vegetated subdivision and turned right at a T-junction. 'We're back on track now,' she said. 'This road ends at Isaac Hale Park – Pohoiki – where we're going.'

Ten minutes later, they arrived at the coast. Driving past public bathrooms, a large grassy area, and a playground, they came to a parking lot by the water. About a dozen other cars were there, several with empty boat trailers hitched behind. 'You should see this place on the weekends,' Jordan said as she pulled into a spot near the small boat ramp. 'You can barely find a place to park.'

'I think we came through here last Sunday with Isaac, didn't we, Kristen?'

'Yeah, we did.' Kristen had jumped out of the car and was

already pulling the surfboard from the back. 'There were a ton of people here that day.'

'Right. I remember now – lots of folks barbecuing and swimming and stuff.'

'Uh-huh.' Kristen set the board down and climbed up onto the breakwater to scan the small bay, over which the rising sun was casting its early-morning rays, then returned to where Jordan and Valerie were standing. 'Looks like a few guys are catching some waves over there, on the far side.' She removed a bottle of sunscreen from her pack and started slathering it over her face and arms, wisely keeping on her white T-shirt.

'Yah, that's where the good break usually is,' said Jordan. 'But watch out for coral. And sharks.'

Kristen momentarily stopped rubbing cream on to her neck, but then shook her head and went on. 'We've got Great Whites back in California. No puny little tiger shark is going to keep me from surfing.' She capped the bottle, replaced it, and took out a bar of wax, which she began to rub over the surface of the surfboard. 'So where you guys gonna be?'

'Down the coast a little bit, 'round the shoreline there.' Jordan pointed to her right. 'There's some rocks you can fish from. You'll probably be able to see us when you're out surfing.' She pulled her phone out of her jeans pocket and checked the time. 'Wanna meet back here around ten thirty?'

'Sure, sounds good.' Kristen removed a towel, baseball cap, and water bottle from her pack and shoved them into a cloth shopping bag, then yanked off her khaki shorts, revealing a blue swimsuit underneath. She folded the shorts neatly and, after adding them to the bag and placing it and her flip-flops behind the breakwater, trotted off toward the boat ramp with the board under one arm. With a quick wave, she dove in the water and paddled off.

'Like a kid in a candy shop,' Valerie observed.

Jordan smiled. 'Not too different from how I am about fishing, actually.' She climbed back into the car. 'So, *hele* on!'

Valerie remembered Isaac using this phrase. '"Let's move," right?'

'Yep. You're a quick learner.'

*   *   *

It seemed to Valerie like an awful lot of gear for just the two of them, but Jordan insisted everything was essential. After driving down to the end of a dirt track, they'd scrambled through a patch of dense jungle to get to her fishing spot on a low cliff overlooking the water. Several spindly ironwood trees provided a bit of shade. They went back for a second load and finally had all the items deposited on the black lava rock: a pair of long bamboo poles, two enormous coils of rope, eight empty plastic jugs, the box of garbage bags, a large metal tackle box, plus a folding beach chair for each of them and a small red cooler.

'Kind of windy here,' Valerie observed, opening one of the chairs and sitting down. Shading her eyes from the glaring sun, she peered out at the water. 'Hey, look, I think I see Kristen!' She waved, but her wife wasn't looking their way.

Jordan knelt down and got to work preparing the lines. 'Okay,' she said, knotting the end of one of the ropes into a large loop. 'This is your lucky day, 'cause I'm gonna teach you the local-style flag fishing, which was invented right here on the Big Island.'

'Cool.' Valerie paid strict attention, not wanting to come across as too much of a neophyte.

Jordan counted off ten arm-lengths of rope and made another knotted loop. 'With this kind of fishing,' she said, 'you can get your line way out into the ocean – hundreds of yards out to sea. That's where the big fish are, mahi mahi, *ulua*, marlin.'

'Can I help with that?' Valerie hoisted herself out of the low chair. 'I'm more likely to remember if I actually do it once.'

'Sure thing.' Jordan showed Valerie the knot she was using and then watched closely as she made her first attempt, nodding when she was done. 'Not bad.' She picked up the second coil. 'Oh, and you gotta make sure to use the poly rope, so it will float, yah?'

They sat next to each other, Jordan's strong fingers deftly forming loops at double Valerie's rate. After a few minutes, she decided it was time to start picking Jordan's brain.

'So,' she asked, 'you grew up in Puna, right?'

'Uh-huh.' Already finished with her rope, Jordan coiled it neatly and reached for her tackle box.

'Well, I was wondering: I heard there's been a lot of avocado theft around here lately. Has it been a problem for a long time?'

Taking out a spool of fishing line, Jordan started cutting lengths and tucking them carefully under the corner of the box so they wouldn't blow away. 'When I was a kid, I don't remember hearing about anything like that. But these days, it seems like it's gotten pretty bad.' The lines cut, she removed a plastic container with small compartments from the tackle box and opened its lid. 'Why do you ask?'

'This woman at a fruit stand was telling me about it, and I was just curious. She said some people have even bought guns because of the thefts. Have you heard of anyone being shot or anything like that because of it?'

Jordan looked up from sorting through a collection of fishing hooks, weights, swivels, and lures, and grinned. 'What, you afraid maybe it's dangerous down here Puna side? 'Cause you don't need to worry – I can protect you.' She flexed her arm, body-builder style, but the effect was pretty much ruined by the sloppy sweatshirt covering any muscles that might be lurking underneath.

'That's good to know,' Valerie said with a laugh. Was she flirting? The way she kept glancing over and then looking away when Valerie caught her gaze certainly suggested an interest in that regard. And she had given Valerie that wink the day they'd met at the Orchid Grill. Had she or Kristen mentioned to Jordan that they were a couple? She didn't think so. But surely Jordan must have noticed the wedding ring on her hand. Then again, maybe not. Or perhaps she simply didn't care.

Well, Valerie could absolutely play that game, too; it might help move her agenda of pumping Jordan for as much local information as possible. 'But really' – Valerie touched Jordan briefly on the wrist – 'doesn't it seem a little weird that someone could get shot at over a fruit. Or vegetable – whatever it is.'

'Definitely a fruit, since it's got a seed,' Jordan said, not visibly reacting to the touch. She selected a length of cut line and tied a snap-on swivel to one end and a large hook to the other. 'But when you think about it, they're worth a lot, those avocados – like two dollars each for the big ones. You can get six papayas for that price.'

'Yeah. Plus, avos have got to be the most delicious food known to man.'

Jordan made a face as if she'd just taken a bite of something nasty. 'Ugh. I'm not a fan.'

'Are you crazy?' Valerie couldn't fathom someone not liking avocados.

Jordan just chuckled, then returned her focus to getting the lines rigged. Valerie's loop-tying finally done, she stared out at the water while Jordan worked. The sun was now high enough over the horizon that the glare on the ocean was intense. Fishing her sunglasses from her pack, she put them on and sat forward, squinting down at the group of surfers below. Kristen was easy to spot, her white T-shirt standing out from all the shirtless bronzed torsos. She had just caught a wave and was paddling back out from near the shore.

Jordan set her rigged lines aside and commenced fastening swivels to the plastic jugs – gallon milk and pog containers. 'These are the floats,' she said. 'But you gotta make sure they got their caps on, so they don't fill up with water and sink.'

At Valerie's 'Well, duh!' look, she laughed again. 'Okay,' she added, 'but some people aren't as smart as you.' Another look her way, but this time Jordan kept it there for slightly longer. When Valerie turned to meet her gaze, she smiled and then went back to work.

The floats finished, Jordan reached for the two long bamboo poles and began pacing back and forth over the cliff top, staring at the black rock at her feet. 'Aha!' she said after a minute and jammed one of the rods into a crack in the rock, so that it was standing at a forty-five-degree angle to the ground. Both pieces of bamboo, Valerie observed, had V-shaped crooks at their end.

After finding a similar place for the second pole, she came back over to Valerie, who was lounging in her beach chair, and opened the cooler. 'I use this for the bait,' Jordan said, holding up a box of squid. 'Costs only three bucks and the fish love it.'

'Mmm, calamari! Back home, we deep fry them whole in batter and eat 'em with spicy ketchup.' As Valerie said this, she realized she was starting to get hungry. With a pang, she realized that she and Kristen had neglected to bring anything to eat.

Glancing at Jordan's cooler, Valerie wondered if it might contain any snacks.

'Yah, we cook 'em that way here, too.' Jordan sliced a squid into strips and demonstrated how to attach them to the hooks so they wouldn't fall off. With her cutting and Valerie baiting, the task was quickly accomplished.

'We make a good team,' Valerie said, wiping her fingers on a paper towel.

'Yeah.' Jordan grinned and stood up. 'Now for the fun part.' Yanking a black trash bag out of the box, she held it open and let it fully inflate. 'This is why we want the wind,' she said, twisting the end closed. 'Grab me some duct tape, will ya?'

Valerie located the roll in the tackle box, ripped off a long piece and handed it over. 'So, you have the day off work, or what?' she asked. Jordan taped the end of the bag tightly, trapping the air inside. Then she wrapped it several times with fishing line and knotted it, leaving the line attached to the spool. 'Because it is a weekday,' Valerie added, since she hadn't received a response to her question.

Jordan walked to the edge of the cliff and peered down at the water. 'I'm kind of between gigs right at the moment.'

'Oh, yeah?'

Jordan cleared her throat. 'Yeah, well, I got laid off my job a couple months back.' She lifted the inflated bag up above her head, where it tugged at the line like a kite. 'I was filling in for another guy who was out on disability, but when he came back, they let me go.'

'That's a bummer.'

'Maybe not so much, actually. It's probably about time I found some other line of work that's not so hard on my body. I'm almost fifty, you know.'

'I wouldn't have guessed,' Valerie said. Which was true; the woman had the look of someone at least ten years younger. 'So what was it you did?'

Releasing the bag, Jordan let it be taken by the offshore wind, unspooling the line as it wafted out to sea. 'I was a pipe-fitter at BigT,' she said. 'You know, that new geothermal plant?'

TWELVE

At Valerie's gape-mouthed expression, Jordan shook her head. 'What? You surprised that a woman would work in the trades?'

'No. It's not that. It's just that, well, I bet there aren't that many female pipe-fitters, is all. Especially here in Hawai'i. So yeah, I guess I was just a little surprised. But I think it's totally cool.'

Jordan laughed. 'Well, you're right about that. I'm pretty sure I'm the only one here on the island, though there are a few women electricians and plumbers. We get together sometimes to share our war stories.' She turned back to her fishing apparatus and concentrated on the inflated plastic bag, which the wind continued to carry offshore, pulling the fishing line with it.

Digesting the news of her previous employer, Valerie watched as Jordan cut the line and tied it to the loop at the end of one of the ropes. This could be the break she'd been hoping for – Jordan would surely be able to explain about geothermal plant explosions. And there was a good chance she'd even know something about Daniel Kehinu, since she'd worked for the same company as the missing man.

But Valerie could tell this would not be the best time to start bombarding her with questions. Jordan was cautiously letting the rope out, and each time she came to one of the loops they'd made, she would snap on a float and a baited line and let them fall into the water. After the last loop was past, she allowed another long length of rope to go out to sea and then hooked the rope over the V at the end of one of the fishing poles, ran it down the shaft, and tied off the rope at the base of one of the scraggly ironwood trees.

Finally looking Valerie's way, she nodded at the pole. 'You watch this one while I get the other going. If any of the floats start to sink or bounce around a lot, lemme know, okay?'

'Will do.' Valerie moved her chair next to the pole and sat

back down, keeping an eye on the floats, but also watching as Jordan inflated another garbage bag and released it into the breeze. She followed the bag as it floated over the azure sea, getting smaller in the distance as Jordan let out the rope and attached floats and hooks. Occasionally, it would lose altitude and bounce on the water, but then fly back up again, like a toy balloon on a stick.

'Some people think it's cheating, doing flag fishing,' Jordan shouted over the wind as she let out the last of the rope and ran it down the bamboo pole. 'But I think they're just jealous, 'cause of how good it works.'

'You ever lose the bags,' Valerie asked, 'when they rip on something or just fly off?'

'Sometimes, sure. But usually by then the hooks are far enough out so it doesn't matter.'

'But don't you worry about the bags ending up in the ocean, you know, where they could hurt a fish or seabird or something if it eats one?'

She just shrugged by way of answer, and Valerie chose not to pursue the topic further. For the time being, at least, both the bags seemed to be securely fastened.

Tying the second rope off to another tree, Jordan brought her chair next to Valerie's and plopped down. 'Okay, now we wait,' she said, stretching out her long legs with a satisfied sigh. Almost immediately, she sat up, yanked off her hoodie, and tossed it aside. 'Gets warm once you sit down, yah?'

She was right. In the low chairs with the vegetation at their backs, they were blocked from the wind, and the sun felt delicious on Valerie's skin.

'You thirsty?' Jordan opened the cooler and held up two bottles – one of water and one of Primo beer. Valerie managed a quick look inside the cooler, but was disappointed to see it didn't contain anything besides the bottles and squid.

'Thanks.' She accepted the water. 'It's a little too early for me for beer.'

'Not for me.' Jordan popped the Primo and took a long drink.

Valerie sipped some water and then turned in her chair to face Jordan. 'So you said you used to work at the new geothermal place – BigT, right?'

'Uh-huh.'

'Did you read in the newspaper about that explosion there last week?' Valerie asked.

'Huh-uh. I don't read the paper. Why? What did it say?'

'Not much. Just that there was one. And there hasn't been any follow-up story, so that's about all I know.'

Jordan took another drink of beer. 'Stuff like that happens all the time,' she said. 'It was probably a blowout – when the gases are vented by accident.'

'How does it work, anyway, getting the geothermal energy. Do you know?'

'Sure. I worked on the wells and piping, so I better understand it.' She set down her beer. 'It's all about getting the steam, 'cause that's where the energy comes from. First they drill these wells that are super deep – like a mile down or something – to bring everything up. It's a mixture of steam and gases and what they call "brine," which is all the stuff that's dissolved in water. Then they separate out the steam, which goes through a generator to create the power, and all the rest of the stuff is re-injected back into the ground.'

'What causes the blasts?'

'Well, you gotta understand that all those geothermal fluids are under a hell of a lot of pressure when they bring 'em up, and they're really hot – like six hundred fifty degrees. So if a pipe breaks or leaks, *bam*!' Her hands flew apart in demonstration. 'It blasts out into the air instead of being re-injected like it's supposed to be. They call that a "blowout." And some of the stuff in that brine – hydrogen sulfide, ammonia, arsenic, even mercury – it ain't good news.'

Valerie frowned and nodded. 'So if someone wanted to really cause a problem, blowing up one of those pipes or wells would be a good way.' Jordan had raised the bottle to her lips, but stopped, turning to look at Valerie. 'I know, I know,' Valerie said, 'you're wondering why I'm asking all these weird questions. I'm not planning on blowing anything up, if that's what you're thinking.'

'Glad to hear it.' Jordan chuckled and took the sip of beer the question had interrupted.

'It's just that . . .' Valerie picked up a rock lying next to her chair and rolled it between her hands. It was smooth and warm

from the sun. 'Okay, here's the thing. I was down at the lava
flow last weekend and – I know this is really bizarre, but I swear
to God it's the truth – I saw a body there, being covered over
by hot lava.'

'No way!'

'Yeah way.' She studied Jordan's face, but couldn't tell if the
look was one of disbelief or simply astonishment. 'The thing is,
I went down there with my friends – Kristen and that other guy
you met at the restaurant, Isaac – but they weren't with me when
I saw the body, and I'm pretty sure they think I just imagined
the whole thing.'

'Damn, girl. That's gotta be crazy-making.'

'You said it. But then the next day, there's an article in the
paper about an explosion at BigT that happened the night before
I saw the body, and a few days after that, a guy's reported missing
who works at BigT.'

Jordan was giving Valerie one of those 'And?' looks.

'So don't you see? I've got to figure out who that guy was
that I saw in the lava. No way am I going to go through life
having them think I'm just on some freaky fantasy trip.' Hurling
the rock out into the water, Valerie felt the anger rise up inside
her once more.

'Did you see the face or anything you could identify the body
by?'

'Huh-uh. Just a boot and part of a pant leg is all.'

'Oh, too bad . . .' *Was that a slight flicker of the eyebrows?*

'*No*,' said Valerie with some heat. 'Don't *even* try to tell me
it could have been just a shoe and some clothes. It was definitely
a person.' And then, more softly, 'And you really don't want to
know how I can be so sure about that.'

Jordan stared at her for a moment, her brow furrowed, and
then shrugged and looked back out at the ocean, sipping her
Primo.

'Anyway . . .' Valerie picked up another rock. 'I was hoping
maybe you could help me, being from around here and all.
Especially since you actually worked at BigT. Like, for example,
any chance you know Daniel Kehinu, the man that's gone
missing? He's a night watchman there – at BigT.'

Jordan shook her head. 'I think I know who he is, but I've

never met him or anything. I woulda been gone from work by
the time his shift started.'

''Cause I have this idea. What if Daniel Kehinu is the guy I
saw down at the lava? And what if he was killed by that explosion last week and whoever did it dumped his body down at the
lava? You gotta admit it would be a great way to hide a body.'

'Yeah.' Jordan nodded, continuing to stare out to sea. 'It would.'

'And I know lots of folks have gripes against the whole
geothermal thing. Like, for example, those Pele's Children
people—'

'They're a bunch of nuts, those guys.'

'Nutty enough to try to blow up BigT?'

'Maybe, but I'm sure that thing you read about in the paper
was just another accident. They happen a lot more than people—
Ho!' Jordan jumped up and ran to the cliff's edge. 'I think we
got a bite!'

Sure enough, two of the plastic jugs near the middle of one
of the lines were bouncing around like crazy and getting pulled
under water.

'Looks like a big one!' Yanking on a pair of leather gloves
she'd left next to the tackle box, Jordan grabbed the now-taut
rope and began hauling it in, hand over hand. The fish had other
plans, however, and after about six tugs she had to let the rope
back out. Whatever had taken the hook made a run for it. But
whenever the line started to slacken, Jordan would tighten it up,
keeping the fish constantly working but not yet attempting to
pull it in.

'Gotta tire it out!' she shouted over her shoulder, and then let
out the rope again as the fish continued to fight. There was a
flash of silver as it leaped out of the water and Valerie was able
to make out a rounded head.

'It's huge!' She jumped up too, and made her way carefully
to the edge of the cliff.

'Yeah – an *ulua*,' Jordan answered. 'About forty pounds, looks
like. Not that big actually for one of 'em, but it's a strong buggah!'
She started hauling in the rope again. 'I think he's starting to
lose some steam.'

After working it for another ten minutes – it seemed like ages
to Valerie – Jordan finally landed the fish. Valerie stared at the

writhing beast while Jordan went to her tackle box, returning with a hammer which she used to put the poor thing out of its misery.

'Are they good to eat, the *ulua*?' Valerie asked as Jordan crouched down and made a long slice down the fish's belly.

'Not as *'ono* as mahi mahi, but it's not bad.'

'Fried in butter and ginger like you told me yesterday at the market, I bet it would be great even if the fish tasted like cardboard.'

Jordan tugged at the entrails, cutting away the strands that remained attached to the cavity and then tossed it all into the ocean. 'I could cook this one like that for you if you wanted,' she said, ripping several sheets of paper towels off the roll and wiping the fish guts off her hands.

'Wow, that sounds great. But it'll feed a lot more than just us.' Sizing up the *ulua*, she calculated how many steaks it would make and came up with somewhere around twenty. 'Hey, I've got an idea. My sixtieth birthday is next Thursday—'

'No way! You don't look that old,' Jordan interrupted with a grin.

'Yeah, right. Flattery will get you everywhere. Anyway, we're having a party that evening – it's a potluck at Coconut Island – probably starting around five. How would you feel about coming along and bringing it with you? Oh, but would the fish last that long?'

'Sure, as long as I freeze it till then. My grandparents have a big chest freezer, so that shouldn't be any problem. It can be your birthday present.'

Jordan pulled two beers from the cooler, offering one to Valerie. This time she did not refuse.

THIRTEEN

'You've been drinking.' It was a statement, not a question. 'And it's only, what' – Kristen consulted her watch – 'eleven thirty.'

'Aw, c'mon, all I had was two beers.'

'Uh-huh . . .'

'Look, it was really hot, and we'd just caught a huge fish, so to celebrate—'

Kristen waved her hand and laughed. 'I'm just busting your chops, Val. You know I so don't care if you have a couple brewskies before noon. We're on vacation, and I'm actually thrilled to see you finally enjoying yourself.' She picked up the menu and shot Groucho brows over its top. 'But I do need to do some catching up with you.'

They were back at Raul's, Valerie's third time within a week. Jordan had dropped them off at their rental car in Pāhoa, and when Valerie had told Kristen how famished she was, Kristen had suggested lunch at the Mexican place. Which was more than fine with Valerie.

They'd been quickly seated next to a threesome just getting their food. The tables were close together, and craning her neck to see around a man in what must have been a size XXXL green-and-white philodendron leaf motif shirt, Valerie was able to get a peek at the dishes being set down on the table. Something slathered in a red sauce – enchiladas, probably – for the big guy, and a plate of what appeared to be chiles rellenos with rice and beans for the woman next to him. The man across the table had already started on his taco salad, which looked enticing, topped as it was with generous slices of avocado and a good dollop of sour cream.

'Before I forget,' Kristen said as she perused the menu, 'after lunch, let's stop by that thrift store you told us about. I could use some more Hawaiian shirts in my collection.'

'Aloha shirts,' Valerie corrected her.

'Right.' She closed the menu and swiveled in her chair. 'Can you see what beers they have on tap?'

'Bud . . . Longboard lager, it looks like . . . and something else I can't read.' Valerie picked up her menu and studied it. The fish tacos she'd seen the guy at the bar eating the other day were tempting, as was the taco salad. Deciding to wait to make her final decision until the waitress came for the order, she set the menu back down.

Kristen was typing something into her phone. 'Great,' she said, and slipped it back into her shirt pocket. 'Today's tide chart. It says it'll be halfway between low and high in mid-afternoon, perfect for snorkeling. So you wanna head down to the Kapoho tide pools again after we check out the thrift shop?'

'Sure. It'll be fun to see some fish up close after spending the morning trying to hook the poor things.'

'How was the fishing, anyway?' Kristen asked. 'That was some nice catch you got there.'

'Yeah. It's like a forty-pound *ulua*, which is Hawaiian for some kind of jackfish. Jordan was pretty vague about what exactly it's called in English. But whatever it is, I can tell you it put up quite the fight. Not that I had anything to do with it, other than as a spectator. Oh, and she said she'd freeze it, and then cook it and bring it to my birthday party next week.'

'My, aren't you two becoming friendly.' Kristen eyed her curiously. Valerie couldn't imagine she'd be jealous, but there appeared to be something bothering her.

With a laugh, Valerie just shrugged. If her wife hadn't been acting so peevish about her investigation of the body in the lava and the disappearance of Daniel Kehinu, she'd have told her the truth about why she wanted to hang out with Jordan. But Valerie wasn't going to go there now; she really didn't want another scene – especially here, in a public place. 'She's friendly,' she said, instead. 'And knows a lot about local culture. It's fun hanging out with her, is all.'

'Uh-huh.'

Time to change the subject. 'So how was the surfing? From where I was, it looked like the waves were pretty good.'

'Yeah, not bad at all. The current was a bit gnarly, but once

I watched the other guys for a while, I was able to figure out the break and get some nice rides.'

'Are the locals territorial about the waves?'

'The ones I've run across have actually been way better than in L.A. This guy out there today, he even held up on one of the best waves all morning so I could catch it. You'd never see that out at the Redondo breakwater back home. Aha.' This last remark was directed at the waitress coming their way.

While Kristen was ordering – beef enchiladas and a pint of Longboard lager – Valerie frantically weighed the pros and cons of the fish tacos versus the taco salad. The waitress took Kristen's menu and turned to her, and she could feel her pulse quicken from the pressure. 'Uh . . . I guess I'll have the taco salad.' At least it had the appearance of being healthy. But then she immediately worried she'd made the wrong choice.

'Anything to drink?' the woman asked.

'Just water, thanks.'

The server dropped their orders off at the kitchen window and then headed for the bar. Kevin was there again this morning and was busy loading up a tray with cocktails in a variety of garish colors – green, yellow, and blue. Curious as to who else would be starting happy hour so early in the day, Valerie watched the waitress collect the tray and was surprised to see the drinks delivered to the people at the table next to theirs, who she'd assumed to be on their lunch break from work. Clearly not, she decided, eyeing the empty glasses being replaced by the new. Or maybe their jobs simply didn't require a high level of attention to detail.

The big guy – who was just finishing up his plate of enchiladas – had been talking but fell silent when the waitress arrived and served their fresh round of drinks. 'To all things green,' he said after she left, raising his chartreuse-tinted cocktail.

The man with the taco salad speared an avocado slice and held it aloft. 'Green gold,' he said, and the three of them laughed. Leaning across the table, he pointed his fork in the direction of the bar. 'You talk to Kevin yet?' he asked, voice low. 'You find out yet what kine?'

This grabbed Valerie's interest. Shushing Kristen, who had started to speak, she too leaned forward, pretending to study the map of Mexico on the wall behind their table. Mr XXXL swallowed a large bite before answering. 'Sharwil.'

The woman with the chiles rellenos nodded agreement. 'Right. And no worries – gonna be primo, like Puna butter.'

The younger guy ate his forkful of avocado, chewing thoughtfully as he watched Kevin pull a pint of beer. 'I heard dat the oddah one, he gone missing. That could screw the deal up, yah?'

'No worry, beef curry,' said the big guy, punching him lightly on the shoulder. 'Kevin, he got one kind of green stuffs, we got the other.' He rubbed his fingers together in the universal sign for money. 'Dass all it takes.'

When their talk turned to the woman's car troubles, Valerie finally sat back and turned to face Kristen. 'What?' she mouthed, frowning.

'I'll tell you later,' Valerie whispered.

She shook her head. 'Whatever.'

Their food came, which gave Valerie a few moments to process what she'd just heard while Kristen concentrated on attacking her enchiladas.

'Sharwil,' the guy had said. That was the name of that amazing avocado variety she'd tasted at the road-side stand. 'Greengold' was one of the other kinds she'd had for sale. And 'Puna butter' certainly described the creamy flavor and texture of those avos Valerie had bought and taken home to use for her grapefruit and avocado salad.

So her hunch had to be right: Kevin and Daniel *were* stealing avocados from the farms in Puna, and the people at the next table were there to purchase some of their ill-gotten wares. Like those avos she'd seen on the produce cart outside Raul's kitchen, which had been missing their stems. *Kevin and Daniel must provide them to the restaurant, too, which is why they can sell their guacamole and chips for such a cheap price.* It all made sense.

But could it have anything to do with Daniel's disappearance?

Kristen had started talking about snorkeling, how it was better in the morning when the sea was calm, but Valerie only half listened as she crunched her iceberg lettuce and taco shell.

The table next to them paid their bill and stood up to leave.

'See you in a few, Charmaine, yah?' the big guy said, and the two men went out the front door. The woman walked over to the bar, spoke briefly to Kevin, and then followed the guys outside. After watching her leave, Kevin said something to the busboy who'd come to clear the tub of dirty dishes from behind the bar, then slipped out through the door into the kitchen.

'Be right back,' Valerie said to Kristen. 'Gotta pee.' She walked sedately toward the restrooms, but once out of Kristen's sight, dashed to the end of the hallway. Looking out the screen-door window, she had a full view of the parking lot behind the restaurant. Kevin was heading for a blue pickup truck in the far corner of the lot. The woman who'd just left the restaurant was already there, waiting for him. Valerie could see the two other guys standing by a small car at the opposite end of the lot, smoking cigarettes.

Valerie and Kristen's rental car was parked two spaces down from the truck. But did she have the keys, or did Kristen? *Yes – she patted her front pocket – they were there. Good.* Taking a deep breath, she opened the screen door and stepped outside.

Kevin looked up when Valerie approached, but she kept her gaze fixed directly ahead and walked straight to the car, unlocking the trunk and opening it. Pretending to search for something inside, she strained to listen in on their conversation.

Low murmuring was all she could hear. *Damn.* She shut the trunk and went to the driver's side door, closer to where they stood. As she opened the door, she glanced – nonchalantly, she hoped – in their direction and then slid quickly into the seat. She'd been expecting to see a box, or perhaps a large bag, that could contain avocados. But from the glimpse she'd managed to catch, it had looked an awful lot like a plastic bag in Kevin's hand. The kind of zippered bag that would hold drugs. Contraband drugs like marijuana.

Valerie thought back to the day they'd passed the store in Pāhoa with the pipes and marijuana-leaf flags in the window. Hadn't Isaac made some crack about 'Puna butter'?

So the people in the restaurant hadn't been talking about avocados at all.

She drummed her fingers on the gearshift, thinking. But why, then, had the big guy talked about 'sharwils'? She chanced a quick look over to where Kevin was laughing with the woman. 'Charmaine,' the guy had called her. And then she got it: 'Char will,' he had said, not 'sharwil.'

Valerie laid her head down on the steering wheel. *Idiot!* What kind of moron would imagine rings of top-secret avocado thieves plying their nefarious trade at Mexican restaurants around the Big Island of Hawai'i? And now, here she was – just like Kristen had said – a *haole* girl from California sticking her nose where it had no business going, witness to some drug deal going down, deep in the heart of Puna. *Stupid, stupid . . .*

Slouched down with eyes closed, trying to make herself as invisible as possible, she considered her options. Drive away and come back later for Kristen? *I don't think so.* Stay and wait until after the deal went down, hoping they didn't notice her prying eyes? *Not likely.* Get out of the car right now and walk resolutely back into the restaurant, as if nothing in the world were amiss? *Not an attractive prospect.*

There was a sharp rap at the car window. Sitting up slowly, Valerie turned to see who it was, already knowing the answer.

FOURTEEN

M anaging a smile, Valerie lowered the window. 'Hey, Kevin. What's up?' He was alone; she could see the woman he'd been talking to heading back across the lot towards her friends.

He did not smile back. 'Why'd you follow me out here?'

'What do you mean?' Valerie asked, hoping he'd take the anxiety in her voice for mere confusion or surprise. 'I wasn't following you. I just needed to get something from the car.' Looking around, she spotted a map of the Big Island on the passenger seat and seized hold of it as if it were manna from heaven. 'We're thinking of going to the Kapoho tide pools after lunch and I wanted to figure out how close they are. Though snorkeling after a huge meal probably isn't the best idea. My mom always made me wait an hour after eating before going swimming, because she was worried I'd get a cramp and drown or something. So we may do something else first, before driving down there . . .'

Kevin just continued to stare at Valerie – arms folded, eyes hard – as she rattled on and on. Laughing nervously, she opened the enormous map and attempted to fold it so it showed their location in Puna.

He did not appear to be taken in by her story. 'Why is it you're so interested in me, anyway? I saw you watching us just now. You a cop or something?'

This suggestion was so ludicrous that it produced a genuine laugh from Valerie and made her temporarily forget the delicate situation she found herself in. 'Right,' she said. 'I came all the way from California to bust you for selling a few grams of pot.' But then she immediately regretted allowing her sarcastic devil side to overcome the more cautious and diplomatic angel side. *Great. Now I've admitted that I know what he was doing.*

Kevin just nodded, however, drumming his fingers on the car door. 'So why *are* you so interested in me?' he persevered. 'And

Daniel. I don't get it.' He leaned through the open window, inches from Valerie's face. 'And I sure as hell don't like the way you seem to be stalking me.'

She scooted a little to her right, putting some space between their two heads. 'Okay, look, you want the truth?'

He nodded. 'Yeah, the truth would be nice.'

'Fine.'

She told him about seeing the body down at the lava flow, then reading the story about Daniel Kehinu's disappearance, and the timing of the two which matched perfectly. 'I wouldn't care that much – not that Daniel's disappearance isn't important or anything – except that no one seems to believe that I saw that body in the lava. Or part of a body, rather. It was just a boot and lower part of a leg I saw; the rest was already covered by the time I got there. Anyway, my friends all act like I'm some kind of nutcase, and the only way I figure I can prove my sanity is by finding out who it was I saw out there.'

Daniel stood back up, giving Valerie some breathing room again, and let out a breath. 'Well, I gotta say I'm relieved. Not about your story – which is pretty damn creepy – but to learn it's not *me* you're after. 'Cause the way you'd been acting, I was starting to worry you were some kinda stalker, if not a narc.'

'I'm most definitely neither of those things.'

'So, you really think it might be Daniel you saw in the lava?' Kevin was frowning once more, but this time it was a concerned rather than angry look.

'I don't know. Maybe. That's what I'm trying to find out.'

Neither of them spoke, Kevin staring out at the row of raphis palms along the edge of the parking lot, she at her clenched hands on the steering wheel. 'But maybe I'd have better luck answering that question,' Valerie said after a bit, 'if you'd tell me what you know.'

Kevin turned to her, eyebrows raised. 'Know about what?'

'Well, for one, whether Daniel was involved in' – she nodded in the direction of the blue truck two spaces down – 'you know, *that.*'

Kevin laughed. 'You some *lolo*, sistah.'

'So, what? You don't think there's any possibility they could be connected?'

He shook his head. 'No way his disappearance has anything to do with the small time *pakalolo* sales we do. But I will tell you what might.' He leaned down again on the door. 'Daniel had a monster fight with his wife right before he went missing. He'd been seeing someone else, and Faith found out about it. Daniel came into the restaurant afterwards—'

'When was this?'

'Lemme see . . .' Kevin scratched his chin and thought. 'It would have been, what, last Thursday, around five or six in the evening?'

'Okay. Go on.'

'So anyway, he came into the restaurant and he was really pissed off, madder than I've ever seen him. He was drinking beer – which he never usually does before work – and going on and on about leaving her, maybe even moving off island. Oh, and it looked like he'd been in a fight, too – he was all bruised around one eye. I asked if his wife had done it, and he just laughed.'

Black eyes were becoming *de rigueur* on the Big Island, Valerie mused. 'I don't think Faith did it,' she said. 'She told me the husband of one of the women he's been seeing beat him up.'

'You talked to her?'

'I was at the thrift shop and met her there.'

'Huh.' Kevin grinned. 'Well, I'm glad I'm not the only one you've been stalking.' Valerie got the feeling he was reassessing her, based on this new information. Thinking maybe she had more going for her than he'd previously thought.

'So, you think Daniel might actually have left?' she asked. 'And that's why he disappeared?'

'I doubt it. He'd never make a decision like that so fast. He's the kind of guy who takes weeks to decide what color he's going to paint his garage floor.'

A man after her own heart.

'But I gotta say,' Kevin went on, 'I'm starting to get a little worried myself. The first few days, I didn't think it was any big deal. He's gone AWOL before. But the fact that he still hasn't contacted me, and it's been almost a week now.' He shook his head. 'It's weird. There's something wrong with that.'

'Is there anyone you know who has a grudge against Daniel? Did he ever talk about anything like that?'

Kevin snorted. 'Besides Faith, and all his girlfriends' husbands and boyfriends, you mean?'

'Well, like, did he ever double-cross anyone with regard to your . . . uh, business . . .?' A noncommittal stare was Kevin's only response. 'Or . . . I've heard lots of folks are pretty upset by the whole geothermal thing. Would people have been mad that he took a job there?'

This at least produced a nod. 'That's possible.'

'But you haven't heard anything specific.'

'No, huh-uh.'

'What about the woman he was seeing – the one Faith found out about? You know anything about her?'

'Not much. Daniel never talks to me much about his flings. But . . .' Kevin drummed his fingers on the car door again. 'Right. I think he might have met her down at MacKenzie. It's one of his favorite fishing spots. I kinda remember him saying something about her camping down there, maybe?'

'MacKenzie?'

'The state park, down on the Red Road.' Kevin's phone rang and he extracted it from the pocket of his tight black jeans. 'Yah, be right there,' he said to the caller and then shoved it back into his pocket. 'Gotta jam; Ramón's wondering where the hell I am.' He turned to go.

'One more thing,' Valerie said. 'Daniel wore work boots, right?'

'Sure, I guess so.'

'Did they have green laces?'

She couldn't read Kevin's reaction – though he definitely had one. His eyes narrowed and his jaw clenched a couple of times. It took a moment for him to answer. 'I dunno,' he finally said. 'I guess I never really paid attention to his shoes.' Swallowing, he added, 'But given the reason you likely asked me, let's hope not,' and then walked quickly back to the restaurant.

'You did *what*?' Kristen nearly dropped a forkful of blood-red enchilada onto her white shirt. As Kristen would surely have blamed her for the resulting stain, Valerie was relieved to see her recover from the food fumble and manage to maneuver the cheesy bite safely back on to her plate.

Given the length of time she'd been gone, Valerie had felt

obliged to admit what she'd been up to outside. But she knew Kristen would not be pleased, and steeled herself for the coming lecture. Wiping red sauce off her fingers with a paper napkin, Kristen pushed her plate aside and leaned across the table.

'Do you have *any* idea,' she hissed, 'how dangerous it can be to mess with a drug dealer? It would be bad enough back home in your own element, but here – in a completely foreign culture? Are you *crazy*?' She glanced around to make sure no one else was listening and then lowered her voice even more. 'Some of the biggest pot-growers in the whole state operate out of Puna, and they are not likely to take kindly to some chick from California poking her nose into their business. I know to you it may seem all peace, love, and aloha around here, but scratch beneath the surface and there's some ugly stuff going down. Last time I was on the island, a tourist – a woman from the Mainland – was murdered by some local dudes.'

'So that Daniel guy could have been murdered over a drug deal, you're saying.'

'What I'm saying is *you* could be killed. Ohmygod, Val, just listen to yourself for a second!' Shaking her head impatiently, Kristen pulled her plate back in front of her and ate the last few bites of enchilada, refusing to meet her wife's gaze.

Valerie was well behind Kristen on her lunch and hurried to catch up, but it's hard to eat a taco salad quickly – all that lettuce takes some serious chewing. Kristen ordered a second beer while Valerie finished her lunch. Since Kristen still wasn't talking, Valerie spent the time contemplating how to broach the subject of visiting MacKenzie State Park so she could look for Daniel's paramour. A variation on the line she'd tried on Kevin seemed ripe for re-use.

'Oof. I'm full,' she said, and set her fork down on her cleaned plate. 'I probably shouldn't have eaten that whole thing.'

'Yeah, me neither,' Kristen responded. Thank goodness she wasn't going to give her the silent treatment for the rest of the afternoon. Not only that, but she was playing right into Valerie's hand.

Inflating her belly as far as possible, she placed her palm across it. 'Maybe we should wait a while before snorkeling. Swimming doesn't sound all that appealing right now, with this

full stomach. I wouldn't mind going back to MacKenzie beforehand – you know, that place we visited with Isaac with the
crashing waves? As I recall, it's not too far from Kapoho.'

'Sure, okay. It's still early.' Kristen consulted her phone. 'Not
even one yet, and high tide's at six. But we should probably get
a move on.' She drained her beer and stood up. 'I'll get the
check.'

Passing by the bar on her way out, Valerie looked to make
sure Kristen was occupied with paying the bill and then got
Kevin's attention. 'I'm on my way down to MacKenzie,' she said
in a low voice. 'Thanks for your help.'

A slight nod of the head was his only response.

FIFTEEN

'I still want to check out that thrift store before we head down to the Red Road,' Kristen said as they stepped out onto the raised wooden sidewalk in front of the restaurant.

'Sure, no problem.' *And while you're looking at shirts, maybe I can talk to Faith again*, Valerie mused. Now that she knew more about what Kevin and Daniel had been up to, perhaps she could get more information out of Daniel's disgruntled wife. 'C'mon,' she said. 'It's this way.'

Valerie led Kristen down the block, studiously resisting the urge to glance into the shop windows displaying marijuana paraphernalia. No sense getting her started on that subject again.

A cloud cover had moved in but, if anything, it was hotter than earlier. The air was still and muggy, and it was a relief to enter the thrift store, which had an enormous fan blowing full blast down the center aisle. Placing herself directly in front of its breeze, Valerie waited for her body temperature to come back down to normal while she scanned the store for any sign of Faith.

Good. She was at the back, sorting through a shopping cart full of new donations. Kristen had located the aloha shirts and already had several slung over one arm as she flipped through the hangers on the long rack. Now was the time.

'Hey, Faith.'

She looked up, frowning as she tried to place Valerie, then remembered who she was and frowned again. 'Oh. You again,' she said, extracting a Hello Kitty lamp from the cart and setting it on the floor next to a set of barbells.

'So, I thought you might like to hear what I just caught Kevin doing,' Valerie said. Since Faith clearly was not interested in talking to her, she figured the situation called for an attention-grabbing opener.

This one seemed to work. Setting down a stack of jigsaw puzzles, Faith turned to face Valerie, hands on hips. 'Okay, I'll bite. What was he doing?'

'He was in Raul's parking lot, selling pot to some customers. And I'm pretty sure Daniel is in on it, too. The buyers were sitting next to us at lunch, and I heard them mention him.'

Faith started going through a wad of clothes, separating the shirts from the pants and laying them in neat piles. 'I'm not surprised,' she said, shaking out a brown silk Tommy Bahama shirt with more force than necessary. It looked to be about Kristen's size; Valerie would have to point it out to her. 'He seemed like he might have had more cash than normal lately.'

'When did that start – his having more money?'

'Beats me. The only reason I even suspected was 'cause I noticed he'd bought some new fishing gear – a brand-new rod and an expensive Shimano reel.'

'Oh, yeah?' Valerie prompted her.

'He probably didn't think I'd notice the new things, but my brother's into fishing, so I know what that stuff costs. Daniel isn't about to tell me, though. He wants to keep all the money for himself, selfish bastard.'

Valerie glanced over to check on Kristen, who was busy trying on shirts in front of the store's cracked full-length mirror. 'You think his disappearance could have anything to do with his dealing pot?' she asked.

'If he stole from 'em, it might.'

'Would he really steal from his good friend Kevin?'

Faith rolled her eyes and hefted a cardboard box full of coffee cups from the shopping cart. 'Friendship don't mean that much when you're talkin' about the kind of money those dealers . . .' She trailed off, then set the box back down and turned to face Valerie. 'Wait, I just thought of something. When Daniel first took that job at the geothermal plant, he made some joke about not letting the weed farmers know. I asked what he meant, and he told me about how the geothermal companies go exploring all over Puna to look for the steam vents or whatever it is they're looking for, and those weed guys, they don't want nobody going into their jungle. So they really hate anyone who's got anything to do with geothermal – they're afraid they gonna run 'em out of business.'

'If that's true, why would Daniel have gotten involved with them, after he was already working at the plant?'

'I never said he was all that smart.' Faith toyed with the mugs in the box, lifting one out and examining its design – a royal flush poker hand with the words 'California Hotel & Casino' printed underneath. 'Maybe he thought they wouldn't find out. But it's hard to keep anything a secret 'round here. Everybody knows everybody else's business through the coconut wireless.' She replaced the cup, picked up the box again, and set it down next to the Hello Kitty lamp and barbells.

Valerie considered the implications of what she'd just heard. If Daniel had been selling marijuana, and his suppliers subsequently discovered he worked at the geothermal plant, they would have double the reason to be furious – for his working there and his hiding the fact from them. Killing him would act not only as punishment for the betrayal but also as a warning to others in the trade. And by dumping the body in the lava flow, even if he were discovered – by some unlucky person, say, such as she – those not in the know would be led to believe it was someone connected with the Pele's Children movement who'd done it, taking the heat off the true culprits.

Kristen had finally decided on a shirt and was now at the check-out counter paying. 'I gotta go,' Valerie said to Faith. 'But thanks for your help. Oh, and can I take this?' She extracted the brown silk shirt from the pile of clothes and held it up.

'Yeah, go ahead,' Faith answered, and went back to sorting the donations in the shopping cart.

'Nice find, babe. Thanks.' Kristen fingered the fabric of the brown silk shirt as they headed out of Pāhoa and then tossed it and the other one she'd purchased into the back seat. 'So, what were you and that woman talking about, anyway?'

'Nothing much. I was just asking if she was from around here and if she knew Isaac. She is, but doesn't.' Valerie didn't like lying to Kristen, but she also didn't want another lecture from her. Stopping at the signal, she waited for the green light before going straight, down Highway 132 towards Kapoho and the Red Road.

At MacKenzie State Park, they left the car by the picnic pavilion and walked down to the cliffs. The sea was much calmer than it had been the previous Sunday, sloshing gently against the black rock face. 'Wanna go up the coast a little?' Valerie asked.

'Remember how Isaac said there was a nice walk to a grove of coco palms?'

'Sure, why not?'

The path hugged the water on the left, winding through stands of tall, wispy ironwood trees and gaping pits in the ground – lava tubes, Kristen called them. Valerie kept her eye out for any signs of camping and had to contain her excitement when she spotted several tents pitched on the few flat spots along the rocky coastline. Their flaps were zipped shut, however, and no one appeared to be about.

After a while, the scenery abruptly changed, and they both stopped in their tracks. 'Ohmygod, it looks like a set from *Gilligan's Island*!'

'Totally,' said Kristen, gazing upward.

The towering coconut palms were so thick they blocked the sun, and there was a sudden hush, as if the ocean had been commanded to silence. The only sound was the rustle of the sea of deep green fronds above them.

'Yikes. Check *that* out.'

Kristen looked where Valerie was pointing. 'Whoa. They look almost like *skulls*.'

Someone had stacked fallen coconuts into massive piles – each at least six feet high, with hundreds of coconuts in each one.

'Yeah,' Valerie said. 'Like all those skulls piled up in the Catacombs in Paris. Creepy. I wonder who did it.'

Kristen walked to the nearest pile and picked up one of the coconuts. All of them were brown – no ripe, green fruits were to be seen. 'You know,' she said, 'I was reading in the guide book about this place. MacKenzie Park was built by convicts, who had to clear all the dense jungle 'round here and move tons of massive lava rocks to level the ground. A lot of them died doing the work – from exhaustion, heat, disease, I'm not sure exactly what – and were buried all around here in unmarked graves.' She held the coconut aloft in one hand and gazed at it, emulating the gravedigger in *Hamlet*.

'Apparently, a lot of the locals believe the park is haunted by the convicts' ghosts,' she went on. 'Grizzled old men who wander around at sunset with pick axes.' Kristen lowered her arm and turned the coconut over in her hands. 'And that's not all. There have been a series of murders here too, including a couple of campers not too long ago who were severely beaten and then left outside their tent, dead.' She tossed the coconut back onto the pile. 'I don't know why anyone would want to camp here, after reading about stuff like that.'

'I'm not afraid to camp here.'

They both started at the sound of the voice behind them.

The man laughed as Valerie and Kristen turned to face him, then set down his daypack. 'It's the most beautiful spot on the island,' he continued, 'and I've yet to see any sign of ghosts.' He was scrawny, with stringy blond hair and several days' growth on his chin.

A lot like what those convicts must have looked like, was Valerie's thought.

'Sorry to scare you,' the man said, 'but I just couldn't resist.'

'You didn't scare me,' Kristen said. 'I was just startled. And I don't believe in any of that stuff. I just think it's interesting cultural history, is all.'

The man continued to smile, scratching at his beard. Valerie doubted he was taken in by Kristen's bravado. 'You camping here now?' she asked.

'Yep.'

'How long you been here?'

'Over a week.' He leaned forward and added in a stage whisper, 'But don't tell anyone, 'cause you're supposed to leave after five nights.'

'Have you met any of the other people camping here?' Valerie jabbed a thumb down the trail. 'I saw several different tents back there.'

'Yeah, most of 'em, I think.' The camper extracted a metal canister from his pack and drank from it. 'We hang out together at night sometimes. Why? You looking for someone?'

Kristen was frowning at Valerie. *Yeah, why* do *you ask?* was what she figured Kristen was thinking.

Oh, well, no avoiding it. She was simply going to have to risk another lecture from her wife. 'I am – a woman who's been camping here. Kinda looks like me, or so I'm told. Though probably younger than I am. I think she was camping alone, but she may have been hanging out with a local guy.'

The man nodded, screwing the cap back on the bottle and replacing it in his pack. 'Sure, I seen her around – and that guy you're talking about, too. Though not for a while. I've been wondering what happened to her, actually, 'cause her tent's still here.'

'Could you show me which one it is?'

Kristen was shaking her head and staring at Valerie, but she didn't say anything.

'I could do that.' He hefted his pack. 'C'mon, it's down here.'

They followed him back the way they'd come, Kristen grabbing Valerie by the shirt sleeve and hissing, 'What the hell, Val?'

She shook off her grip. 'Just let me do this, okay?'

The man stopped at an orange-and-gray tent pitched about ten yards off the trail. 'It's this one,' he said. 'But like I said, I don't think she's been back for at least several days. Maybe she's staying with that guy. I dunno . . .'

'Did she tell you her name, or anything about her?'

'It's Amy,' he said after a pause, as if he'd been sizing Valerie up, deciding whether to answer her question or not. 'I don't think she's a local, but she didn't say much about herself.' He scratched at his scraggly beard again; perhaps the new growth itched. 'She was pretty interested in the turtles, though. Asked me if I'd seen any around here.'

'What about the guy she was with?' Valerie asked. 'Did you talk to him?'

'Huh-uh. Once he started coming around, I didn't talk to her none. Seemed an awful lot like they wanted to be alone.'

Valerie stared at the tent for a bit and then made up her mind. 'I'm gonna check it out – go inside.'

'Val!' Kristen grabbed her arm once more. 'You can't do that. It's breaking and entering!'

'Into a tent? C'mon, Kristen; don't be such a cop.'

'Wait, you're a cop?' It was the camper's turn to look startled. Valerie noticed he was clutching his daypack just that little bit tighter.

Kristen shook her head and glared at Valerie.

'No, she's just a know-it-all, which is far worse,' Valerie said, then unzipped the flap and crawled through.

SIXTEEN

S he was immediately hit by the stink of rotting organic matter and had to suppress the urge to gag. Breathing through her mouth to minimize the smell, Valerie took in the contents of the small tent. Most of the space was taken up by a double-bed-size air mattress with a pillow and a thin sleeping bag lying in a heap on top. An open suitcase lay in the corner, along with a pair of red-and-black flip-flops and two canvas shopping bags.

These contained food: a loaf of nine-grain bread; a half-eaten jar of peanut butter; partially consumed packets of cheddar cheese and luncheon meat, the meat and cheese so covered in green mold that they were barely identifiable; three shriveled, black bananas; and two overripe avocados (both with their stems, she couldn't help noticing).

Valerie breathed a sigh of relief. The cause of the stench was far more benign than what her paranoid brain had been imagining.

But the state of the foodstuffs made it clear that the tent's occupant must have indeed been gone for at least several days, and that she had not intended to be away for so long. Either that or she had no idea how quickly perishables could go bad in the tropics.

She turned to the suitcase. All the clothes inside were neatly folded except for a pair of olive drab shorts and a yellow beach towel, which had been thrown carelessly on top. A search through the pockets of the shorts revealed nothing but a stick of lip balm and a wad of tissues. She examined the inside of the waistband: size 8, the same that Valerie wore.

Kristen poked her head into the tent. 'Pee-yew!' she said. And then, 'How much longer you gonna be? Someone might find us snooping here.'

'Just a minute more; I'm almost done.' Valerie dropped the shorts back onto the bed and rummaged through the rest of the clothes in the suitcase: a pair of jeans (nothing in the pockets), a black one-piece bathing suit, three T-shirts, several knit tank tops, socks, a bra and underwear, and a couple of flowered blouses.

Valerie pulled out the T-shirts; one can learn a lot about a person from what they choose to display on their chest. Unfolding the first one, she chuckled. 'Got Poi?' it read. The second bore a stylized drawing of a turtle, similar to the ones on the aloha shirt she'd bought at the thrift store the other day. The last shirt had a logo of a wave, volcano and moon, with the words 'School of Ocean and Earth Science and Technology' written underneath. She repeated the name to herself several times, to try to commit it to memory.

The only other items in the suitcase were a toiletry kit full of the usual shampoo, soap, and toothpaste items, as well as a couple of paperback novels, both thrillers. She'd been hoping to find a purse or daypack containing something that could more specifically identify the woman – Amy, the camper had said her name was. But it made sense that she would have taken anything valuable like a wallet or cellphone with her when she went out and about.

Returning to the blow-up mattress – which had lost about half of its air – Valerie yanked off the rumpled sleeping bag. Underneath sat two additional books: *Beaches of the Big Island* and an academic volume about sea turtles. She flipped through the pages on the chance their owner had used something intriguing like a business card or boarding pass as a bookmark. No such luck; just a plain white scrap of paper marked her place in the turtle book.

'C'mon Valerie!' Kristen called with some urgency from outside. 'Let's go!'

Tossing the sleeping bag back on the bed, she gave one last look around the tent and then crawled outside. Kristen, hands on hips, was tapping her foot dramatically. The guy was still there, too. 'Find anything interesting?' he asked.

'Maybe.' Valerie zipped the flap closed. 'From the state of the rotten food she left behind, I think you're right that she's been gone for a while. And I'd say she is indeed interested in sea turtles. Either of you ever heard of the School of Ocean and Earth Science and Technology?'

Both shook their heads.

Kristen started down the path back toward the car. 'Let's get out of here,' she said, not looking back. 'I'd really like to get to Kapoho before high tide.'

Valerie smiled at the camper, who continued to clutch tightly to his daypack, eyes wide. 'Well, thanks for your help,' she said, and then trotted to catch up with Kristen. Rounding a bend, she glanced back at the man. He was still staring after them.

'I'll drive,' Kristen said as they approached the car. Valerie tossed her the keys and waited while she unlocked the doors. Kristen hadn't said a word during the entire walk back, but once settled in the driver's seat, she took a deep breath, ready to speak.

'Wait.' Valerie held her palm out. 'Before you start in on me, just let me explain.'

Kristen leaned back against the faux leather seat and exhaled loudly. 'Fine,' she said, placing her hands on her knees and staring straight ahead. 'Let's hear it.'

Valerie told her everything. About going back to Raul's alone and learning from Kevin that Daniel's wife Faith worked at the thrift store. How Faith had ranted about Daniel's philandering and laughed at his resultant black eye, seemingly unconcerned about his disappearance. And how today Kevin had told her he was finally starting to get worried and that he was the one who'd sent Valerie down to MacKenzie – that he thought Daniel's most recent girlfriend had been camping at the park.

'So that's why you wanted to come back down here.' Kristen continued to stare out the windshield.

'Yeah.' A light rain began to fall, and Valerie rolled the window halfway up. 'And there's more.'

'Great.'

She recounted what Faith had said about local marijuana growers not taking kindly to folks working for the geothermal companies, particularly when it was one of their own. And how Jordan used to work at BigT and what she'd said about explosions being a common occurrence.

'Is that the only reason you wanted to go fishing with Jordan – to pump her for information?'

'Well, I *was* actually interested in learning how they fish around here. But, yeah . . . I guess that was the main reason.'

With an abrupt shake of the head, Kristen rolled up her window as the rain began to come down harder.

And then Valerie told her about eavesdropping on the dancer Keoni after the hula show, and how she'd heard him boast about hot lava and TNT. Kristen listened in silence, the muscle in her jaw tensing and unclenching as Valerie talked.

'Right, that's all,' she said when she'd finished. 'Now you know as much as I do.'

Kristen started the engine. 'Okay. Let's go snorkeling.'

So once again Valerie found herself in the car with Kristen, neither of them speaking. That made twice within the space of just four days. Up until six weeks ago – before Charlie's death – driving with Kristen had pretty much always been a lively, chatty affair, with the one interrupting the other in a constant race to come up with the cleverest *bon mot*, the remark most likely to set the two of them off in a fit of laughter.

Which made today's drive all that more uncomfortable – and sad.

Valerie switched on the radio, letting the lilting strains of a slack-key guitar and falsetto voice fill the silence. As they turned back onto the Red Road, passing under the canopy of ironwood and coco palms, she tried to analyze from Kristen's point of view what was happening between the two of them.

It was true that the whole point of their trip to Hawai'i had been rest and relaxation. More specifically, it was meant as a respite for Valerie from the lingering trauma of her brother's death – not to mention her own brush with the same. So she had to admit it made sense that Kristen would find Valerie's becoming obsessed with yet another death to be completely contrary to the predetermined plan of action.

And, Valerie reflected, gazing out at the blue-beyond-blue waters to her right, there was nothing Kristen hated more than a change in 'The Plan.'

Now, that's not fair, she chided herself. This was supposed to be about seeing Kristen's side of the matter.

The rain had now let up and Valerie unrolled the window to inhale the moist air. It tasted of red dirt and seaweed, floral perfumes and decomposing vegetation. *Okay, so why else would*

Kristen be reacting so strongly against my need to discover the identity of the body in the lava?

She knew the answer, of course. She'd known it from the very first, when Kristen had seen the terror in her eyes after witnessing that human leg being enveloped in searing red lava. She just hadn't been able to admit it until now.

Kristen *had* believed her.

But at the same time, she had to be afraid for Valerie – fearing how it would affect her psyche, the search for the truth of what had happened out there on the lava flow. For not only would it mean reliving the grisly scene she'd witnessed that morning at Kalapana, but because of the similarity between the two events, it couldn't help but also rekindle the trauma and heartache of Charlie's death in that fiery crash.

Which was, in fact, what had happened. Kristen's fears had been spot on.

Valerie turned to look at her wife, ready to smile and break the ice, but Kristen kept her eyes on the road, jaw set, with no response to the conciliatory gesture.

Fine. Valerie returned to gazing out the window and watched as they passed Isaac Hale Park, where she'd been fishing just that morning. Whatever her gallant motives might be, Kristen could sure be one stubborn cuss.

And besides, Valerie mused, feeling the irritation well up once again, *she has yet to even acknowledge* my *needs,* my `desires.* Assuming she did believe Valerie had seen an actual body down at the flow, could Kristen truly not appreciate how acting as if Valerie had merely imagined the whole thing would make her feel crazy? Didn't she realize that by trying to 'protect' her, she was just making it that much worse?

Kristen had commenced humming along with the pop ditty now playing on the radio – a habit Valerie normally found charming but which annoyed the hell out of her right at that moment. *How can she sit there so calmly while I'm writhing inside with frustration?*

Clearly, the only way to get beyond this whole mess was to solve the mystery on her own. And since their stay on the Big Island was already half over, if she wanted to do so, she needed to get cracking.

Okay, so what new facts had she learned today at MacKenzie Park?

Valerie mentally ticked them off. First of all, Daniel and this Amy person did seem to be having some sort of relationship – and the fact of it was apparently one of the few things about which both Kevin and Faith were in agreement.

In addition, it appeared the camper they'd met was correct that it had been several days since Amy had returned to her tent. This was significant, since Daniel had also gone missing in the past week – though it sounded as if he'd disappeared before she did. It was possible, of course, that the camper's hunch was correct, and they were simply shacked up together in some love nest.

On the other hand, it could mean something far more sinister.

As they passed the warm swimming pond, steam rising in wisps through the coco fronds overhanging the geothermal pool, Valerie imagined possible scenarios. What if Amy, in a fit of jealousy, or maybe even in self-defense – say, if Daniel had attempted to push for more than she'd wanted – had ended up killing him? She'd certainly be loath to return to her campsite after committing such an act, and it would make sense for her to have gone into hiding, or returned to wherever she came from, simply abandoning the tent and her belongings.

But given that she apparently had the same small build as Valerie, would Amy be tall or strong enough to lug the dead weight of a corpse all the way out to the lava flow? *Not likely*, Valerie concluded, thinking back to how difficult it had been simply walking across that treacherous lava field. Amy would have needed help.

But that didn't exclude her from suspicion; she could easily have known someone in the area to help. And they had seen two figures – not one – from a distance that morning out at the flow.

Then again, what if it had been Faith? Who was to say she didn't discover her husband *in flagrante delicto* with Amy, and then react in a rage, taking them by surprise and hitting them over the head with, say, a heavy rock – there were certainly a lot of those on this island. And she, too, could have secured the assistance of another to help dispose of the dead lovers.

And then Valerie was struck by a gruesome thought: What if the body she'd seen had not been the only one out at the flow? What if *two* people had been buried by lava that morning?

SEVENTEEN

'*H*umu . . . humu . . .' Valerie began, but then trailed off. Sachiko helped her out and finished the mouthful-of-a-word, separating the syllables as one would when instructing a pre-schooler: '. . . *nuku-nuku-āpu-a'a.*'

'And *that's* what they picked as the state fish?'

Sachiko nodded and laughed. 'But most people just say "*humu.*" We only use the whole thing when we want to impress the tourists.'

'Like me.'

Continuing to chuckle, Sachiko took a sip of her white wine. 'Right.'

Isaac emerged from the kitchen onto the lānai balancing two wooden bowls along with a cocktail and sat down – not next to Sachiko on the couch, Valerie noted, but in the chair across from her. He offered around the larger bowl and they all took a handful of edamame – steamed soybeans.

'I was just telling Sachiko about snorkeling down at Kapoho today,' Valerie said, sucking out a pair of the salty legumes and tossing the bright green pod into the empty bowl on the coffee table. 'We saw a couple of *humus* – it's a kind of triggerfish, right?'

'Mmmm,' Isaac said as he swallowed his soybeans. 'Da name means "triggerfish with a snout like a pig" in Hawaiian.'

'Well, I didn't notice its snout, but they sure have trippy colors.'

Isaac grinned and helped himself to another handful of edamame. 'So, where's Kristen?' he asked. 'She's not usually one to miss out on *pau hana* time.'

'Probably checking her email. She'll be here soon, I'm sure. But we weren't about to wait for her.' Valerie raised her gin and lime. '*Ola loa.*'

'*Ola loa,*' repeated Isaac, and they clinked glasses.

Sachiko frowned. 'Oh, "long life." I like it.'

'Kristen kind of made it up, I think – as a toast, anyway. But I don't think it's a traditional Hawaiian one.'

'Okay, then. *Ola loa*,' said Sachiko, holding up her glass. She took a drink of wine and then glanced at her watch. 'So when do you think we'll be eating?' she asked Isaac.

'Oh!' Valerie jumped up from her chair. 'That's me – I'm doing a barbecue tonight. You need me to get it started?'

'It's just that I have a lot of work to do at home afterwards, so . . .'

'No worries, everything's already pretty much done but the chicken, and that'll just take a few minutes to cook, since it's boneless breasts. Isaac, if you turn on the grill, I can go get the salad ready.'

But then she noticed Isaac wasn't paying any attention to her. He was looking at Sachiko, a hangdog expression on his face. 'You no gonna stay tonight, babe?'

'Uh, I guess I can go start the grill,' Valerie said. Best to leave them alone for the moment.

She made her way down to the gas barbecue under the carport overhang, turned the burners on to high and then headed for the kitchen, nearly colliding with Kristen.

'Whoa, missy – where's the fire?'

'Sorry,' Valerie mumbled, too embarrassed to admit that the reason she hadn't seen Kristen coming through the door was she'd been craning her neck, spying on Isaac and Sachiko.

Kristen started for the lānai but Valerie stopped her. 'You might want to hold off a bit; they're having a relationship moment.'

'Oh.' She turned back. 'A whole lotta that going on 'round here lately,' she said with a half-smile.

'Yeah.' Valerie stared at the vinyl flooring for a moment before raising her eyes to meet Kristen's. 'Look, I've been thinking about . . . everything. And, well, I guess I understand where you're coming from.'

'It's just that I'm worried about you, hon.'

Valerie nodded. 'I know.'

Kristen took her by the hand. 'But I get that my trying to discourage you in all this has gotta be hard. That instead of helping you deal with the loss of Charlie, it's actually having the opposite effect. So . . .' She shrugged. 'I guess I'm just kind of at a loss as to what exactly to do.'

'Well, maybe try to put yourself in my position a little bit?

You know, imagine if it had been you who'd seen what I did out there in the lava? That would be something. Even if you don't actively help me try to figure it all out.'

'Okay,' she said, squeezing Valerie's hand. 'I'll do my best to be more supportive, I promise. And hey, for starters, can I give you a hand with dinner?'

'Sure.' Valerie opened the fridge and extracted the chicken, which had been marinating in sesame oil, miso, ginger, and sake. She handed the pan and a pair of tongs to Kristen. 'Once the grill's hot, you can throw these on. They'll only need a few minutes per side, so be sure to keep an eye on them so they don't dry out.'

'Right-ee-o.'

'And here's a clean plate to put 'em on when they're done.'

'Thanks.' Kristen leaned over and kissed Valerie on the lips, then looked her in the eye. 'You know I love you. Even if I can be kind of a pain sometimes.'

'I know,' said Valerie with a grin. 'About both those things.'

Once Kristen had left, Valerie grabbed a fork and poked the Russet potatoes baking in their jackets in the oven. *Good, more than done.* Switching off the oven, she set to work preparing the ingredients for the salad: thinly sliced celery, chopped dates and toasted walnuts, slivers of Pecorino cheese. The dressing – a simple red wine vinaigrette with a dash of orange juice for a touch of sweetness – was already made, sitting in a ramekin on the counter.

The salad prepped, she gathered plates, flatware, and napkins, and headed for the dining room. *Maybe Kristen's right*, she thought as she laid them out on the table. *Maybe this whole thing is making me worse.* It was certainly true that ever since seeing that boot in the lava, she'd been dwelling much more on what had happened to her brother.

But simply stopping her investigation wouldn't excise from her brain the vision of Charlie in that burning car, she reasoned. If anything, it was taking her mind *off* that horrible memory, providing somewhere else to direct her focus.

As Valerie came back to the kitchen to fetch a stick of butter for the baked potatoes, Kristen returned from the grill bearing a platter of glistening chicken breasts, their crispy golden skins adorned with caramelized grill marks. 'Where would you like me to put this?'

'On the table,' Valerie said. 'And you can call Isaac and Sachiko to dinner.' Giving the dressing one last vigorous whisk, she tossed the salad, grabbed the potatoes from the oven and plopped them in a bowl, then joined the others at the table.

No. I can't give up now, she decided. *Not when I feel so close to a breakthrough.*

Back downstairs after dinner, Valerie flopped onto the bed, opened her laptop, and thought back to that T-shirt she'd found among Amy's possessions at MacKenzie State Park. What exactly had it said? School of . . . something. Was it 'Ocean Sciences'?

She typed this into the Google search bar. A school at Bangor University in Wales came up at the top of the query results. Not likely.

But the second entry was more promising: the School of Ocean and Earth Science and Technology, at the University of Hawai'i, Mānoa. *Yes*, that was what the shirt had said. And she recognized the logo of the volcano, sea, and moon. But where the heck was Mānoa? *Ah*, she realized as she read about the school – that was the name of the University's Honolulu campus.

Clicking on the home page's 'Directory' link, Valerie typed the name 'Amy' into the search box. Nothing.

She returned to the main page and studied it further. 'Academic Departments' was one of the menu options. The first department that came up was the Graduate Program in Marine Biology. If Amy were connected to the school, based on her interest in sea turtles, it seemed a good bet that this would be hers.

Yes. Their page had a link for 'People.' Once again, she typed the name 'Amy,' but to no avail. Under the search box was a list of faculty, but scrolling through it, she saw that none had that name.

Maybe she's a student. But search as she might, Valerie was unable to find a list of the program's students anywhere on the website. Shutting the computer, she lay back on the pile of pillows. A gecko chucked softly from somewhere in the room, and outside the window above her bed, the coquí were performing their nightly serenade. Upstairs, someone walked heavily across the living-room floor. That would be Isaac. The steps continued toward the other side of the house, and a door creaked shut.

Sachiko must have left for the night.

The steps recrossed the floor, and after a moment, the muffled voices of Isaac and Kristen could be heard through the hardwood panels of the ceiling above Valerie.

And then she heard the train.

That was what Isaac called the sound of the trade-wind rains as they swept upslope, because of how you could hear them coming – sometimes a full minute before they actually arrived. Valerie listened with a smile to the deep thrumming from afar, growing louder and louder until finally it hit: a tremendous pounding on the metal roof, as if a giant in the sky had upended a truckload of gravel atop the house.

And then it stopped, as suddenly as it had begun. Setting her computer on the bedside table, Valerie shut off the light and watched as ghostly clouds chased across the sky, illuminated by the waxing moon. A solitary coquí sang a hesitant note. Another piped up in answer, and before long the chorus had returned, accompanied by the steady patter of water dripping off the ti plants outside her window.

A few minutes before two o'clock the next afternoon, Isaac and Valerie pulled into the parking lot of the East Hawai'i Community Center, in an industrial area across town. It had been gray and rainy all day long and was pouring buckets when they arrived at the center.

During the drive over, Valerie apologized for not being more lively the night before, but Isaac just shook his head. 'I didn't even notice. But then again, I wasn't in the best of moods myself last night.'

'Yeah . . .'

They fell silent after that, listening to the rhythmic slapping of the windshield wipers until they arrived at the hula class. Several young men dashed inside from their cars, dodging deep puddles in the parking lot, and Valerie and Isaac chased after them into the large room, kicking off their slippahs and lining them up against the wall with all the other shoes. Other guys were already inside, moving chairs against the wall and cleaning the hardwood floor with large dust mops. They were all young and exceedingly fit. Valerie looked around for Keoni and spotted him on the floor, stretching his legs. The bruising around his eye had diminished, but his face was still noticeably discolored.

A large mirror ran along one of the walls of the room, above which the Hawaiian state flag and a long wooden canoe paddle hung. Luana stood next to the mirror, talking to a boy who couldn't have been much older than fifteen. She appeared to be the only other woman in the room besides Valerie.

'It's a men's *hālau*, I gather?'

Isaac nodded and turned to face her. 'You sure you want to do this? 'Cause I could just say you wanted to come watch the practice, if you've changed your mind.'

'No. I want to do it.' Valerie started towards Luana, but was only halfway there when the teacher clapped her hands and called out, 'Okay, everyone, *e hele kākou*! Let's get going!'

The dancers dropped their daypacks and gym bags along the wall and took their places on the floor, facing the mirror. Most wore board shorts, and about half were shirtless.

Isaac shrugged as Valerie walked back to where he was standing. 'Sorry I was so late getting home from work,' he said, and pointed to some red plastic chairs at the back of the room. 'You wanna watch and talk to her at the break?'

'Sure.'

Luana started with some group stretches and then announced they were going to work on the hula they'd started learning the previous week. Coming over to switch on the music, she noticed Isaac and Valerie for the first time and bent to kiss Isaac on the cheek. 'Gonna dance with us today?'

'No wayz,' he said with a smile. 'So much easier just to watch da young braddahs do all da work for a change.'

The song and dance were modern, with slack-key guitar and falsetto singing rather than an *ipu* and chanting, and with smooth, swaying movements and smiles from the *hālau*, as opposed to the violent stomping and grimaces Valerie had seen the other night during the ancient hula.

She watched, enchanted, as they ran the routine over and over – Luana stopping now and again to correct a hand movement or comment on timing – and found herself disappointed when a break was finally called. How had she ever imagined that the hula was just some dippy gimmick for the tourists?

'Do they have any *hālaus* on the Mainland?' Valerie asked Isaac as the group sat down and sipped from their water bottles.

'Absolutely. There are even a couple from California who've danced a bunch of times at the Merrie Monarch.'

She had heard enough about this annual hula festival in Hilo to know that merely being invited to participate was an enormous honor. *Maybe I should check out some hula when I get back home.*

Standing up to stretch her back, Valerie scanned the room for Luana, only to see her heading their way. 'So, you liked the hula the other night so much you wanted to come back for more, yah?'

Valerie stood, and they gave each other a quick hug. 'I do really like it, it's true. I think you've got a convert.'

'I have a beginning class that meets Tuesday nights, if you're interested,' she said with a wink.

'Oh, God.' Valerie let out a laugh. 'You wouldn't want me; I'd be a hazard to the other dancers. Best I stick with being a spectator. Anyway, I'll be heading back to the Mainland the end of next week.'

And then as she said this, it hit her just what that meant. Her trip to Hawai'i was more than half over. And there was so much she still wanted to do: hang out more at the beach, go snorkeling again, visit the National Park and the tropical gardens, see the waterfalls . . .

And, of course, solve the mystery of the body in the lava.

She touched Luana on the arm. 'Can I ask you about something?'

'Of course.' Curiosity showed in the teacher's eyes.

'It's about the dancer we talked about that night at the Palace Theater, Keoni.' Valerie glanced over to where he was standing, right as he burst out laughing. The two men with him laughed, too.

'Uh-huh?' Luana's expression became even more quizzical. 'What about him?'

'It's just that . . . well, that night at the Palace, I overheard him talking. And what he said got me kind of nervous.' She stopped, suddenly embarrassed.

'Go on,' Luana said, leaning closer to her. 'What did he say?'

'I don't know exactly, but it was something to do with explosives. I distinctly heard him say "TNT." It had to do with how he got his black eye. And then he said something about it happening down at the lava flow.'

Luana pursed her lips and turned to stare at Keoni, but didn't speak.

'Tell her about the body,' Isaac prompted, nudging Valerie's shoulder with his. 'And the explosion you read about.'

This got Luana's attention. She looked back at them, eyes wide. 'What body? What explosion?'

Valerie sighed and told her story for what seemed like the millionth time. 'So,' she said when she'd finished, 'when I heard Keoni bragging about using TNT, I figured he might be the one who caused the explosion at BigT that was in the paper. And then I heard him talking about being in a fight down at the lava flow, and I remembered how you'd said he hadn't shown up for your performance last Friday night – which is the same night I think the guy in the lava died. Well, you could see how that could make me wonder if maybe Keoni was the one who . . .' She trailed off, not able to actually say it, to accuse the student of being a killer.

Luana shook her head. 'My goodness. This story you're telling me, it's not so easy to take it all in.' She looked at Isaac with a frown, as if to ask, 'Is this gal for real?'

He shrugged in response. 'I know it all sounds strange,' he said, 'but I believe her. I didn't actually see the body, but I saw Valerie right after she saw it, and I can tell you she was plenty freaked out. And I also saw the newspaper story about that explosion at BigT. Plus, this guy Daniel that she's talking about? He really does work at da plant, and he really is missing.'

Luana stared at Keoni again, thought a moment, took a deep breath, and strode off towards the dancer.

She was going to confront him about it *now*? Right here at the rehearsal? What if he really *was* a murderer? Valerie gave Isaac a nervous look, then the two of them hurried to catch up.

EIGHTEEN

'Could I talk to you for a moment, Keoni?'

The dancer grinned. 'Sure, Aunty.' But the smile quickly disappeared when he saw Luana's stern expression. The two guys with him saw it too, and slipped away.

Keoni glanced from Luana, to Isaac, to Valerie and frowned, likely wondering why the hell the two others had come over with his *kumu* to talk to him. He wiped his damp brow, and Valerie thought she could detect a sour muskiness radiating from his body.

'I wanted to ask you where you were last Friday night, when you should have been at our performance.'

He hung his head. 'Sorry, Aunty.'

'Does it have anything to do with that bruise on your face?'

He didn't answer and just continued to stare at his feet. Luana let him stew, not saying anything further. After a moment, he looked up, working his jaw back and forth. 'What have *they* got to do with it?' he asked in a surly voice, nodding at Valerie and Isaac.

'This is Isaac, who used to dance with this *halau* – and who never once missed a performance, I might add. And this is his friend Valerie. They're here because Valerie overheard something you said Wednesday night at the Palace – something rather disturbing.'

Uh-oh, was Valerie's thought. *Now I'm really in it.*

But Keoni merely looked at Valerie again and shrugged. 'I don' recognize her.'

'She heard you talking about how you got that black eye,' Luana continued. 'How you got into a fight with someone down at the lava flow in Kalapana.' She turned to Valerie for confirmation. 'Is that right?'

'Uh . . . right.'

'Huh?' said Keoni. 'I nevah said dat.'

'You did,' Valerie interjected, the insinuation that she might be lying now overtaking any fears she had of the young man. 'I heard you say it. Maybe not those precise words. But I distinctly heard you say . . .' She thought back to what exactly she'd heard that night. 'You were down at "the hot lava" – that was it.'

He smiled. 'Now *dat* sounds like something I could-a said, 'cause I was dere Friday night.'

'You were?' Valerie and Luana exclaimed simultaneously.

'Yah. It was my girlfriend's birthday and we went dere for a few drinks. I'm real sorry I missed da performance, Aunty, but she woulda nevah forgave me if I didn't spend dat night with her.'

'So you *were* down at the lava flow Friday night,' Valerie said.

Keoni frowned and shook his head. 'I nevah was dere; I told you so already.'

'Wait, you just said . . .' Valerie turned to Luana, confused. The teacher shrugged and shook her head, as if to say, *I don't understand, either.*

But then Keoni snapped his fingers and laughed. 'I get it! Da Hot Lava – it's a *bar* down Keawe Street. That's where we were – not down Kalapana side, where da real flow is.'

'Oh.' Valerie could feel the blood rush to her cheeks and hoped her Hawaiian suntan would hide the resultant flush. 'But what about the TNT?' she insisted.

'TNT?' Keoni repeated.

'Yeah, you were talking about how you used TNT the night you got your black eye.'

Keoni shook his head once again, a blank look on his face. He turned to Luana. 'I dunno what she's talking about. Why would I have TNT . . .' And then he laughed again, much louder this time. So loud that others in the room turned to look. 'Ho! That is *so* funny!' He dissolved into a fit of the giggles, crouching and slapping his leg over and over again.

'*What* is so funny, Keoni?' Luana finally grasped him by the arm and the dancer stood back up, panting and wiping his eyes.

'Not T-*N*-T,' he said, trying to get control of the chuckles that continued to slip out. 'I was talkin' 'bout da T-*M*-T!' And then he burst out laughing all over again. 'I no can believe you thought it was TNT,' he managed to articulate between giggles.

'Uh, what's TMT?' Valerie asked softly, wishing she were

anywhere but there, in front of twenty handsome young men, all staring at her with wide grins on their faces.

'It's the Thirty Meter Telescope they want to build on Maunakea,' said Isaac. 'Remember I told you that a lot of native Hawaiians are opposed to it being constructed there? I'm guessing Keoni is one of those, yah?'

He nodded. 'Dat's how I got dis,' he said, pointing to his eye. 'There was these astronomy guys at Da Hot Lava dat night, goin' on and on about how great da TMT was gonna be for da community an' all. I got sick of listenin' to them, an' we kinda had words . . .'

'More than words, I'd say.' Luana was frowning, hands on hips.

'Sorry Aunty,' Keoni said once again.

Valerie asked Isaac to take her home as soon as Luana called the *hālau* back to order for the second half of their practice. No way did she want to sit there with all those guys watching her, knowing what a fool she'd just made of herself in front of them.

Kristen was in the kitchen whipping up a banana and yogurt smoothie. 'How was the surfing?' Valerie asked once she'd shut off the blender's blaring motor.

'Sloppy. I probably shouldn't have gone out once it started raining so hard, but whatever . . .' She took a drink straight from the blender jar, leaving a creamy white mustache above her upper lip. 'How was the hula class?'

With a quick glance at the two women, Isaac grabbed the jar of peanut butter from the cupboard and a spoon from the dish drainer and made a quick exit.

'Embarrassing,' Valerie said.

'What, did they make you join in?'

'Very funny.' Plopping down at the kitchen table, she smoothed out the cloth napkin sitting there in a crumpled heap. 'I just had something completely wrong, is all.'

Kristen took the seat across from her, and Valerie handed her the napkin. 'What did you have wrong?' she asked, wiping her mouth.

'Promise you won't give me another lecture?'

Kristen set down the blender jar, splayed her hands on the

table and stared at them. After a moment, she sighed, slapped both palms on the Formica surface, and looked up at Valerie. 'Fine, I promise. No lecture.'

'Okay. Remember what I told you that dancer Keoni said during the reception after the hula show the other night?'

'Uh . . .'

'That he talked about being down at the hot lava, and I heard him mention "TNT"?'

'Oh, right.'

'Well, that was the reason I wanted to go to the rehearsal today, to talk to his hula teacher – Luana, the woman we met that same night – about what I'd heard him say.'

'Uh-huh.' Kristen sipped her smoothie, eying Valerie over the jar.

'I'd been so sure he'd been up to something,' she went on. 'I mean, it makes so much sense that someone from Pele's Children would have been who put that body there. Did you hear what that woman said during the show, about how Pele took revenge on her sister when she thought she'd stolen her betrothed?'

'I gotta admit I sort of glazed over during a lot of that part.'

'Well, she said that the way Pele got even with her sister was by covering her forest with lava and turning her best friend to stone. Sound familiar?'

Kristen raised her left eyebrow, Vulcan-style, and downed the rest of her drink.

'That's right, Mr Spock. It's the exact same thing that happened to that body I saw – it was covered in lava, and, hence, turned to stone.'

Kristen stood up and walked to the sink. 'So I take it you did talk to that guy's *kumu hula* today about what you heard him say?'

Valerie nodded. 'Yeah, but it turns out the "Hot Lava" he was talking about is a bar—'

'Oh, right. I've seen it,' said Kristen as she rinsed the jar. 'It's a sort of dive place downtown.'

'I sure wish you'd mentioned that earlier; it would have saved me from making a royal ass of myself in front of the entire hula class.' Valerie watched Kristen dry the blender, replace it on the base, and hang the dish towel back on its hook. 'Not only that,' she continued, 'it wasn't TNT – the explosive – that Keoni was talking about. It was TMT – that telescope they're building.'

'The Thirty Meter Telescope.' Kristen sat back down. 'Hey,' she added as Valerie leaned forward and put her head in her hands. 'It's okay. Anyone could have made the same mistake.'

Valerie clenched her eyes shut, willing the tears to stay put. 'I just feel . . . so *stupid*.' Kristen reached over to touch her arm, and that simple gesture of sympathy was all it took. Out they poured, turning quickly to violent sobs. Coming to Valerie's side of the table, Kristen put her arms around her wife's shaking body and held her tight until the tears subsided and her breathing started to return to normal.

Valerie sat up and wiped her eyes, managing a half-hearted smile. 'Sorry about that. I just seem to be so emotional lately.'

Kristen gave her shoulder one last squeeze and returned to her seat. 'Look,' she said, 'just because that hula guy didn't set off that explosion or dump that body in the lava doesn't mean your theory is completely wrong. It might still have been one of those Pele's Children types, or someone else with similar beliefs who did that stuff.'

Valerie couldn't believe what she was hearing. 'So, what? You're actually encouraging me now?'

Kristen's hands went up in surrender. 'I know, I know. But there's two things. First off, I can't stand to see you like this any longer. This trip was supposed to help you maybe take your mind off Charlie – at least for a while – but ever since that day down at the flow, if anything, you've only been *more* unhappy. Even when you're trying to put on a good face, it's obvious you're miserable inside. And I'd say it's become pretty darn clear that my trying to stop you from obsessing about it isn't helping any. So . . .'

'If you can't beat 'em, join 'em?'

She shrugged. 'I dunno about that. But I do have to say, what you were talking about just now? About that body being covered by lava and turned to stone – how it's just like in that story about Pele and her sister?' She shook her head. 'I have to admit there is something kind of . . . well, strangely similar about the two.'

'So you're gonna help me?' Valerie asked, gracing her with the toothiest matinee-idol smile she could muster.

'Let's just say I'm willing to give you moral support. And maybe some advice.'

'Well, that'll certainly be an improvement on how you've been up till now.' Valerie dipped her head in a mock bow. 'So, *Sensei*, how do you advise me to proceed? 'Cause I've hit dead ends everywhere I've looked so far.'

'Seems to me your best lead at this point is that woman who was camping down at MacKenzie State Park.'

'Amy? But I already Googled the school I think she may be associated with and came up with a big fat nothing.'

'So call them and talk to a real live person.' Kristen pulled her phone from her front pocket and consulted the screen. 'Good. It's not five yet, so someone should still be there. What's the name of the school?'

'The School of Ocean and Earth Science and Technology, at the University of Hawai'i, Ma . . . Ma something. I forget.'

Kristen typed in the name. 'Here it is. Mānoa.'

'I think their Marine Biology Department is our best bet,' Valerie said. 'What with her big interest in sea turtles.'

Kristen nodded, typed some more, and then punched in a number. When she heard the line ringing on the other end, she held the phone out to Valerie.

'Aloha,' said a woman's voice through the tinny speaker. 'May I help you?'

Valerie grabbed the phone. 'Uh, hello? Hi. I'm calling about someone I think may be associated with your department. I'm not sure if she'd be on the faculty or a student, but her first name is Amy. I was wondering if you could maybe look up the name and—'

'All our faculty is listed on our website,' she said, rather brusquely to Valerie's mind. 'And if she's a student, I'm afraid we're not allowed to give out their contact information.'

'I didn't see her listed as faculty on your page.' Valerie was trying to decide if going the whiney route would be the best tactic in this instance. 'Could you at least tell me if you have any current students named Amy?'

'I'm sorry, but I really can't do that.'

'But I just—' The line went dead. 'Well, that sure didn't work. Maybe she didn't appreciate getting a call right before quittin' time on a Friday afternoon.' Valerie handed the phone back to Kristen. 'But I've got another idea. Be back in a jiff,' she said, and headed downstairs.

Valerie grabbed her laptop and pulled up the School of Ocean and Earth Science and Technology website once again to scan the list of faculty. They were listed by specialty, such as oceanography, geochemistry, biology, microbiology, and geology. Picking one of the biology professors at random, she clicked on her email link and typed a message:

Dear Professor Hamasaki,

I'm trying to find a woman named Amy who I think may be a grad student with your department. She's interested in sea turtles and has been camping at MacKenzie State Park here on the Big Island for a week or so, but she hasn't been back to her campsite for several days, so I've been unable to track her down.

I know this all probably sounds rather strange, but if you do know who she is, I'd truly appreciate if you'd write me back.

Mahalo!
Valerie Corbin

Perhaps the mysterious aspect of the message would prompt a response. Valerie closed the laptop and headed back upstairs for cocktail hour.

NINETEEN

Saturday morning.

Had it really been a full week since the hike out to the lava flow – since Valerie had watched that leg and boot become entombed forever in molten rock?

She'd promised herself the previous night that she would make a good-faith effort today not to obsess about the body in the lava, or about Daniel or Amy. That she'd do her utmost to spend the day simply having fun, acting like a real tourist enjoying a tropical vacation with her spouse.

But the front-page article in the morning paper was not helping. Valerie had been unable to resist reading about BigT's proposal for an additional geothermal location down in Puna and the locals' vehement opposition to the plan, which in turn brought to mind once more the questions that had been plaguing her all week: Just who had been killed and then dumped down at the flow? And by whom? And *why*?

The three of them – Isaac, Valerie, and Kristen – were again seated in Isaac's kitchen, breakfasts and newspaper sections spread out across the red Formica table. Valerie finished the story and folded up the front page, then took a bite of sweet papaya chunks tossed with tangy yogurt and fresh lime. Leaning back in her chair, she closed her eyes and took a few deep breaths. *Relax. Just let it go, Valerie . . .*

'Ho!' Isaac's exclamation startled her out of her attempt at meditation. 'I forgot! Da canoe races are today,' he said, pointing to the headline on the sports page. 'Starting at nine, down at da Bayfront – we should go check 'um out!'

Kristen looked up from the crossword she was working on. 'Really? That would be way cool, don't ya think, Val?'

'Absolutely,' she agreed. It sounded like an excellent way to get her back on her 'have some fun' track. 'Let's do it.'

*   *   *

The Bayfront was hopping, and they drove all the way to the far end of the parking lot before finding a spot for Isaac's car. Heading down the long, narrow beach toward the crowds, Valerie kicked off her flip-flops to walk barefoot in the mixture of red dirt and black sand. After a night of hard rain, the storm had finally petered out, and the fierce morning sun was causing the still-dripping palm fronds to shimmer in its light. Waves were crashing over the breakwater, but inside the bay, the ocean appeared calm.

A few outrigger canoes were already floating in the water, but most were still on the beach, lined up in rows with their teams gathered about at their sterns. Several groups of stragglers hurried to lug their heavy six-man craft out from the canoe houses along the Bayfront down to the edge of the beach.

As they passed the various teams, they could hear coaches giving pep talks to their crews. 'Long, powerful strokes,' Valerie heard one say.

'Don't forget, it's all about timing!' another shouted.

They stopped at a table set up in the middle of the teams, and Isaac spoke with the woman there, who was checking off names on a clipboard. 'I got some friends racing today,' he said to Kristen and Valerie after they'd finished talking. 'Their club is over there.' He headed farther down the beach, and the two women tagged along.

More crews were starting to move their canoes out to the water, and as Valerie watched them, she saw that different-colored flags had been set up in the ocean, not too far offshore. 'Is that where they'll be racing?' she asked Isaac as they walked, indicating the flags.

'Yeah. Today is a regatta – short sprints. They start over there.' He nodded toward the three canoes already out in the water to their left, being held steady behind a line of flags by people floating at their bows. 'Then they go 'round those flags dere, and come back to where they started. There'll be a bunch of heats, and den the final runs. Oh, there's the guys I know.' Isaac took off at a trot toward a group of muscular men standing around a green-and-yellow canoe.

'I'm gonna go get a cup of coffee,' Kristen said, and started for a table with a hand-lettered sign reading 'Kea'au Canoe

Club – 'Ono Grindz.' Two pre-teen girls were nearly hidden behind a stainless steel coffee urn and plates piled high with donuts and Spam *musubi*. 'You want one?'

'No, thanks.' Valerie turned to follow after Isaac, but then stopped and squinted into the sun. Was that who she thought it was?

A large man who'd been blocking her view stepped away, and she saw that it was indeed Kevin, the bartender from Raul's. He'd been talking to several other people, but it looked like the group was breaking up. Valerie trotted to catch up to him as he walked toward one of the canoe houses.

'Kevin.'

He turned at the sound of his name and waited for her. 'Howzit?' he said as she came up to him.

'I thought that was you. Are you here to race?'

'Yeah.'

So she'd been right about his rower's physique, though at the moment it was hidden by a baggy long-sleeved T-shirt with a drawing of an outrigger canoe and the words 'You deserve a good paddling.' Not something she'd want emblazoned across her own chest, but she did chuckle.

'I just wanted to let you know what happened when I went down to MacKenzie the other day,' Valerie said. 'That woman you told me about – Amy is her name – she is, in fact, staying down there. But I guess she hasn't been back to her campsite for a while – several days at least.' She told Kevin what the camper they'd met had said and about what little she'd learned from looking in her tent.

'Huh,' was his only response.

'So, you hear anything about Daniel yet?' Valerie asked.

'Not a word. And I really don't get why he wouldn't have contacted me by now. It makes me pretty nervous, actually.' He dug his big toe into the sand and gazed out at the tiny island on the far side of the bay, its numerous palm trees swaying in the light breeze. Catching her watching him, Kevin nodded at the island.

'You know,' he said, 'Coconut Island's Hawaiian name is Mokuola – the island of healing. In ancient times, it was a place of refuge for warriors, or for other people who'd broken the laws of *kapu*. If they could swim out to it without getting caught, they'd be pardoned for whatever crimes they'd committed.' He sighed. 'If only it were still that easy.'

'You been committing crimes you need pardoning for?' Valerie asked, and he shot her a quick look and then returned his gaze to the bay. She laughed. 'Oh, yeah, there is that one involving green-colored herbs, but I doubt the ancient Hawaiians would have considered that a mortal sin.'

'Unless it was reserved for the chief or *kahuna*,' Kevin said.

'Well, if that's the case, it wouldn't hurt for you to get your sorry ass out to Coconut Island. It might still work; you never know. And at least there's now a bridge, so you wouldn't have to swim. The good news for me is I'll be hanging out there this Thursday evening – it's my big six-oh birthday celebration. So if I've unknowingly committed some sort of taboo while here, I should be safe.'

Kevin smiled and then glanced towards the canoe house.

'I should let you go,' she said. 'Good luck in your race.'

'Thanks. Take it easy.' Flashing her the shaka, he turned to go.

Valerie went in search of Kristen and Isaac and found them down by the water. The first race was about to start. Five canoes bobbed about in the ocean in a row, each with a swimmer holding it in place behind its flag. Six women sat in each canoe, their paddles extended, ready to stroke. A man on shore dropped a flag, and they shot forward, digging their blades into the water in unison, like the wheels of a powerful steam locomotive. Shouts of 'hut, hut, *ho*!' carried across the water, signaling the paddlers to switch sides.

In what seemed like mere seconds, they reached the flags at the far end of the course and did one-eighties around them to race back home. The number-three canoe cut it too close and its outrigger ran over the flag. 'Disqualified,' Isaac said, shaking his head. 'Too bad.' Its paddlers let up after their foul, but the four other canoes ratcheted the tempo up a notch, the women leaning so far into their strokes that their chests appeared to touch their legs.

Two canoes were neck and neck coming into the finish, but the number four inched ahead at the last second to take the win.

A group of women standing a little ways from them jumped up and down and cheered wildly.

Valerie realized she'd been holding her breath. 'Wow. Exciting!' she said.

'Yah. I love da canoe races.' Isaac grinned, then walked off down the beach.

'I'm gonna go look for a bathroom,' said Kristen, downing the last of her coffee. Valerie nodded absently, watching Isaac as he stopped to chat with one of the women who'd cheered the winners of the last race and then wandered on, exchanging pleasantries with just about every other person he met. He was talking to an older Hawaiian-looking man whose neck was draped with several elaborate flower leis, when Valerie again spotted Kevin, standing behind the man Isaac was speaking with.

She moved closer to get a better look. Kevin was gesturing dramatically with his arms and yelling at someone – a short, rotund woman with shoulder-length hair. And then Valerie let out a little gasp. It was Faith, the woman from the thrift store. Daniel's wife. And she and Kevin were going at it like two snarling junk-yard dogs.

She was trying to decide whether to approach closer and risk being noticed when Kevin leaned over, getting right into Faith's face. Faith shrieked something in response to whatever he'd just said, and then stalked off, leaving him panting and glaring in her direction.

Should I try to catch her? But Faith was already in her car, backing out and zooming away. *Damn.* Maybe she could find out from Kevin what the hell that had all been about. But by the time Valerie turned back, he was sprinting after a bunch of guys carrying a canoe down to the water's edge, yanking off his shirt as he went. He was coming Valerie's way but didn't appear to see her.

As Kevin darted past, she spied the large tattoo inked on the back of his right shoulder – it was the green, yellow, and red flag of the Hawai'i sovereignty movement.

'Anyone hungry?' Isaac asked at around one o'clock. 'This is gonna go on all afternoon, but I have no need to stay till the end. We can check out the results in the paper tomorrow morning.'

Valerie's hand shot up. 'I am!'

'You're always hungry,' said Kristen with a laugh, then turned to Isaac. 'I have no idea how she keeps that girlish figure.'

'I'm blessed with good genes, is all. Which is very lucky, given how much I do adore my food. So, where do you want to go eat? Oh, I know – how about The Speckled Gecko? I've been wanting to try it out . . .' Valerie trailed off, realizing this might not be a time Isaac was eager to visit his girlfriend's place of employment.

But he seemed to like the idea. 'Sure, we could do that. I wouldn't mind having an excuse to see Sachiko, actually. You know, gauge how she's feeling about . . . things.'

They walked to Isaac's Subaru and drove along the coco-palm-lined Bayfront back to town. The restaurant was busy on this Saturday afternoon, but they lucked out and were seated after a wait of only ten minutes. The server led them to a table in the covered outdoor area, handed them menus, and then left to take another table's order.

'Wow, this is great.' Valerie swiveled in her chair to take in their surroundings. Planter boxes of pink ginger, waxy-leaved philodendron, and parrot-beaked heliconia dangling from tall stalks separated the dining area from the sidewalk beyond, and a fountain spouting water from its dolphin mouth provided soothing background music, as well as a cooling mist to offset the warm, humid day. On the far side of the lānai stood a wood-carved bar with six stools and rows of liquor bottles lining the shelves behind.

Kristen and Isaac were busy studying the offerings. 'I'm getting the *lau lau*,' Isaac announced.

'Oh, yeah? What's that?' Valerie searched the menu for the item.

'It's a traditional Hawaiian dish – pork and fish wrapped in taro leaves and then steamed. A lotta times, people use a cheap kine fish, but dey make it here with butterfish – it's *'ono*-licious!'

Kristen tapped her menu. 'Well, I'm gonna get the jerk chicken. I could use something spicy to go with this heat,' she added, fanning herself with the sheet of card stock.

They both looked at Valerie, who was scanning the lunch

specials with a critical eye. The Thai noodle salad with chicken, cucumber, and peanut sauce sounded enticing, as did the Kalbi ribs. But then again, the *lau lau* plate lunch that Isaac was getting also looked good.

She was saved from having to make a hasty decision by the approach of Sachiko to their table. 'Hey, Isaac,' she said, holding his eyes for a moment before turning toward the two women. 'What're you guys up to today?'

'Been to the canoe races and worked up an appetite watching the paddlers do all dat strenuous exercise.' Isaac flashed a nervous grin, and Valerie observed that his thumb was tapping out a rapid cadence upon his right thigh.

When Sachiko returned his smile, the thumb slowed its pace. 'Ah, good fun,' she said. 'So, you going home after lunch, or off to some other adventure this afternoon?'

Isaac glanced at Kristen and Valerie. 'Probably just go home,' he said. 'I wouldn't mind having an afternoon off, maybe watch some baseball. But you two could go out and do something if you wanted.'

''Cause, well, I was thinking maybe between shifts I could come over to the house . . .' Sachiko paused. 'So we could, you know, talk.'

Isaac's four other digits joined in the tapping. 'Uh, yeah, babe. That would be great.'

'Okay, then. Well, I'd better get back to work. See you in a bit.'

Isaac watched as she headed back to the indoor part of the restaurant, then let out a long breath.

'Good news or bad, you think?' Kristen asked, and he merely shook his head.

'Who knows? But I kinda just lost my appetite.'

TWENTY

Back at the house after lunch, Isaac and Kristen headed for the living room to watch the end of the Dodgers–Giants game on TV. 'Oof, I can barely move,' Isaac proclaimed, stretching out on the couch and patting his stomach.

Kristen plopped down on the faded brown easy chair by the window. 'Yeah, I was pretty sure you wouldn't have any problem eating,' she said. 'Though I was a bit surprised when you ordered dessert, too.'

'I nevah can resist their molten chocolate cake. But in this case, I think maybe I should-a.'

Valerie, who'd followed them into the room, squinted to read the score on the screen: L.A. was ahead twelve to two, in the bottom of the sixth inning. 'Well, this doesn't look terribly exciting,' she said with a snort. 'Guess I'll go downstairs for a bit.' She left them to their game and headed to their studio.

Time for a little research.

Sitting at the desk, she fired up her laptop and typed 'Hawaii sovereignty movement' into the search box. Numerous articles popped up, but one near the top caught her eye: 'Hawaiian Sovereignty – Goals and Strategies.' A quick scan of the piece told her that while all involved in the movement agreed that the overthrow of the Hawaiian nation in 1893 had been illegal, there were multiple viewpoints regarding possible solutions. The goals and strategies listed in the article ran the gamut from implementing something similar to the status Native Americans were accorded on the Mainland, to out-and-out independence from the United States with a full restoration of the Hawaiian monarchy.

She clicked on another link. The current sovereignty movement, this article said, had its roots in the Hawaiian Cultural Renaissance that occurred in the 1970s in conjunction with a rise of interest in the Hawaiian language and traditional arts and music, as well as the successful voyage of a replica of an ancient double-hulled canoe from Hawai'i to Tahiti using only Polynesian navigation techniques.

'But today in 2018,' she read on, 'some adherents of the sovereignty movement are seeking to reestablish traditional Hawaiian culture as a way of life on the islands, with certain of the more radical factions willing to force these old ways upon the status quo.' The banning of geothermal power on the Big Island as well as the decommission and deconstruction of all the telescopes atop Maunakea were two examples the author provided.

Valerie stopped reading and gazed at the mynah birds squabbling as they pecked berries from the palm tree outside her window. So, she wondered, did that mean that someone who had the sovereignty flag tattooed on his body was likely to subscribe to those more radical beliefs? *And more to the point*, she asked herself, *could Kevin have killed Daniel because his friend had betrayed the cause by starting to work at the geothermal plant?*

She was about to click on another article when she noticed a new email message in her mailbox. It was from Professor Hamasaki:

Aloha, Ms. Corbin,

It's interesting timing that you wrote when you did, as I do have a graduate student named Amy Krauss. She's been on the Big Island for a couple of weeks, surveying and mapping tide pools along the south-east coast of the island, where green sea turtles can become stranded after storms and heavy rains. But I'm concerned, as she hasn't answered any of my emails from earlier in the week.

She could, of course, simply be off the grid – or more interested in things other than messages from her professor. Nevertheless, if you do have any information about her, I'd love to hear back from you.

Thank you,
Judith Hamasaki, Ph.D.
Professor of Biological Oceanography

Valerie sat back in her chair and closed her eyes. *Oh, boy.* So it sounded like Amy was indeed missing. What did that mean? And what on earth was she going to write back to Professor Hamasaki? 'I think your grad student may have either killed her lover and dumped him in the lava, or she may be dead herself,' hardly seemed an appropriate response.

She leaned forward again and held her hands over the keyboard, deciding what to say. Something vague would have to do, at least for now:

> Thanks for writing back so quickly. I'm afraid I don't have any information regarding Amy Krauss's whereabouts. It's just that someone I know was wondering how he could contact her, and it occurred to me that you might have that information. I'll be sure to let you know if I hear anything further.

Hitting send, Valerie stood to stretch, then looked up as Kristen came down the wooden stairway.

'Total blowout, that game,' Kristen said. 'And Sachiko just showed up, so I figured I'd see what you were up to. She and Isaac are hunkered down in his bedroom to talk, and I'm guessing it may be a while before we see them again.'

'Ah. Well, I wish them the best.' Valerie pointed at her computer screen. 'Check out the email I just got.'

Coming to stand next to her, Kristen bent to read the message. 'Creepy,' she said when she'd finished. 'So maybe her disappearance *is* related to Daniel's, just like you thought.'

'Maybe so. But it still doesn't answer the big questions: Could it have been one of them I saw in the lava? And if so, who killed them, and why?' Valerie closed the lid of her laptop. 'I was hoping the professor would give me a new lead, but all this email does is make things even more confusing.'

'Well,' Kristen said, giving Valerie's shoulder an affectionate pat, 'I'm amazed she wrote back at all. I mean, for all she knows, you could be some freako stalker trying to find this Amy gal.'

'True. Which just goes to show how worried she must be about her student going AWOL, to have responded to my message.'

Kristen nodded. 'And who knows, maybe the prof will hear from Amy in the next day or so and let you know.'

'Right. I'm not holding my breath for that to happen.' She walked to the bed and lay down, stretching out her legs. 'So, what do you feel like doing with the rest of the afternoon?'

Kristen peered out the window. 'Looks like it's still sunny. You interested in heading out to Richardson Beach for a couple of hours, let Isaac and Sachiko have the house to themselves? It's supposed to have a nice black sand area to hang out on, and I read that it's the best place to snorkel in Hilo.'

'Sounds good. And we can stop at the store on the way home to pick up some wine for dinner. Maybe some nice Champagne, in case it turns out to be good news for Isaac, and a bottle of cheap red for if it's not.'

Sachiko's car was gone when they returned home from the beach. Valerie and Kristen let themselves in through the studio's private entrance, and by the time they'd showered and changed clothes it was five o'clock – time to head upstairs for cocktail hour.

Isaac was in the kitchen, humming to himself as he chopped vegetables. *Ah, must be good news,* Valerie thought as she listened to his tuneful rendition of 'Over the Rainbow.' At the sound of the two women entering the room he set down his knife, and when he turned to face them, she saw that he'd been crying.

Uh-oh, maybe not . . .

But then she noticed the smile, which seemed to bear no relationship to the tears streaking his cheeks. *What the . . .?* As he stepped toward them, arms extended, Valerie wasn't sure what to think.

Until she spied the mound of chopped yellow onions on the cutting board. *Aha!* With a laugh, she returned his happy embrace.

'Well, looks like we should break out that Champagne we bought,' Kristen said, and headed back downstairs to retrieve the bottle. Once they were settled on the lānai, the bubbly opened and poured, she turned to Isaac. 'So, I take it she said yes?'

He chuckled. 'You make it sound like a marriage proposal. But yeah, the short answer is, she did agree to move in with me.'

'Huzzah!' Valerie raised her glass, and the three toasted his good news.

'Okay, so what's the long answer?' Kristen asked. 'Inquiring minds want to know.'

Isaac tasted his Champagne. 'Wow, this is good.' He picked up the bottle and examined the label. 'French, even. Must be expensive. Thanks.' Leaning back in his chair, he took another sip and rolled it across his tongue, making a show of savoring the frothy liquid.

'We're waiting . . .' Kristen prompted.

'Okay.' Isaac leaned forward and set his glass on the wicker coffee table. 'So it turns out she wasn't opposed to the *idea* of us living together. She just needed to figure out how it would work – how she wanted it to work, anyway. And so she wanted to come over this afternoon to discuss all that. You know, where she could put her things and how she could have her own space . . .'

'She wanted to make sure she'd have "a room of her own,"' Valerie said, making air quotes.

He nodded. 'Right. And I said she could have the second bedroom upstairs as her own room for an office an' all her stuff.'

Kristen chuckled.

'What?' Isaac looked at her, confusion in his eyes.

'Val was referencing Virginia Woolf,' she said. 'I'm guessing it's not just about the actual *room* for Sachiko. It's about her independence, her sense of self, separate from the guy she's gonna be living with.'

He frowned. 'But I would nevah try to take that away from her.'

'Yeah, and I'm sure she knows that,' Valerie chimed in. 'But it's also about how the world views her – how it views the woman in a relationship with a man. You don't know what it's like to be at a restaurant when the waiter automatically hands the check to the guy you're with, or looks to him when asking what kind of wine you want for dinner.'

'No, you're right, I don't. And that totally sucks. But her moving in with me won't make any difference to stuff like that.'

Kristen lay a hand on his arm. 'But it will change her status – from an independent woman who currently lives alone, with her own separate life, to a woman who's moved into her boyfriend's house. Which will be a huge difference for her, no matter how great you are about the whole thing.'

Isaac's shoulders slumped.

'Look,' she went on. 'I'm not saying it's a bad idea for you two to live together. It's a wonderful idea. And she did say yes, after all. All I'm saying is that you should understand some of the other impacts – how big a change it will be to her life. And maybe, I dunno . . . let her know that that's something you get.'

He shook his head slowly as he stared at the glass in his hand, then lifted his eyes to Kristen's. 'She did ask whether I'd want her to always tell me her schedule, and when she was goin' out with her friends and stuff like that. I said I didn't need to know her every move, but that I wouldn't want to have to worry if she didn't come home when I expected her. I guess maybe that was the wrong answer . . .'

'I don't think so. Remember, she did agree to move in with you. And it makes sense that you'd want to let each other know your plans so the other wouldn't have to worry. Val and I do that for each other, and I bet most couples do. It's just common courtesy.'

Valerie nodded agreement. 'I'm sure it's all going to be fine, so buck up, mister. It's a celebration, after all.' She raised her glass to Isaac once more, then drained its contents. 'So when's the big move?'

'Well, she has to give a month's notice on her apartment, so it'll be sometime around the end of May. Which is actually good, since it gives us both time to get ready for it all. I, for one, gotta start getting rid of some da stuffs I got all over the place. Hey,' he said with a smile, 'you know anyone wants a barely used, ten-year-old elliptical machine?'

It was after nine before the three of them dragged themselves into the kitchen the next morning for breakfast and – more important – coffee. The celebratory bottle of Champagne had been followed by the cheap red they'd also bought 'just in case' to go with Isaac's delicious onion frittata, and then he'd insisted on after-dinner brandies to finish off the night.

No one was talking much, but Valerie caught snatches from across the table of the same tune Isaac had been humming the previous afternoon. 'Someone's still in a good mood this morning,' she said, turning the pages of the Sunday paper but paying little attention to its contents.

He glanced up with an embarrassed smile. 'Sorry. Am I bugging you?'

'Not at all. You have a nice voice, actually. I only wish I felt half as chipper this morning, is all.'

But now with the spotlight on him, Isaac grew quiet, and Valerie wished she'd held her tongue. It was nice hearing him hum, and it had helped sooth her own inner turmoil – the result of not only her continuing unease regarding the unsolved mystery she'd taken upon herself but also the headache and simmering nausea she'd awoken to.

With an internal shake of the head (an actual shake would have set her temples throbbing), she focused once more on the newspaper open before her. The weekly *Volcano Watch* had an intriguing headline: 'A Busy Time at Kīlauea Volcano's Summit and East Rift Zone.' Valerie read the first two paragraphs, then sucked in her breath.

'Whoa, you guys,' she said. 'Check this out. It says here that since April twenty-first, high lava lake levels within' – she paused, trying to get her mouth around the Hawaiian name – 'Halemaʻumaʻu at the summit of Kīlauea Volcano have produced multiple overflows of lava on to the crater floor, with *spectacular* views from the Jaggar Museum overlook in the National Park.' She set down the paper.

Isaac was nodding vigorously. 'Oh, yeah, I heard about dat yesterday from a guy I know. He went up to the Park a couple nights ago and said it was amazing – that you could see the lava flow real good from the overlook. I meant to tell you, but this whole thing with Sachiko kinda distracted me.'

'And get this,' Valerie said, jabbing a finger at the article. 'Puʻu 'Oʻo – that's the cone that was spouting the lava we saw last week down in Kalapana, right? Anyway, apparently it's been inflating and expanding steadily since mid-March, "with the west pit lava pond level rising," it says, and they predict that means there'll be new breakouts of lava from new vents on the cone.'

Kristen shoved back her chair to get more coffee. 'Cool,' she said. 'What d'ya say to heading up to the National Park this afternoon to see that overflow of the crater?'

'I'm in!' Valerie shot her hand up like a kid in a classroom.

'It'd be great if you could come with us, too,' she added, turning to Isaac. 'And if you were willing to act as tour guide, that would be even better.'

'Sounds awesome. I'd love to see that overflow. It hardly ever happens. An' I can ask Sachiko if she wants to join us. She doesn't get off work till around two, but since we wouldn't want to arrive at the overlook till it starts to get dark in any case, that'd be okay, right?'

'Absolutely.' Kristen added milk to her mug, then sat back down. 'We can head up there around three, maybe go for a short hike or something, grab a bite to eat, and then check out the view of the lava.'

'Perfect,' Valerie said. 'It's a plan.'

The three returned to their silent newspaper reading and coffee sipping. Valerie flipped through to the end of the first section, folded the paper back up, and stared absently at the front page.

And then she blinked and looked again at the headline of the lead article, which she'd managed to miss earlier in her hungover daze: 'Body Discovered on BigT Property Identified as Missing Man Daniel Kehinu.'

No. She shook her head, immediately regretting the action, and took a deep breath before reading the article. Then she folded up the paper once more and lay her head upon the table.

'What's wrong?' asked Kristen. 'Are you okay?'

With a moan, Valerie sat back up and shoved the newspaper across the table. 'They found his body – Daniel, the missing guy. They think he died of a heart attack at work, but no one found him till yesterday 'cause he apparently staggered off into the bushes and fell into a big lava crack.'

'Really?' Kristen picked up the paper and studied the article. 'Well,' she said, passing the section on to Isaac once she'd finished reading, 'at least we now know what happened to the guy, so that's something.'

'But don't you see? This means, since we now know it wasn't Daniel's body down there in Kalapana, that the two events – his death at BigT and whatever happened to whoever I *did* see being covered in lava – are obviously unrelated.'

Valerie put her head down once more on the table.

'I'm back to square one.'

TWENTY-ONE

Kristen knew better than to argue with her wife, to try to convince her otherwise. Not right now, anyway. Valerie needed time to come to terms with what she'd just learned, to absorb and process the information. So she merely gave Valerie a squeeze on the shoulder and headed out to the lānai with her cup of coffee.

Isaac sat for a moment staring at the newspaper article, then he too stood, mumbled something about the ball game starting in a few minutes, and retreated to the living room.

After about five minutes, Valerie joined Kristen outside. 'You were right,' she said, sinking onto the tropical-print sofa next to Kristen. 'I was an idiot to imagine I could solve the mystery of who it was I saw out there in the lava. What the hell was I even thinking? I'm such a dope.'

Kristen scooted closer to Valerie and wrapped her arm about her shoulders. 'No, you're not. Given the circumstances, it's actually pretty amazing how much you figured out about Daniel, and about who might have a good reason to want to see him dead.'

'Hrumph.' Valerie slumped down on the couch, clearly not convinced. 'A fat lot of good that does, since he apparently died of natural causes. Who cares if people had grudges against the guy? It's all irrelevant. And now I have no leads whatsoever about who it was that I actually saw out there in the lava. I've completely failed.'

'I don't know about that—' Kristen began, but Valerie cut her off.

'And my whole life is pretty much pointless,' she went on. 'I have no idea what the hell I'm going to do when we get back home. Even if Eddie keeps Chez Charles up and running now that Charlie's gone, there's no way I could go back there to work. It would be too hard. Every time I walked in the door, it would only remind me of my brother.'

Valerie stared out at the mass of tropical foliage surrounding Isaac's back yard – a tangle of yellow hibiscus, red ginger, and giant tree ferns, all intertwined with thick vines attempting to choke out everything else. 'I wonder what it would be like to live here – in Hawai'i,' she said after a bit.

Kristen turned to face her. 'Really? Because I've been thinking the same thing. But it never occurred to me that you'd even consider leaving L.A. Are you serious?'

'I dunno . . . maybe.' Valerie shrugged. 'I mean, now that we're both retired, it would make sense, I guess. The hardest part would be leaving our friends.'

'But, hey, if you move to Hawai'i, you know they'll come visit you,' Kristen said with a laugh. 'Especially if you have a guest room. And it's not as if we have a ton of friends still there, in any case. Seems like most of them have left town for cheaper locales.'

'Hawai'i's pretty expensive, too. If we were to move, it'd probably be better to go someplace cheaper, like Arizona or Oregon.' She glanced at Kristen. 'I know what you're probably thinking – that we could build on Charlie's lot for not all that much money. But I don't think I'd want to do that.'

'Yeah, well, it sounds like the property's awful barren, anyway, from what you said – not to mention pretty far away from any real town.'

'True, but that's not the only reason. I mean, this trip has in fact ended up being good for me with respect to Charlie. Like, I'm not thinking about him every other minute the way I was before. And I can see that as even more time passes, it's gonna get easier for me, getting used to him being gone.' Valerie blew out a slow breath. 'It'll be tough not having my brother around, but I know now that I'm gonna be okay. That said, though, I also don't think it'd be such a good idea to actually live on his land.'

'Agreed – on all counts. And I can't tell you how happy I am to hear that you feel you're doing better.' Kristen wrapped her arms around Valerie in a tight hug. 'But you know,' she said, releasing her and sitting back, animation shining from her eyes, 'you're actually wrong about how expensive property is here. I've been checking out the real estate ads in the local paper, and you can get a three-bedroom house here in Hilo for far less than our place is worth. If we were to sell our house in Mar Vista, we could buy something way nicer here – or get something about the same, and then have the extra money to invest.'

'Really? Huh.' Valerie looked out across Isaac's lawn toward the backyard neighbor's house with its classic white-washed wood siding and green metal roof.

Kristen continued to talk excitedly, going on about fee simple property sales – which were apparently not a given in Hawai'i as they were on the Mainland – and how they could ship their car and possessions over on a barge. But Valerie was only half listening. Could they really move here? Of course they *could*. But would she *want* to leave the hustle and bustle of Southern California for a small, slow-paced town like Hilo?

The idea sent a pleasant yet rather scary shiver through her body.

She glanced at Kristen, who was smiling back at her. 'Hey, even if all we do is talk about it,' Kristen said, 'it's fun to fantasize, right?'

'It is. And it's a nice way to take my mind off what a dork I've been about the whole Daniel Kehinu thing.'

'Like I said before, I so don't think that's true. I think it's impressive how much you've learned over the past – how many days?' Kristen calculated in her head. 'It's only been a *week* since Isaac took us down to Puna and to the Orchid Grill. Jeez, girl, maybe you should become a PI in your retirement.'

'I don't think so,' Valerie said with a snort. 'For all my sleuthing, in the end, all I unearthed was information utterly unconnected to the body I saw. Who knows who it actually was?'

Kristen shook her head. 'That's not necessarily true. There could still be a link. After all, we now know this Amy gal has gone missing. Maybe she's the one you saw in the lava.'

'Yeah, right. What are the chances of that coincidence happening?'

'But what if it wasn't a coincidence? What if they are, in fact, connected – Daniel's death and her disappearance? We do know that they were probably sleeping together, or at least hanging out with each other.'

Valerie frowned, then sat up and reached for her mug. 'Okay ... so maybe Amy killed Daniel, and then went into hiding afterwards? They could have been up at BigT together and, I dunno . . . they got into some kind of altercation and she shoved him into that lava crack?'

'That works,' Kristen said. 'Oh, but wait. Didn't the article say he died of a heart attack?'

'Yeah, but they could be wrong about that. Or maybe he had a heart attack during a fight, or when he fell into the crack.' Valerie sipped her coffee as she imagined possible scenarios. 'But that still doesn't answer the question of who I saw in the lava.'

'No,' said Kristen, 'it doesn't. But it still could be true, and the body you saw totally unrelated to it.'

'Which brings us back to square one again.' Valerie let out a long breath and sank back into the couch. 'What about Jordan?' she said after a bit.

'Jordan? You think she could be involved?'

'Well, it is a little . . . odd, you know, how she took such an interest in us?'

'You mean in you,' Kristen said with a grin. 'I just assumed she had the hots for you, is all.'

'Ha ha,' Valerie replied. 'I doubt she's interested in an old lady like me.' Though she had, of course, had the exact same thought during their fishing adventure.

'But seriously,' Kristen went on, 'I was wondering about that too, and it occurred to me that if she *is* a lesbian – and my gaydar definitely perked up when I first met her – maybe she doesn't have a lot of other gays in her life. That Trevor dude at the Orchid Grill that Isaac went to school with, and the guy Jordan was eating lunch with that day, they sure didn't strike me as LGBTQ. So maybe she's just jonesing to hang out with "family," you know?'

'I suppose. But she did used to work at BigT, so even though she said she didn't know Daniel, she could be lying. And also, she's really into fishing, so she could have known him that way, too.'

Kristen laughed. 'You have any idea how many people are into fishing on the Big Island? Probably half the population, I'd say. But okay, fair enough. She can be one of our suspects. So who else do we have?'

'I'm thinking Faith has to be up there pretty high. Maybe she killed Amy. Thinking she was sleeping with her husband would be a pretty strong motive – remember how angry Pele was with her own sister? And then someone helps Faith dump the body down at Kalapana afterwards. We did see those two people there that morning. Oh.' Valerie put her hand to her mouth. 'And I just thought of something else. I saw Faith and Kevin arguing yesterday down at the canoe beach, and they were really going at it. And I just realized that, as next of kin, Faith could have just that morning learned about their finding Daniel's body. So what if she was confronting Kevin about it – what if she thinks Kevin had something to do his death?'

'Maybe he does have something to do with it,' Kristen said. 'Do you know if he has a girlfriend?'

'Kevin? I have no idea. He's never mentioned one. But I suppose it's possible that if he does, he could have thought that Daniel had put the make on her – or that Daniel, in fact, did so. Faith said lots of guys were super pissed off at Daniel 'cause of that behavior. He was apparently the local Lothario, the Don Juan of Puna.'

'Or maybe Daniel was stealing some of the pot that they were selling, and Kevin found out.' Kristen suggested.

'Maybe. . . .' Valerie chewed her lip. 'But I have to say, Kevin did seem genuinely worried about Daniel's disappearance. And once I told him why I was so interested in the whole thing – and about what I'd seen out in the lava – he got a whole lot friendlier to me.'

'Well, that certainly doesn't mean he didn't do it,' Kristen said. 'It could mean the exact opposite – that he's buddying up with you only because he's worried you'll find out the truth about him, and he wants to learn what exactly you know.'

'You mean it's not simply because of my charming personality?'

'Well, there's definitely that, too,' Kristen said, patting Valerie on the knee.

'Okay, let's say it could be Kevin. If so, then I'm thinking a more likely reason would be anger about Daniel taking that job at BigT. When I saw Kevin at the beach yesterday, I noticed he had a tattoo of the Hawaiian sovereignty movement flag on his shoulder. I read up about it after we got home, and a lot of those sovereignty guys are apparently pretty radical, you know, like the Pele's Children group. So I wouldn't be surprised if he was opposed to the geothermal plant. Maybe he confronted Daniel at work and ended up shoving him into that lava crack.'

Kristen nodded. 'Yeah, I like it.'

'And maybe Kevin and Faith were even in on it together,' Valerie went on, warming more and more to this new theory. 'Since I know she was none too happy with Daniel about his escapades – not to mention that he was hiding from her the extra money he was making from the pot deals. And she certainly had reason to be super mad at a woman who was sleeping with her husband.'

She sat back up and turned to face Kristen. 'So, how about this? After Kevin kills Daniel, he and Faith go confront Amy at her campsite, and she ends up dead, too. Who knows? They could have convinced her to hike out to the lava, like we did. She was, after all, visiting from O'ahu, so seeing hot lava would be pretty exciting. Maybe they whacked her on the head with a big rock and then just dragged her body in the path of the oncoming flow. The perfect crime.'

Kristen gazed out at the hedge of pink ginger as she pondered the idea. 'Okay,' she said, 'so what would they have been arguing about yesterday during the canoe races, then, if Faith was in on the whole thing with Kevin? It couldn't be that she'd just learned about Daniel's death and was confronting him about it.'

'Good point,' Valerie said, thinking for a moment. 'It's possible Faith saw me and Kevin talking together at the beach beforehand. And, well, if the two of them *were* in on all of it, maybe they aren't too happy about me poking my nose into everything.' She swallowed, then turned toward Kristen. 'So maybe they were arguing about what to do about *me*.'

From their table in the Volcano House restaurant, the view of the gaping mouth of Halema'uma'u was impressive – and would have been even more so, had a gray haze not been obscuring most of the massive caldera.

'It's 'cause of all the volcanic activity going on right now,' Isaac said, digging into his mound of fettuccine Alfredo speckled with chunks of smoked salmon. 'Usually, you can see the crater way more bettah. But check it out.' He pointed with his fork out the picture window. 'See that dark-gray, blobby mass near the edge of the big hole? That's the hot lava spillover, I betcha. Once it's nighttime, you'll be able to see the glow.'

The four of them had spent the afternoon hiking through Kālauea Iki, the much smaller pit crater adjacent to the National Park's main summit caldera of Halemaʻumaʻu. The trail had taken them through an other-worldy tree fern forest along the rim of the bowl. They then hiked the trail down the walls of the crater and across its red-and-brown Mars-scape floor, which sixty years earlier had been a molten lava lake. Even now, parts of the surface were warm to the touch, with steam from heated rainwater rising eerily from cracks in the crater floor.

Sachiko took a bite of her cheeseburger, then turned to peer out at the voggy view. 'I read online that the lava lake within Puʻu Oʻo has also been rising the past few days. Kinda exciting. I wonder what Pele has in mind for us all.'

'Are you guys at all anxious?' Valerie asked. ''Cause it seems a bit nerve-racking, wondering whether at any minute your house could be inundated by hot lava.'

'Nah. I think we're pretty safe where we live,' Isaac said with a wave of the hand. 'It'd have to be a flow from Mauna Loa – a whole different volcano – to get to us, and it's been pretty quiet for a while. Plus, the lava would have to travel a long ways to reach Hilo. Now, if I lived in the East Rift Zone, which is directly down-flow from Kīlauea Volcano, that would be anoddah matter . . .'

'Where's the East Rift Zone?' asked Kristen.

'Down Puna side,' he said. 'Pāhoa, Leilani Estates, Kalapana . . .'

Valerie set down her pulled-pork slider. 'Yikes. That's a lot of populated places.'

'They know the risk,' Isaac said with a shrug. 'That's why the property down dere is so much cheaper than Hilo side.'

'Huh,' was Valerie's only audible response. And the unease that had crept over her upon hearing what Isaac had said remained throughout the rest of their dinner, as they watched the clouds of gray smoke rise from the menacing caldera outside the restaurant window.

By the time they'd finished eating, the sun was nearly down, and the sky had turned a deep, electric blue. They drove along Crater Rim Drive till they reached the turnoff for the Jaggar Museum, and were lucky to snag one of the last remaining spaces in the parking lot.

'Busy tonight,' Sachiko observed as she shrugged into a pale-blue puffer coat.

Kristen grabbed a bomber jacket from the trunk and handed it to Valerie, then pulled out a bulky parka for herself. 'And chilly, too. Thanks for loaning us these coats, Isaac. It's obvious we'll be needing them.'

'Yah, at four thousand feet, it gets pretty cold up here at night, especially when the wind kicks up.'

They made their way over to the Jaggar Museum building, with its displays of seismology monitors and equipment, as well as cultural exhibits about ancient Hawaiians and the fire goddess, Pele. After taking turns jumping up and down to see who could make the needle of the seismograph on display move the farthest (Kristen beat Isaac by a hair), the four moved outdoors to the lookout area.

The now-inky sky was bursting with stars, and a couple of bright planets hung just above the horizon. Once Valerie made her way through the crowd of visitors on the observation deck to its rock wall edge, however, she forgot all about the celestial objects above. The eerie earthly goings-on were far more spectacular.

Below her, the crater's gaping mouth was a roiling lake, spilling over its edges onto the caldera floor. Plumes of smoke and steam rose from the crater, at times obscuring the view, only to be swept away once more to reveal the ghostly sight before them.

But the scene wasn't the mass of bright-orange liquid Valerie had been expecting. Rather, soot-dark geometric shapes were outlined by threads of hot magma, which continually split apart the jagged chunks of cooled rock floating atop the lake's surface. It was like a writhing patchwork quilt of black fabric with orange stitching, stretched out across the length of the caldera.

'Wow,' said Kristen.

'Uh-huh, pretty awesome,' Isaac agreed.

Valerie merely nodded, too mesmerized to speak. The wind

changed direction, and she zipped up her leather jacket, coughing as the acrid air hit her lungs.

And that was all it took. The combination of witnessing once more the fearsome lava beast – spread this time over acres and acres of land – along with the tang of sulfuric fumes, transported her instantly back to that morning out at the Kalapana flow. Standing there at the Halema'uma'u overlook, she saw again in her mind's eye the gruesome scene of hot lava flowing over the leg, only to be lost forever under a blanket of hard rock.

Who was it she'd seen? And why did they die?

She had to discover the truth or the perishing flames would never leave her mind.

TWENTY-TWO

That night, Valerie lay awake for over an hour, listening to the rain drum upon the metal overhang outside the studio window. It had been dry when they left the Park, but by the time they passed through Glenwood on their drive back down the mountain to Hilo, it was coming down in bucketfuls.

The four of them had all gone straight to bed, and within minutes, Valerie could hear Kristen's even breathing, punctuated by the occasional soft snore. She herself, however, was too amped up to fall asleep. Instead, she listened to the rain, so hard at times that she worried it might break the window, and tried not to think about that body in the hot lava. Nor her brother in the burning car.

She finally dropped off to sleep well after one a.m., and when she awoke the next morning, she was alone in bed. She slid her palm under the covers next to her. Cold: Kristen had been up for a while. The sound of voices came through the ceiling, so others were still at home. Rousting herself from the comfort of the warm bed, Valerie showered and dressed, before heading upstairs to join them in the kitchen.

Sachiko and Kristen were at the Formica table, and Isaac stood near the door, looking through a stack of papers on the counter. 'Ah, here it is,' he said, extracting a page and sliding it into his briefcase. 'My list of extra credit homework the kids can do to bump up their grades before the end of the semester.'

'Do many take you up on it?' Kristen asked.

'Mostly just the ones who already got a lock on an A,' he said with a grin. 'But at least I give 'um the chance, yah? Okay, well, gotta jam. Everyone have a good day while I'm off molding the minds of our future world leaders.' Leaning over to give Sachiko a kiss, he threw the shaka to Valerie and Kristen, then dashed out the door into the rain.

As Valerie helped herself to coffee from the machine, Kristen and Sachiko recommended an earlier discussion. 'So, are you

going to bring all your furniture over here, or sell some of it?'
Kristen asked.

'Oh, I'm bringing all of it. It's mostly things that belonged to
my grandparents – beautiful carved wood pieces that are way
nicer than Isaac's stuff from Target,' which she pronounced 'tar-
zhay,' as if it were in French. 'So he'll have to get rid of some
of his own things if there isn't room for all mine. But he's okay
with that; it's part of our deal.'

'Ah. Way to go, sistah.' Kristen raised her mug in salute, and
Sachiko laughed.

'The main thing we have to decide is if we want to rent a
moving truck, pay someone to move it all for us, or just borrow
someone's pickup and do it ourselves. You don't happen to know
anyone with a big pickup truck do you?'

'Right,' said Kristen. ''Cause we know *so* many people here
in Hilo.'

'Actually, I have this memory that maybe I do know someone
here with a truck,' Valerie said, pulling out a chair to join them
at the table. 'Now, who was it . . .?' She thought a moment, then
snapped her fingers. 'I know. It's Kevin, the bartender. I saw him
go out to his truck in the parking lot the other day when Kristen
and I were there. But I guess that won't help any, since it's not
as if I know the guy well enough to ask him to loan you his
vehicle.'

'No worries; we've got a month to figure it all out.' Sachiko
squinted at the clock on the stove, then let out a sigh and stood.
'I guess I should get going, too. I promised my mom I'd help
her shop for a new washer and dryer this morning.'

After she'd gone, Kristen turned to Valerie. 'So what's on for
today? We could go to the Lyman Museum or something. Or it's
probably clear on the other side of the island – we could go back
to Hāpuna if you wanted.'

But Valerie didn't answer. She was still thinking about Kevin's
truck. It had been dark blue, as she recalled . . .

'Earth to Val,' Kristen said, waving her hand in front of her
face. 'You listening?'

'Sorry. I was just thinking about something else.' She turned
to face her wife. 'Wasn't that truck we saw at end of the road
before we hiked out to the lava flow a dark-colored one?'

'Uh . . . I'm not sure. I wasn't really paying much attention.'

'I'm pretty sure it was – either black or maybe brown . . . or dark blue.' She gave Kristen a meaningful look. 'Like Kevin's truck is.'

'Oh.' Kristen sat back in her chair as she considered this possibility. 'Is his truck the same size as the one we saw down there at the flow?'

Valerie nodded. 'I think so.'

'Huh. Well, I guess that shows he *could* have been there, but just how many dark-colored pick-ups would you guess are on this island?'

'True. But I'm thinking it totally makes sense he *was* there, like we talked about. Him and Faith, getting rid of Amy's body.'

'Okay. So how do you prove it?'

'Aye, and there's the rub.' Valerie tapped her thumb on the table and stared out the window at the palm fronds blowing about in the rain. 'Here, lemme check something.' She pulled her phone from the pocket of her khaki shorts and tapped the screen. 'Darn,' she said after finishing her search. 'Raul's is closed on Mondays. I was hoping we could go back down there today and take another look at his truck. That maybe there'd be some kind of clue or something.' She shook her head. 'It just seems like Puna's the key. Everything leads back to there.'

'Well, let's go back down there and just snoop around, then. Isaac says the weather tends to be better down in Puna than here in Hilo, so it might not be raining. We could go check out the tide pools again and have lunch in Pāhoa afterwards. Who know? Maybe something interesting will turn up.'

Valerie leaned across the table to give Kristen a soft kiss. 'And this is why I love you so very much.'

An hour later, the two women were stretched out on beach towels, trying to make themselves comfortable on the hard – and occasionally jagged – lava rock of the Kapoho tide pools. Kristen's forecast about the weather had been correct, and they were now drying off under the fierce tropical sun after a swim through the pools of dazzling corals and rainbow fish.

'Did you see that black-and-white-and-yellow one I was

pointing at right before we came in? With the super long top fin?' Valerie examined the plastic-coated fish identification card they'd brought out with them. 'Oh, here it is – a Moorish idol. What a fabulous name.' She set the card down next to her, draping an arm over her eyes to block the blazing sun.

'I think I missed it,' said Kristen. 'I was too busy gawking at all that pink and purple coral, and those itty-bitty fish – wrasses, I think they're called – wriggling in and out of it. Totally amazing.' She sat up to take a drink from her water bottle. 'So where do you want to go for lunch?'

'How about the Orchid Grill, that place Isaac took us the first day down here? I wouldn't mind getting some of that crispy glazed chicken you had. Not to mention . . .' She turned to Kristen with a devilish grin. 'He did originally suggest it as the best place to nose around down here, since it's such a local hangout.'

'Sounds good to me. And I'm actually getting pretty hungry. You dry yet?'

'Dry enough. Let's go.' Valerie slowly got to her feet. Her knees weren't as strong as they'd once been, and using her hands to help push herself up was tricky on the sharp rock. Draping the towel over her shoulder, she slipped on her flip-flops and grabbed her mask and flippers.

They made their way carefully over the black lava, then walked up the road to where they'd left the car. Once there, Valerie checked her phone. 'It's only eleven thirty,' she said. 'Would you be up for taking the long way to Pāhoa? I'd love one last drive along the Red Road before we leave the island.'

Kristen unlocked the car and settled into the driver's seat. 'Sure,' she said. 'Good idea. I'd like to see it again, too.'

From Kapoho, the road took them first through a bleak lava field, on past the thermally fed pond where they'd swum that day with Isaac, and to Isaac Hale Park, where Jordan had dropped Kristen to surf during the fishing expedition. As they drove past where Jordan had parked that morning, Valerie looked for her old Volvo, but the area was empty.

They continued along the road, which now plunged into a tropical rainforest – through towering ironwood trees and groves of stately mangos, whose intertwining branches formed a kind of primordial cathedral above, all draped with countless vines threatening to completely block out the sun.

Neither of them spoke. They weren't returning to California until the coming Saturday, but as they drove along the winding coastal route, the reality of their impending flight hit Valerie hard. Time to truly *savor* their surroundings.

The Red Road ended at Kaimū, and Kristen made a hard right onto Highway 130, back toward Pāhoa. After about ten minutes, as they passed a road on the right, Valerie turned to read the sign painted on a rock wall at the intersection.

'Wait! Hold up,' she said to Kristen. 'This is where Jordan lives with her grandparents. I remember she came down this road that morning to pick up those garbage bags for fishing. Would you be willing to swing by her house?'

'Okay . . .' Kristen glanced behind her, then made a U-turn. 'So what exactly do you think you'll find?' she asked, turning left onto Leilani Avenue.

'I dunno. Maybe there'll be a dark-colored truck there.'

'But we know she drives a yellow Volvo,' Kristen said. 'We rode in it with her that morning.'

'Yeah, well, maybe her grandparents have a truck. Or maybe we'll see something else that could be a clue.'

Kristen shook her head. 'Whatever. You're the boss. You remember how to get there?'

'I think so. Here, hang a left. I think it's a little ways down on the right. Yeah, that's the house. I remember those two short, fat palm trees out front.'

'Bottle palms,' Kristen said, but Valerie paid no heed. She was peering down the driveway at the two-car garage, whose door was fortuitously open. Parked inside were two vehicles – a small red sedan and a black SUV. Next to the garage was Jordan's battered old Volvo. No truck in sight.

'Damn,' said Valerie.

'Oh, well.' Kristen patted her on the knee. 'C'mon, let's go eat.'

Lunch was delicious but similarly unproductive. As Valerie savored her mammoth plate of Korean chicken, mac-and-tuna salad, white rice, and cucumber with sesame-ginger dressing, she studied the other patrons. No one she recognized, and no one with the look of someone who'd committed a murder and then dumped the body into a lava flow – though what that look would be, she had no idea.

Afterwards, she checked out all the vehicles in the parking lot – including a classic but battered turquoise-and-white convertible T-Bird that seemed rather out of place in Puna. The only dark-colored truck she spied was one of those monster trucks, with its wheels jacked way up high – definitely not the one she'd seen at the end of the road that morning.

'Wanna walk around town a bit?' Kristen asked. 'I wouldn't mind checking out some of the stores to look for presents for folks back home.'

'Sure, why not?'

They made their way down the raised wooden sidewalk, glancing into shop windows along the way. As they passed the True Hope Mission thrift store, Valerie paused to peer through its open door. No sign of Faith.

'You wanna go in?' asked Kristen, but Valerie shook her head.

'Not unless you want more aloha shirts.'

'No, I'm okay. I already got enough for one trip.' But at the next window down, Kristen stopped. 'Oooh, look at those beautiful carved fish,' she said. 'I bet they're koa. Let's go in here.'

The pieces were indeed koa and, although pricey, exquisitely crafted and small enough to fit easily into their suitcases. After purchasing three – a Moorish idol, a *humuhumu* and some sort of wrasse – they continued along their way, past shops offering organic food, computer repairs, and hemp clothing. As the two stood checking out tropical landscapes on display in the window of a small art gallery, the sound of a revving engine made them both look. A cherry-red truck came barreling down the street, its speakers booming a staccato bass line.

'There sure are a lot of Toyota Tacomas roaming this island,' Kristen observed as it sped past. 'That's like the twentieth one I've seen in just the past few days.' She turned to face Valerie. 'I wonder if that's the kind of truck that was there at the lava flow.'

'Could be,' Valerie said, watching the red truck recede into the distance. 'It was about that size, I'd say.'

Kristen started once more down the sidewalk. 'Too bad, if it's true, since there are so many of them around. Makes it pretty hard to track down.'

'Yep,' was all Valerie had to offer in response.

At the end of the next block, the shops ended, so they started across the street to head back down the other side. Before making it to the curb, however, they heard the gunning of an engine once more. 'Uh-oh, I think he must be back,' Kristen said, breaking into a trot. 'What a jerk.'

But then a black car came careening around the corner, aimed directly at Valerie, who had yet to reach the sidewalk. Grabbing her by the wrist, Kristen yanked Valerie out of the way mere seconds before the car passed over the exact spot where she'd been standing.

Gasping, the two of them stood and stared at the back of the car as it sped away. 'Did you get the license plate, by any chance?' Valerie asked.

'No. And the sun was in my eyes, so I didn't get a good look at the driver, either.' Kristen shook her head. 'But – and I know this sounds crazy – I swear the woman driving looked kind of like that gal from the thrift store.'

'Faith?'

'Right. Though I could be totally imagining it.'

'Huh.' Valerie frowned. 'Well, I couldn't tell what make of car it was, either, other than being some kind of SUV. It went by way too fast. But didn't we just see a black SUV parked in the garage at Jordan's house?'

Valerie could see Kristen's eyes widen for a moment, then relax. 'Then again, the only thing there's probably more of on the Big Island than Toyota Tacomas is black SUVs,' Kristen said with a short laugh. 'So good luck with that.'

They stood a moment longer, then turned and headed back down the sidewalk, no longer much interested in window shopping. When they got to the block with the thrift shop, Valerie kept an eye out for black SUVs, but there were none anywhere near the store.

Of course, if it was Faith trying to run me down, she rationalized, *she wouldn't be so stupid as to then park the car on the same street she knew we'd be walking down, would she?*

Back at their rental car, Kristen popped the trunk so they could set their bags inside. 'What now?' she asked.

'Well, we could go—'

At a sudden shaking of the asphalt beneath her feet, Valerie jerked her head up, poised to dart away from what she was sure would be an oncoming black car. But there was no car – nothing moving, in fact – in the now near-empty Orchid Grill parking lot.

Kristen let out a chuckle. 'Just an earthquake,' she said. 'Like we're not used to them from all the ones back home.' Slamming shut the trunk, she stepped forward toward the driver's side door.

And then the earth shook again – much harder this time.

TWENTY-THREE

The route from Hilo to South Point travels up and over the mountain pass between the Mauna Loa and Kīlauea volcanoes, then back down through the arid Kaʻū Desert into the green, rolling hills of Pahala, along the black sand beaches of the southeast coast, and then finally along a twisty, rutted road through windswept grasslands to Kalae, the southernmost point of the fifty United States.

After this almost-two-hour drive the next morning, Valerie and Kristen were happy to climb out of the car and stand atop the tall cliff overlooking the vast Pacific Ocean. Gazing in wonder at the crystalline water – so clear that the schools of shimmering yellow tang appeared to be suspended in glass – they shook out their legs as they thankfully inhaled the salty sea air.

'Look, there's someone way down there!' Kristen shouted over the wind.

Valerie turned to see the tiny form of a swimmer rise up from the depths, then break the surface of the water. In one hand he held a mesh bag, and in the other was some kind of pale-colored sea creature.

'Whoa, it's an octopus,' said Kristen. 'He must be one of those free divers I've heard about. Did you know that some of them can hold their breath for like ten minutes?'

The diver maneuvered the wriggling cephalopod into the bag, readjusted his face mask, then dove once more into the blue, blue water. They watched as he descended, his body growing smaller and smaller, until he was a mere speck.

'I wonder how he gets in and out,' Valerie said, peering over the side of the cliff. 'Oh, check it out. There's a ladder.' Fastened to the face of the red rock was a long metal ladder, reaching almost – but not all the way – to the surface of the ocean. As Valerie took a few steps closer to the edge, a surge of water brought the level up over the bottom of the ladder, then quickly back down once more.

'Yikes,' she said. 'Getting in wouldn't be so hard, but the timing for getting *out* looks tricky. And scary.' She glanced back over her shoulder at Kristen. 'You wanna change into your swimsuit?'

'Ha. No, thanks. But I wouldn't mind going to a beach where you don't have to take your life in your hands to go swimming. You ready to move on with the day's activities?'

After examining the ruins of the ancient Hawaiian *heiau* and taking the requisite selfies in front of the 'Southernmost Point in the USA' sign, they climbed into the car and headed back up the winding road past giant wind turbines to the small town of Nā'ālehu. There, they made a quick stop to purchase two loaves of Portuguese-style sweet bread (one plain, one guava) from the southernmost bakery in the United States, before continuing on their way back north to Punalu'u Beach.

Once sprawled out upon their hibiscus-print towels set atop the glistening black sand, Valerie pulled from her daypack the sandwiches she'd made that morning before leaving the house. 'This is yours,' she said, handing one to Kristen. 'It doesn't have any mustard.'

'Thanks, babe.'

They munched their ham, avocado, and Swiss sandwiches while watching the stream of tourists descend from an enormous bus that had pulled into the parking lot right after them. Many of the women wore stylish sun hats, and the men mostly favored short-sleeved button-down shirts tucked into their khaki slacks.

'Definitely not American,' Valerie observed. 'Too well dressed.' As the tour bus people made their way across the sand towards them, she heard snatches of Japanese. 'Ha. I was right.'

Soon after the group reached the edge of the water, a woman with a pink tennis visor let out a squeal, causing all those around her to come running. She was pointing at what looked to be a large black rock lying on the sand. But from the reactions of the people around her, it was clearly no rock.

'It's a turtle!' said Kristen, jumping up.

She and Valerie made their way over to the cluster of people and saw that not one but four fat sea turtles lay lazing in the sun. At an exclamation from one of the men in the group, all eyes turned toward the water. '*Mite!*' he shouted, pointing to the right of an outcropping of rock just offshore.

A small black head popped up out of the water. 'Oooooh!' cooed the crowd in unison. Another turtle head broke the surface and then two more.

'Oh, wow.' Valerie used her hand to shield the sun from her eyes, staring in delight at the comic-book-like faces bobbing about in the water. 'I read there were often turtles here, but this is amazing!'

After a few minutes, they returned to their towels and to their sandwiches – which, after being left unattended on the breezy beach, now closely resembled their name. Doing her best to brush the black granules from her nine-grain bread, Valerie took a cautious bite, then washed it down with a drink of water from her flask. 'You think these are the same kind of turtles that Amy person is studying?'

'Probably,' said Kristen. 'I'm pretty sure the only other kind they have on the island is super rare. Why do you ask?'

'I don't know. Seeing them just reminded me of her, I guess.' Valerie turned to watch another group of tourists now encircling the quartet of sea turtles.

'So, what do you think?' Kristen asked after a bit. 'Any chance Amy really did kill Daniel and is now hiding out somewhere?'

Valerie finished chewing her mouthful of sandwich as she thought. 'But if that were the case,' she said, 'why wouldn't she resurface again, now that they're saying he died of natural causes?'

'Well, maybe she hasn't seen the paper and doesn't know he's been found. Or maybe she *has* resurfaced. There's no way we'd know if she had. It's been, what, three days since the professor wrote you that email? And it's not as if she's got any duty to write you again if she has in fact now heard back from Amy.'

'True . . .'

'You still think it was Kevin. Or Kevin and Faith.'

'I have no idea,' Valerie said, running a hand through her hair. 'Maybe.' She unscrewed her water bottle and took another long drink. Frowning, she went on. 'Okay, so you said the person who almost ran me over yesterday looked kind of like Faith. Are you sure it was a woman?'

'Well, the person had shoulder-length hair like hers, but I

suppose it could have been a guy. There are a lot of hippies in Pāhoa, after all.' Kristen laughed. 'Maybe he was just stoned and didn't see us.'

'But with hair that length' Valerie persisted, 'it could also have been Jordan, driving her grandparents' car.'

'Yeah, I suppose so.'

'Or it's completely unrelated to anything to do with us – just a driver distracted by her cell phone or whatever. But it doesn't really matter, since it's not as if we'll ever know for sure.' Popping the last bite of her sandwich into her mouth, Valerie yanked off her T-shirt. 'C'mon, let's go swimming. Maybe we can see some of those turtles up close and personal.'

It was after five when the two finally returned from their day's adventures. Not bothering to check their email or social media, they took hurried showers before heading upstairs. 'Sorry we're late for cocktail hour,' Kristen called out as she emerged into the kitchen. 'Did you start without us?'

No answer.

But then they heard the sound of the television coming from the living room – an unusual occurrence, since Isaac rarely watched anything at this time of day. He was staring at the flat-screen TV, his face rigid, and didn't appear to notice the women come into the room.

'What happened?' asked Valerie, her voice quiet. 'Something bad?'

On the screen was a young man with a microphone and a map behind him. 'I'm not sure,' Isaac said. 'Maybe it's no big deal, but they're saying the crater in Pu'u O'o collapsed yesterday afternoon.'

'Oh! That must be what caused those earthquakes we felt.' Valerie glanced at Kristen, who nodded.

'And that's not all,' continued Isaac. 'Today there's been a bunch of gas emissions along the East Rift Zone causing these *booms*, dey say. An' now a big crack has opened down in Leilani Estates with tons of steam coming out of it.'

'Whoa.' Valerie sucked in her breath. 'That can't be good.'

'No,' he agreed. 'Probably not.'

*   *   *

The next morning, Wednesday, Valerie checked online as soon as she was up, but discovered no new information about the volcanic activity down in Puna. By the time she made it upstairs, Isaac had already left for work, so the two women were left to themselves in the house.

'Well,' said Valerie, once she'd helped herself to coffee and made her way out to the lānai to join Kristen on the couch, 'we've got three days left. Tomorrow will be largely filled by shopping and then my fabulous birthday party. So, is there anything left on your list that we should do today?'

'Not really. We've done a good job on it, actually. We could just laze around here, if you like. It's been a pretty busy couple of weeks, so I'd say we've earned it. But how about you? What would you like to do?'

'Other than solving the mystery of the body in the lava, you mean?' Valerie attempted a smile, but it was half-hearted.

'Hey, I'm willing to do whatever you want,' said Kristen brightly. 'Is there something else you want to investigate?'

'That's so sweet. But no.' Valerie slumped down on the aloha-print couch. 'I've pretty much run out of sleuthing ideas at this point.'

'Okay . . . well, I have an idea for an activity, then. Let's see if that realtor who took you to Charlie's property last week can show us some houses in Hilo today. Not that we'd necessarily be looking to buy, but we could get an idea of the market.'

Valerie's smile was genuine this time. 'Yeah, that sounds fun. Good idea.' Sitting back up, she pulled out her phone and opened her contacts. 'Here, I'll give her a call.'

'Do you remember how many bedrooms that red house with the really cute kitchen had?' Valerie stood on her tiptoes to reach for a bottle of chile verde salsa, then set it into the squeaky shopping cart she and Kristen were pushing around the KTA grocery store.

It was the following morning, and she and Kristen were doing the shopping for Valerie's birthday party that afternoon out at Coconut Island. Since the meal would be *al fresco* picnic-style, they were focusing on finger foods and items that wouldn't be too messy on paper plates.

'Uh . . .'

'You know, the one with that super-cool Wedgewood stove?'

'Oh, yeah,' said Kristen. 'Two bedrooms, one bath.'

'Right. Too small, I'd say. Though I sure did love all that vintage, 1930s-era tile.' Valerie grabbed a bag of tortilla chips, then turned down the next aisle and stopped before a cooler filled with packaged sushi. 'This looks yummy,' she said, picking up a container of salmon, cream cheese and green onion rolls. 'And maybe one of the ahi kind, too. How many are we going to be, again?'

'Just us four, right? You, me, Isaac, and Sachiko.'

'Oh, and I invited Jordan, too, so maybe five. But if she does come, she said she'd bring that fish she caught, so I guess we don't need more than one of these.' Valerie replaced the second box of sushi and pushed the cart on.

'So, what did you think of the house-hunting, anyway?' Kristen asked as they made their way down the liquor aisle. 'I mean, I know we talked a little about it last night, but were there any you'd actually consider living in?'

'You mean, would I actually consider moving here – for real?' Valerie stopped walking and turned to face Kristen. 'I'm not sure . . . It's a fun fantasy, to leave L.A. and move to a tropical paradise. But how realistic is it, really?'

'Well, it's not like there's much keeping us there any longer . . . I mean . . .' Kristen trailed off.

'Right.' Valerie stared blankly at the display of tequila bottles and Margarita mix the store had on sale for Cinco de Mayo the coming Saturday. 'Now that Charlie's gone.'

Kristen lay a hand on Valerie's arm. 'I'm sorry. That's not what I meant. I was just thinking about how we're both retired now, so we really do have the luxury of moving. If we wanted to.'

'I know. And hey, maybe it would be the best thing for me. To move away, so I'm not reminded of him every time I turn a corner in Venice or Culver City.' Valerie wiped her eyes and smiled. 'And I sure did love that red house with the cute kitchen. Maybe we could find something like that, but with another bath and bedroom.'

'Maybe we could,' said Kristen.

After stocking up on beer and sodas, they made their way over to the poke counter. 'I don't care how much food we might end up having,' Valerie said. 'We need to get some poke, too. It's nowhere near this good back on the Mainland, so I want to consume as much as humanly possible before heading home.'

There was a long line at the counter. As they waited their turn, Valerie studied the trays of the many varieties on offer: four kinds of ahi – sesame, shoyu, spicy, and seaweed – as well as octopus, mussels, *lomi lomi* salmon, and several others she couldn't identify.

She'd just settled on the sesame ahi and spicy mussels when the woman behind her in line called out to another customer headed their way. 'Toshi – so good to see you!'

'Aloha, Teresa. How are you?' the man answered, giving the woman a warm hug. 'Have you heard about what's going on down in Leilani Estates? Another big crack opened up today, and a lot of people are starting to evacuate. Doesn't your sister still live down there?'

She nodded vigorously. 'Uh-huh, she does. I talked to her dis morning, an' she told me some of her neighbors are evacuating, but she not gonna leave. She says everybody makin' a big deal about nothing.' The woman shrugged. 'I no can do anything about it. If she don't wanna leave, dat's her choice, yah? An' she may be right. Remember last time, when dey all said da lava was gonna cover Pāhoa town and then it jus' stopped.' She snapped her fingers. 'Li' dat.'

Her friend smiled, but his cocked head suggested skepticism. 'Well, I certainly hope she's right. Only time will tell. Look, I've got to get a move on; I'm only on a quick break from work. But it was good seeing you. You take care – and good luck to your sister, too.'

The woman watched him head toward the registers, then took out her phone, thumbed a text, and hit send. *Writing her sister, perhaps?* The furrowed brow and quick shake of the head suggested maybe so.

TWENTY-FOUR

Coconut Island's Hawaiian name is Mokuola, which translates as 'island of life,' and in addition to being an ancient place of refuge for those who'd broken *kapu*, it was also once the site of a temple dedicated to healing. According to legend, those who were sick could be healed by swimming three times around the island. (*Though if you were able to complete this feat, perhaps you weren't truly that sick to begin with*, was Valerie's thought when Isaac told her this fact.)

These days, the island is a popular public park. Families come there to fish, barbecue, play soccer, and splash about its two tiny beaches. In other words, it's still very much an island of life.

Valerie, Kristen, Isaac, and Sachiko arrived at the Coconut Island parking lot at four thirty that Thursday afternoon and hauled coolers, bags of groceries, beach chairs, blankets, and a pop-up canopy across the footbridge to the small island.

'Let's set up over dere,' Isaac said, pointing. They crossed the wide grassy area to a spot to the left of a wood-frame picnic pavilion which was currently occupied by a large family group ranging in age from roughly two to eighty.

While Isaac and Kristen struggled with the canopy, Valerie and Sachiko spread out the blankets and arranged the chairs and coolers. 'Should we pull out the food now, or better to wait?' Valerie asked.

'It's early yet,' said Sachiko. 'Why don't we hold off a bit on the food. But I wouldn't mind a beer in the meantime.'

Valerie handed her a Fire Rock ale and took a Big Wave for herself. 'What a beautiful spot,' she said, wandering over to the low rock wall surrounding the island. Valerie gazed out across the sparkling water back toward Hilo. Several groups of paddlers were out in the bay, heading toward the breakwater with strong, even strokes. And just beyond the low wall, on a spit of smooth, black rock – its lava fingers reaching out into the warm, inviting water – stood a young fisherman in board shorts and rubber slippahs.

In the distance along the Bayfront, Valerie made out the black sand beach with its tiny canoe houses, as well as the brightly painted shops lining Kamehameha Avenue. But what truly made her breath catch were the two massive volcanoes rising up from behind the town: the rounded dome of Mauna Loa to the left and the older, more rugged Maunakea on the right.

'Do you know which of the observatories those are up there?' she asked Sachiko, pointing at several domes that glinted atop the peak of Maunakea in the afternoon sun.

'I'm not sure, but maybe the big white one is the Gemini?'

Kristen and Isaac came to join them, the canopy now successfully erected. 'Nice that the mountains are out this afternoon,' said Isaac. 'Clouds often come in by this time an' cover them up. They must have wanted to give you a birthday present.'

'And a very good present it is.' Valerie smiled as she took a contented sip from her beer. *Yes, maybe I could live here . . .*

'And there's even a cruise ship for you tonight,' he said, swiveling around to face the other side of the island. 'Check it out. Looks like she's getting ready to leave.'

The rest of them turned to look, and Valerie saw the stern of an enormous ship protruding from behind a large building over at the port. As she watched, the ship slowly turned about until its bow was facing the bay.

'C'mon,' Isaac said, striding quickly away. 'We gotta hurry if we wanna watch her go.'

Valerie and Kristen started after him, then stopped. 'Aren't you coming?' Kristen asked Sachiko.

'No, I've seen it a million times. And someone should stay here with our stuff.'

'Oh, okay. Thanks.'

The two women trotted to catch up with Isaac, who led them to the far end of the island, where a grove of hardy ironwood trees sprang from cracks in the lava rock. They took a seat at the edge of the shore, their feet dangling above the dark-blue water which flashed yellow streaks of light in the setting sun.

'You're sitting on the very edge of Mauna Loa right now,'

Isaac said, tapping the black rock with his beer bottle. 'A flow from a couple thousand years ago.'

'Cool,' said Valerie.

'Cool now, but hot then,' replied Kristen with a chuckle. 'Really hot.'

Isaac grinned. 'Well over a thousand degrees Celsius. Which is almost two thousand degrees Fahrenheit, for you non-scientists. But den it cools down real quick, yah?'

Valerie sipped from her beer, trying not to think about the last time she'd witnessed hot lava flow over something and then rapidly cool. 'So,' she said, changing the subject, 'I wonder if I could ask you something that might be kind of . . . personal?'

'Sure,' Isaac said with a grin. 'I got no secrets.'

'Well, it's just that I'm wondering about something. And maybe it's not so much personal as it is . . .' She stopped. 'Okay, at the risk of coming across as culturally insensitive and totally *haole*, I'm just wondering about Pidgin – you know, how you switch back and forth between it and Standard English so easily.'

Isaac nodded. 'Sure. I understand. You're wondering why someone like me, a teacher and a scientist, would use Pidgin when I speak.'

'Right,' Valerie said.

'Okay, so first you need to understand the history of the dialect,' he said, switching automatically into teacher mode. Just as he switched back and forth between Standard English and Pidgin, Valerie observed. 'Pidgin originally developed as a way for the sugarcane workers here on the island to communicate with each other, even though they spoke completely different languages at home – so its vocabulary, grammar, and syntax are derived from those cultures.' He ticked them off with his fingers: 'Hawaiian, English, Japanese, Chinese, Portuguese, and even some Filipino. But later on, it came to be more than that – a way of showing you're part of the local community. So what's totally cool about Pidgin is that it unites all those ethnic and cultural groups; it gives us a sense of solidarity and, I dunno . . . belonging.'

'Which becomes more and more important as tourists and outsiders pour onto the Big Island,' Kristen put in. 'Like us.'

Isaac smiled. 'Nah, you two seem pretty solid to me. But you are right. So even though lots of people think of Pidgin as something only spoken by uneducated people, it's a kind of badge of honor among us locals. A form of community identity. "I'm a local and proud of it" sort of thing, yah? Us against the rest of the— Ho!' He jumped to his feet. 'Dere's da ship!'

Valerie turned to look where he was pointing and saw coming their way the enormous white cruise ship. Blue waves were painted on its prow, and a long row of bright-orange life boats hung from its side. 'Ohmygod, it's the size of an entire city block!'

'Yah, it holds like twenty-five hundred passengers and over a thousand in crew.'

The three of them watched as the great hulk glided past the island, the passengers lining the top deck mere specks gazing back at the receding Hilo Town. Once the ship cleared the breakwater and headed out to sea, Isaac drained his bottle. 'C'mon,' he said. 'I'm ready for another beer.'

As they approached the canopy, Valerie could see Sachiko chatting with two men. *Friends of hers?* But when she got closer, she realized that one was Kevin, the bartender at Raul's.

'Oh, here they come now,' said Sachiko.

Kevin smiled and held out a bottle of Prosecco with a red ribbon tied about its neck. 'Happy birthday!'

'Thanks.' Valerie accepted the gift. 'But how did you know . . .?'

'You mentioned your sixtieth birthday party at the canoe races, so I thought I'd swing by to wish you congratulations. It's quite a momentous occasion, after all.'

'Well, shucks. That's awful sweet.' *Though I'd call it more than merely 'swinging by' to go to the trouble of buying the wine and then coming all the way out here*, was what Valerie was thinking. Did he have some ulterior motive for showing up?

'Hi,' she said to the other man. 'I'm Valerie.'

'I know,' he said with a thin smile and a glance toward the ground. 'You're the birthday girl.'

It was then she noticed the cake sitting in the center of the blanket. It had a shiny chocolate ganache coating and the words 'Happy Birthday Valerie – Old Lady' written in yellow script. Six pink candles were spaced evenly around its edge.

Valerie grinned at Sachiko. 'Ha! So *that's* why you didn't want to go watch the cruise ship go out. You had to go back to the car to get the cake. And I'm guessing *you*,' she said, slapping Kristen affectionately on the shoulder, 'are responsible for the heartwarming decorations.'

'Uh-huh. Each candle is worth ten, since you're now far too old for all the candles to fit on one cake.'

'Well, thank you. I think.' Valerie gave both Sachiko and Kristen a hug, then turned back to Kevin and his friend, who seemed reluctant to provide his name. 'You guys want a beer? We can save the Prosecco to drink with the cake.'

Once they'd all helped themselves to beverages from the cooler, Valerie returned to the rock wall to stare up at the looming form of Maunakea, whose top was rapidly becoming obscured by clouds. Kevin and his friend came to stand by her side, and they sipped their beers in silence.

'I'm so sorry about Daniel,' she said after a bit. 'I read about it in the paper on Sunday.'

Kevin nodded. 'Yeah, that was a shock.'

More silence.

Valerie glanced back at the others hanging out under the canopy. 'Okay, well . . .' But before she could extricate herself and head back to where they stood, Kevin spoke again.

'Uh, look . . . I was wondering if you'd found out anything else. About, you know . . . what happened to Daniel?'

So he *did* have an ulterior motive for showing up.

'What?' she said. 'You don't buy that he died of a heart attack while at work, like they said in the paper?' If Kevin was still interested in what she'd uncovered, did that mean he had reason to believe Daniel had not died a natural death? Or did he in fact know how he died . . . perhaps because *he* was the one who killed him?

She took a step back, glancing again at the trio now sitting in the beach chairs under the canopy.

'No, I mean . . . maybe.' Kevin shook his head. 'I'm not sure what I think, to tell you the truth. But it just seems like there's something off about it all. Like how he ended up in that lava crack? That's pretty weird. And what's the deal with that woman he'd been seeing who abandoned her campsite?'

'Amy,' Valerie offered.

'Right. So why would she go missing at the exact same time that Daniel ended up dying? It just seems weird, is all. And, well, you seem to be pretty good at this whole investigation thing, so I thought maybe you might have some new information . . .'

'Ah, so you didn't come by merely to give me birthday greetings,' Valerie said with a chuckle.

He looked down at his brown-and-green slippahs and shrugged. 'Well, I did also want to—'

'It's okay,' she said. 'I'm actually kinda flattered. And yeah, I have to say those were my thoughts, too, about Daniel's death.' Valerie wondered how much to tell him. If Kevin was lying and was, in fact, a murderer, would sharing what she knew put her in danger? But then again, if she wanted to find out anything from the guy, she'd likely have to give him something first to get him comfortable talking.

'Okay, well, I haven't found out a whole lot,' she said. 'But I did learn that Amy's a grad student in Honolulu, and that she hasn't been responding to any of the emails her adviser has been sending her.'

'Huh,' said Kevin. Both he and his unnamed friend frowned.

'Right. So now it's my turn.' Valerie sat down on the wall, facing the two men. 'What I want to know is, what were you and Faith arguing about that day at the canoe races?'

Kevin blinked several times. 'Uh . . .'

'Look, I saw you two – it was right before your team's heat that morning – and she looked super angry. So what was that all about?' Valerie fixed him with what she hoped came across as a severe look.

'She was just being Faith,' he finally said, and his friend shook his head in a show of sympathy.

Valerie continued to stare at Kevin until he continued.

'Okay, so here's the deal. She'd just been told that morning about them finding Daniel's body, and what does she do? She comes straight to me and demands money for what she thinks he was owed from our . . . side business.'

At this point, the other man threw his hands up in the air. 'Brah! Why you telling this chick about it?'

'It's okay, Derek,' he said to his friend. 'She's not gonna bust us.'

Ah. Derek. And he must be part of their pot-selling crew.

'Anyway,' Kevin went on, 'I was stunned – one, that he was dead, and two, by her stone-cold reaction. Not grief or shock, but "Where's my *money*?"' He spat out this last word as if it were a nasty insect that had flown into his mouth. 'So I told her exactly what I thought: that she's a selfish, callous woman, and even if I owed Daniel any money – which I don't, by the way – no way would I give it to her.'

'And that must be when she stalked away in a huff and took off in her car,' Valerie said. 'Wait.' She closed her eyes and tried to remember what kind of vehicle Faith had climbed into. 'Does she own a black SUV?'

'Yeah, I think she does,' Kevin said. 'Why?'

'Because someone who looked kind of like Faith and was driving a big black car nearly ran me over a few days ago in Pāhoa.'

Kevin and Derek exchanged glances. 'Sounds like her, all right,' murmured Derek.

'What do you mean?'

'He means that she's been acting completely *lolo* ever since learning about Daniel's death.' Kevin blew out his breath, then took a long drink of his Longboard lager.

'Really? Crazy enough to actually try to run me down?'

'Well,' Kevin said, 'she has been telling everyone who'll listen that you're the one Daniel was hanging out with before he died, and that you've been stalking her at the thrift store. So, given how nuts she's been acting lately . . .' With a shrug, he downed the rest of his beer and set the bottle on the ground.

Valerie turned to stare out at a six-man canoe making its way back to the black sand beach. Following her gaze, Kevin shielded his eyes from the sun, which was now poking out from under the clouds as it set behind Maunakea. 'The number-four guy's stroke is way off,' he observed.

Valerie nodded absently. 'So, you think there's any chance,' she asked, swiveling back around, 'given how – what's the best word? – how *wild* Faith's been acting of late, that *she* could have killed Daniel?' She studied Kevin's face to see if he betrayed any particular emotion at being asked this question – surprise, shock, fear? But all he did was furrow his brow as if in thought.

'Mmm . . . I doubt it. First of all, how could she have gotten onto the BigT property? They're pretty strict about letting people in there, 'cause of all the protestors and stuff.'

'True.' Valerie chewed her lip. 'But what if he let Faith in?'

'I suppose,' said Kevin.

And then Valerie had a thought: *What if Daniel had let* Amy *on to the BigT property that night?* She voiced this idea to Kevin and Derek. 'And then maybe he comes on to her super aggressively and she fights back and . . .'

'And he has a heart attack and dies,' Derek finished for her. 'Huh. That works.'

Kevin snapped his fingers. 'Right! I like it. And then she freaks out, worried that she'll be accused of killing him, so she drags the body into that lava crack so he won't be found for a while, giving her time to take off. I bet she's not even on-island anymore.'

The two men grinned at each other like a couple of Einsteins who'd just solved the mystery of dark matter.

'But then who was it I saw being covered with hot lava down in Kalapana?' Valerie asked.

They stared at her a moment, and then Kevin turned his hands palms-up. 'Who says that body has anything to do with Daniel? It's probably completely unrelated – some gang-related killing or drug deal gone bad.' As he turned to head back toward the canopy, she heard him say to Derek in a low voice, 'Assuming it even happened.'

Great. Thanks for that. Killing her own beer, Valerie stood up from the wall to follow them back to the canopy. And then she heard her name called out from afar.

'Yo! Valerie! I brought you the fish!'

It was Jordan, crossing the grassy area from the footbridge towards their group, a large red-and-white cooler in one hand and a six-pack of beer in the other.

TWENTY-FIVE

'I hope you don't mind that I brought a friend,' Jordan said, nodding toward a man who'd come up behind her. 'This is Shane.' He looked familiar to Valerie, and then she remembered he was the guy Jordan had been with that first day they'd met at the Orchid Grill.

Shane bobbed his head in greeting to the group. 'Howzit. And happy birthday,' he added, gracing Valerie with a boyish smile.

'And I'm Jordan, for those who don't know me – bringer of libations and '*ono* kine fish.' She offered beers around, then opened her cooler, releasing the pungent tang of ginger, garlic, butter, and fried fish. 'Here's the baby. And this is only half the sucker. I hope everyone's hungry.'

'I sure am *now*,' said Valerie, salivating at the smell. 'Thanks so much for cooking and bringing it – not to mention doing all the work reeling the monster in.'

Jordan waved her hand. 'Hey, that's the fun part, catching 'em. And besides, it was good fun getting to go out fishing again after so long.'

'Well, I don't know about anybody else,' Isaac said, reaching into one of the grocery bags stuffed with supplies, 'but I sure could eat something right about now.'

At the chorus of assent, Isaac and Sachiko pulled out all the food from their bags and cooler: the poke and sushi, guacamole and chips, a *hulihuli* chicken, slices of pineapple and papaya, and a loaf of the Portuguese-style sweet bread Valerie and Kristen had purchased down at South Point. Kristen passed out plates, forks, and napkins, and after helping themselves to dinner, everyone got settled around the blanket and in the chairs.

Not eager to sit next to Kevin after that last comment he'd made to Derek, Valerie took a seat between Kristen and Jordan. 'Ohmygod,' she said, upon tasting the tender, flavorful *ulua*. 'This is amazing. You have to give me the recipe.'

'I wouldn't really call it a recipe,' Jordan said. 'Ya just season the fish steaks with salt and pepper, grill 'em, then drown 'em in butter that's been melted with about a ton of chopped ginger and garlic.'

'No wonder I like it,' Valerie said. 'My French *grand-père* used to say that even shoe laces would taste good if drenched in enough butter. Not that your fish is anything like shoelaces,' she added, realizing that might have come out wrong. But Jordan merely chuckled as she took a large swallow of beer.

The talk soon turned to what was happening with the volcanic activity down in Puna. 'We heard this morning at KTA that some people are evacuating from Leilani Estates,' Kristen said, turning to face Jordan. 'What about you and your grandparents? Is their house anywhere near where those cracks have opened up?'

Jordan shook her head. 'Huh-uh. That's all happening way down at the bottom of the subdivision, closer to Lanipuna – pretty far away from my *tūtūs.*'

'Well, that's good.' Valerie ripped one of the drumsticks from the rotisserie chicken. 'So how do you two know each other?' she asked Jordan and Shane, then bit into its crispy skin.

'We . . . uh, we've known each other a while.' Jordan glanced at Shane, who was occupied with peeling the label off his bottle of Sapporo. 'You know, long time Punatics,' she said, and let out a short laugh.

'Ah.' *Now, why would she be cagey about something like that?* Were the two of them perhaps romantically involved, and she didn't want Valerie to know? 'So, do you live down in Leilani Estates, too?' she asked Shane.

'Huh-uh. I'm out near Nanawale.'

Valerie had no idea where this was. 'So your place isn't in any danger then, either?'

'Probably not from what's going on right now. But hell, every place down in Puna's in danger from Madame Pele – if not now, then maybe next year or the year after.'

'Right,' Valerie said, thinking once again how nerve-racking it must be to live on an active volcano.

With a grunt, she got to her feet from the low beach chair to help herself to seconds of the gingery fish. By the time she'd plopped back down, the others were discussing a canoe race that Kevin would be competing in the coming weekend. She turned to face Jordan, who – apparently not interested in the paddling conversation – was watching a trio of kids across the island. They followed one another up and off a tall stone tower, jumping enthusiastically into the ocean before clambering ashore to have another turn. 'So I have a question for you,' she said.

'Uh-huh?' Jordan refocused her attention on Valerie.

'You know about those *booms* – the explosions down in Leilani the past few days – right? Well, the newspaper says they're from gas emissions from the volcano, so I'm wondering if maybe that explosion from a couple of weeks back was also from the volcano, rather than a problem at BigT. What'd you think? You know, since you're my local expert on geothermal stuff?'

Both Jordan and Shane immediately shook their heads. 'No way,' said Jordan. 'It couldn't be.'

'Why not? Couldn't it have been a precursor to what's going on now that caused an explosion over at BigT?'

'Nah.' Jordan continued to shake her head. 'That was from a malfunction at the plant, not a gas emission from the volcano. Probably a blowout from a broken pipe.'

'What makes you so sure? I mean, I don't understand why it couldn't be Mother Nature, or rather, Madame Pele, in this case . . .'

'Yeah, but that explosion was a long time before the ground cracks in Puna and the collapse at Puʻu ʻŌʻō,' Jordan countered. 'Plus, those injection wells, they're bad news.' She sipped from her beer as she watched a teenage girl do a forward flip off the stone tower. 'Nice,' she observed, then looked back at Valerie. 'Hey, so speaking of BigT, did you ever find anything out about that night watchman you told me about who was missing, or the body you saw in the lava?'

'You haven't read the newspaper, I guess.'

Jordan shook her head. 'My grandparents get it, but I don't read it myself . . .' She trailed off.

'Hey, no worries,' Valerie hastened to say. 'It's just that last weekend they reported in the paper that the body of Daniel Kehinu – the BigT night watchman who went missing – was discovered in a lava crack on the BigT property. They're saying he died of a heart attack.'

'Oh, wow. No, I hadn't heard. That's too bad.'

'But as far as that body I saw goes, no, I haven't discovered anything about who it might be.' Valerie glanced over at Kevin and Derek, but they were laughing at something Isaac had just said, and seemed to be paying no heed to her conversation with Jordan.

'Ah,' said Jordan. 'Well, at least the mystery of that Daniel guy is solved, so that's something.'

'Yeah.' Valerie set her plate aside to undo the top button of her shorts. Maybe that second helping of fish had been a bad idea. *Oof.* And there was still chocolate ganache cake to come. She stood up. 'Anyone feel like taking a stroll around the island to walk off some of this food before dessert?'

Kristen, who'd been conversing with Kevin and Isaac, jumped up. 'Good idea.'

No one else seemed inclined to join them, so they set off alone. 'What were you guys talking about?' Valerie asked as they headed along the rock wall past the pavilion. The extended family had now settled down around the picnic table with at least a dozen Chinese take-out containers, which they were eating from with chopsticks. 'Did I miss anything good?'

'Nah. Kevin was just telling a long and super-detailed story about some paddling competition he once raced in between Moloka'i and O'ahu. But it was mostly just him going on about his paddling team and then Isaac trying to show how much he knew about the subject, too.' She snorted. 'You know, guys . . .'

'Yup, I know.'

'So you having a good birthday?' asked Kristen.

Valerie took her wife's hand. 'I am. This is a really special place.'

'Yeah, I love Coconut Island.'

'Me too, but I was actually talking about Hilo in general. It's gonna be awful hard to go back to L.A.' Valerie stopped at the tower, where a new cluster of kids stood, deciding whether to prove their valor and plunge twenty feet or more into the ocean below. A boy about ten years old was egging on his older friend, who appeared dubious about the prospect now that they'd actually climbed up there. With a derisive shake of the head, the younger boy let out a Tarzan-worthy yell, took a flying leap, and executed a perfect cannonball with an enormous splash.

At a shout from behind them, Valerie and Kristen turned, expecting to see a proud parent or fellow swimmer cheering on the brave cannon-baller. Instead, they witnessed a group of people crowded around a man holding a cell phone. Valerie and Kristen headed over to see what the commotion was about, and were joined by the others from the birthday party.

'What's going on?' asked Isaac.

'A fissure has opened down in Leilani,' the man with the phone said, scrolling rapidly down his screen.

Other people were now on their phones, logging on to news sites and Twitter for updates. 'They're saying the mayor has ordered a mandatory evacuation of Leilani Estates!' one woman shouted over the din of everyone talking at once. 'And lava's breaching and fountaining from a vent on Mohala Street.'

'Oh, no.' Jordan put her hand to her mouth. 'My *tūtūs*. I gotta get down there and help get them and their stuff out!' She and Shane darted back to the picnic site and began gathering up the cooler and their other possessions.

Valerie and Kristen ran after them. 'You want help?' Kristen asked. 'If you need to move stuff fast, it'd be better to have more hands. The rental car's a hatchback, with a lot of space.'

Jordan looked at them a moment, then nodded. 'Yeah, actually. That would be great. The more, the better. Can you follow me down there?'

'Oh, but wait. What about all this?' Valerie waved a hand toward all the food and supplies they'd brought out to the island.

'No worries,' said Isaac, who'd come up behind them. 'We can take care of all of it. You go and help 'um out. We'll save at least a little of the cake for you when you get back home,' he added with a grin.

'Thanks, man.' Kristen punched knuckles with him, then grabbed her sweatshirt and bag.

Shane had already taken off running toward the footbridge. 'I'm gonna swing by my place to grab some empty boxes and then I'll meet you at your grandparents' house,' he yelled back over his shoulder, and Jordan threw him the shaka.

'Right, brah! Thanks!'

Valerie and Kristen trotted with Jordan back across the grass and bridge to the parking lot. Jordan pulled out first but waited for the other two. Once they'd come up behind her, she took off fast, taking a left out of the Lili'uokalani Gardens onto Banyan Drive, and then speeding down Highway 11 toward Puna.

'I hope we don't get a ticket,' Kristen said, glancing at the speedometer, which was hovering close to seventy mph.

'I bet the cops have better things to worry about right now than tourists driving over the speed limit,' responded Valerie. A black SUV with a blue light affixed to its top came racing past them on the left, closely followed by a marked police cruiser, confirming her observation.

The sun was shining right into their eyes, so low on the horizon that the car's shade was of no help. Driving with one hand shielding her face, Kristen did her best to keep up with the yellow Volvo, which was cutting back and forth between lanes to pass any car doing less than sixty. But then as soon as they made the turn on to Highway 130 toward Puna, the traffic came to a standstill. Gridlock.

Valerie could see Jordan, who was immediately in front of them, pounding the steering wheel in frustration. But there was no option other than limping along in the rush-hour traffic jam.

By the time they finally passed Pāhoa and reached the turnoff to Leilani Estates, it was starting to get dark. A line of cars waited to turn left. Valerie could see why: a roadblock had been erected, with a man in a neon-green safety vest questioning people before allowing them into the subdivision. Several did U-turns and returned the way they'd come – following the stream of cars heading out of the area and up the road towards Hilo – but most were allowed in to drive down Leilani Avenue.

When it was finally Jordan's turn, she spoke for a while with the guard, then pointed back at their car, after which he waved them both through.

Kristen followed her the few blocks to her grandparents' house, and they all climbed out. 'Why don't you wait here till I find out what's going on with them,' Jordan said, and darted across the front yard. The red and black cars were both in the garage, Valerie noticed, and another gray sedan was parked in the driveway.

A man too young to be her grandfather came to the door as Jordan ran up the front steps. He gave Jordan a hug, and the two retreated indoors. Valerie and Jordan waited by their car, listening to the wall of sound from coquís singing all around them. The sharp tang of sulfur hung in the air. After about five minutes, Jordan and the man re-emerged, embracing once more. Jordan then turned and walked across the lawn toward the two women.

'So, what's up?' Valerie asked.

'That's a friend of my *tūtū*s from HPP. They're gonna go with him tonight to his place, but don't want to move anything out right now. They say the fissure's too far away to worry about yet, and if they need to, they'll move stuff later.' Jordan shrugged. 'I tried to convince them to move at least some of their things – like important files and photos and stuff, but they said no. So, whatevahs. I can't make them do it.'

'What about your stuff?' said Kristen. 'We could help you move that.'

'Nah. Almost all my things are in storage in town. All's I got here is some clothes and other small kine stuff. I can move it all in my own car easy.'

The sound of tires on gravel made them turn. 'Oh, here's Shane,' said Jordan, and waved for him to pull into the driveway. Valerie scooted out of the way to allow the vehicle past, but then flinched as she looked up.

Shane was driving a dark-blue Toyota Tacoma truck.

TWENTY-SIX

Nudging Kristen's shoulder, Valerie inclined her head ever so slightly toward the truck. Kristen responded with raised eyebrows and a subtle nod of understanding.

'A friend's here to take them over to his house in HPP,' Jordan called out to Shane as he shut off the truck. 'An' they don't wanna move anything right now, so I guess you came all the way down here for nothing.'

'No biggie. Better safe than sorry.' Shane climbed out of the cab and coughed. 'Dang. Those fumes are intense, even all the way up here. Did you hear anything more about what's going on with the fissure?'

'My *tūtūs'* friend says it's still going, is all I know.' Jordan idly scratched her Hawai'i tattoo for a moment, then flashed a devilish grin. 'Hey, ya wanna drive down there an' see if we can get a look at it?'

'Uh, don't you think it might be dangerous?' asked Valerie. 'Though it would be fascinating . . .'

'Don't worry; we won't get too close. And we can all ride down in Shane's truck, so we won't be clogging the street with a bunch of cars. Whatd'ya say?'

Shane pumped his fist. 'Dude, I'm in!'

Jordan turned to the two other women. 'But you guys can go back up to Hilo, if you want. No worries.'

'What do you think?' Valerie asked Kristen.

'Sure, let's go check it out. It'll likely be our only chance to ever see fountaining lava, so why not?'

'Okay, then.' Shane yanked forward the driver's seat, revealing a tiny bench behind. 'You two can sit in the back. It's kinda cramped, but we won't be going far. Here, lemme get my board out of the way.'

After Shane had moved his surfboard from the back seat to the bed of the truck, they clambered inside and tried to get comfortable – a difficult task for the tall Kristen, whose knees were pressed firmly against the back of Jordan's seat.

It was now dark outside, but while the interior light was on, Valerie took the opportunity to scan the inside of the truck: nearly spotless. The only red dirt and gravel on the floor was that which they had just brought on board themselves. And the area between the two front seats – which in her car back home in California was grimy from years of dust and coffee spills – was clean and shiny.

Could the truck be brand new? But no, she observed: the upholstery on the back of the driver's seat was faded and cracked. It had to be at least several years old.

Jordan and Shane got into the front and slammed their doors, extinguishing the light.

No way did Shane seem the type to maintain his truck in such pristine condition, Valerie mused. It was as if it had just undergone a thorough detailing. *Could it be that he'd wanted to eradicate evidence of something?*

Shane drove back out to Leilani Avenue and turned left. Most cars were coming in the opposite direction, but a few were traveling toward the eastern end of the subdivision as they were. At one point, a man standing on the side of the road hollered at them to stop, that they weren't allowed to go any farther, but Shane ignored him and instead pressed harder on the accelerator.

Several blocks later, the road made a bend to the left . . . and there it was. As one, all four passengers sucked in their breath. Shane hit the brake, pulled over to the edge of the road in front of two other cars, and shut off the engine and lights. No one spoke.

In the distance roared a wall of fire. *Dancing fire*, was Valerie's thought, *just like that hula* hālau *had imagined it to be.* But it wasn't simply flames. It was *liquid* fire, jetting up and shooting fans of molten spray high into the sky, not unlike the plumes of water they'd seen exploding against the cliffs at MacKenzie State Park.

Jordan and Shane got out and flipped their seats forward so Valerie and Kristen could exit as well. Once outside the truck, the heat was intense, even from the distance – at least a hundred yards – that separated them from the fissure. And the roar of the fiery furnace erupting from the blacktop sounded like a thousand blow torches all firing at once.

A group of others stood much closer to the fountaining – dark shapes backlit by the glowing red rampart. Lava slashed across the road, incinerating the thick vegetation on either side. Smoke and steam wafted about, obscuring the view, then clearing as the fire-induced air currents did their own dance. The sulfuric fumes made Valerie's eyes water, and she had to take shallow breaths to keep from coughing.

Shane climbed onto the hood of the truck and leaned back against the windshield. 'Better than any drive-in movie I've ever seen,' he shouted over the noise, his wide eyes reflecting the red-orange glow. Kristen climbed up and sat next to him, while Jordan and Valerie stood staring at the breathtaking display.

But awesome as the sight was, Valerie couldn't help but brood about Shane's truck. *Could it have been Jordan and Shane she'd seen out on the lava field?* she asked herself, taking a couple of steps backward, as if from the heat, so she could covertly study Jordan's face.

Shane's truck could absolutely have been the one parked at the end of the road. If they'd transported a dead body in it, he'd certainly have wanted to clean off any traces of having done so. She glanced into the bed of the truck. It was clean, too, containing nothing but the surfboard and the empty boxes Shane had stopped to get en route.

But why would they want to kill Daniel? And what about Amy? Could she have been the person Valerie saw in the lava? And if so, how did she fit in to it all?

Nothing but more unanswered questions.

Another car pulled up behind the three vehicles, and a man with a large video camera jumped out to run past them toward the fissure. He spoke with the others already there, set the camera on his shoulder, and began filming. After a few minutes, the entire lot of them walked back up the road to the parked vehicles.

'Hey, you guys shouldn't be down here,' called out a man in a hard hat. 'Who knows where it'll blow next. You need to leave, pronto.' With that, the group – several of whom wore long-sleeved

T-shirts with 'USGS' printed on them – got in their cars, did U-turns, and drove off.

'It's okay,' said Shane once they'd gone. 'I think we're safe where we are this far away from it for the time being. Just a couple more minutes, and then we can leave. Sound good?' He glanced at Kristen, who nodded.

'Just a couple more minutes, though.'

Valerie continued her musing. *Okay, so what could Jordan and Shane have to do with whatever happened to Daniel and Amy?* Jordan used to work at BigT. And what had she said at Coconut Island when Valerie had asked her about the explosion? The injection wells at BigT were 'bad news,' were her words.

And then she remembered what the real estate agent, Sandy Spenser, had said about Leilani Estates: that BigT's having been constructed only a half-mile away had caused real estate prices to take a nose-dive in the subdivision. Jordan's grandparents would have been among those affected by the arrival of BigT. And the pipe-fitter certainly was familiar with the geothermal plant – and, based on what she'd said earlier, none too fond of the place.

Another thing niggled at Valerie's brain. Something else that had happened this evening . . . *What was it?*

Right. Why had Jordan said earlier that it was so great to get to go fishing after such a long time? Hadn't she talked about having just spent a couple of nights fishing when Valerie met her that first time at the Orchid Grill? That certainly wasn't a 'long time' before she and Valerie had gone fishing together less than a week later.

So why would she lie about that?

To create an alibi?

The skin along Valerie's neck and shoulders began to prickle, and it wasn't merely the sight of the molten lava wall before them.

That would explain Jordan's interest in Valerie and Kristen, if she'd overheard their conversation that day at the Orchid Grill. Which she must have done, given how she'd specifically come over to their table to talk right after their discussion about Daniel Kehinu and the explosion at BigT.

A touch to her shoulder made Valerie jump.

'Oh, sorry,' said Jordan. 'But I wasn't sure if you heard my question. I think not,' she added with a laugh.

'Yeah, I was just caught up in my thoughts, I guess.' Valerie forced a smile. 'It's all so . . . intense.' She waved a hand in the direction of the fissure. With daylight now fully extinguished, the embers swirling up from the burning vegetation on both sides of the road resembled swarms of demonic fireflies. 'I guess it's all just creeping me out, given what I saw out there in the lava that day . . .'

She turned to watch Jordan's reaction to this last statement. No change in the other's expression. 'What were you going to ask me?'

Jordan stared straight ahead. 'Nothing. It's not important.'

So the mention of the body in the lava *had* affected her. Valerie chewed her lip, wondering how she might get Jordan to trip up and perhaps show her hand. And then she had an idea.

'It's just that watching this,' she said, 'I can't help but remember that leg, burning up in the lava. And the boot . . . and those bright-pink shoelaces.'

Jordan frowned and looked as if she were about to speak, but then clamped shut her mouth, jaw tight. *Had she been about to correct me about the color of the laces, but then caught herself before doing so?*

Valerie stared straight ahead at the fiery fissure, but she could feel Jordan's eyes on her now: wary.

Doing her best to keep her face blank, Valerie tried to recall whether she'd told Jordan about the green laces that day fishing.

No, she decided, *she hadn't*. Other than those who'd been with her out at Kalapana that morning, she'd only provided that particular detail to people who'd actually known Daniel, so she could find out if it had been his boots – and therefore him – buried by the lava flow. Kevin and Faith, yes.

But definitely not Jordan.

Something in Valerie's expression must have changed with this realization, because Jordan's body suddenly tensed. As their eyes met, a spasm of fear crossed over Jordan's face.

Valerie was about to speak, but before she could think of what exactly to say, Jordan took off running down the street away from her – and toward the fissure.

What the hell?

She ran after her. 'What are you doing? Are you crazy?'

Jordan stopped, glancing to either side of the road as if perhaps she could make an escape – either cross-country to her left or down the driveway to her right.

Valerie stopped about ten paces from Jordan, then looked to see how Kristen and Shane had reacted to this sudden development. But although Kristen had now climbed down from the truck's hood, she made no move to follow after them. Perhaps she thought they were merely trying to get a better look at the wall of fire. And no doubt she and Shane couldn't hear what Valerie was shouting, not that far away and over the fissure's roar.

Turning back around, Valerie called out again, 'I know where you and your grandparents live, so why are you trying to run away?'

Jordan stood unmoving, as if undecided what to do, and Valerie approached closer.

'I didn't mean to hurt anybody,' Jordan said after a moment, her body slumping. 'I was trying to help people. I thought if they believed the explosion was an accident, then they'd have to close down the plant.'

'I believe you. Now c'mon back to the truck so we can get out of here. We're way too close to that fissure.' As she said this, a tree about twenty feet behind Jordan ignited, sending an shower of sparks into the air.

But Jordan still didn't move. 'We didn't know they were there until it was too late. And then she got hit by the flying debris, and I guess he must've had a heart attack when he saw she'd been killed. So then we just kinda freaked out, and—'

At the sound of a low rumble, the two women jumped backwards, farther away from each other. Almost immediately, a powerful blast shook the ground. Before Valerie's eyes, the asphalt splintered between them and an enormous crack yawned open across the road, stretching down the middle of the driveway Jordan had been eyeing earlier.

Before Valerie could even wrap her mind around the idea of the earth suddenly ripping open, a cloud of steam erupted from the crack. Her face and arms stinging, she skittered farther back, trying to spot Jordan through the haze. The piercing shriek of several smoke alarms made her jump once more, and when she turned at the sound, she saw that steam was billowing from the windows of the house at the end of the driveway.

The new fissure was running straight under the building.

Whoa.

At the sound of her name, Valerie spun about to see Kristen and Shane come running her way. Kristen grabbed her wife by the shoulders. 'Are you okay?'

'Yeah, but Jordan isn't. She's trapped over there.' Valerie pointed across the curtain of sulfuric steam.

'Ohmygod.' Shane stared at the gaping crack, his body frozen. 'Wha–what are we gonna *do*?'

'I know,' Valerie shouted. 'The surfboard!'

It took a moment for Shane to comprehend, but then he hurried back to his truck, returning a minute later with both the surfboard and another bulky item under his arm.

'Ah, good idea,' Valerie said as he set down the board and folded what she now saw was a blanket into a tight bundle.

'Jordan!' Shane shouted, hurling the blanket through the steam. 'Wrap this around yourself and as soon as we get the surfboard set, walk across it – quickly but carefully! And watch out for the fin!'

Shane pulled his T-shirt up over his face, then knelt and shoved the board across the fracture.

The three of them waited for what seemed like ages. Had Jordan taken off running again, or was she merely steeling herself in preparation for crossing through what was essentially a wall of boiling water?

Finally, as if emerging from the gates of hell, a shrouded figure stepped from the makeshift wobbly bridge onto the pavement, collapsing in Shane's arms.

While he and Valerie helped Jordan back to the truck and into the front seat, Kristen retrieved the surfboard and ran after them. She set the board down among the boxes, then hopped into the bed of the truck, joining Valerie, who was leaning back against the cab. 'No reason to waste a perfectly good surfboard,' she said, and Valerie just shook her head.

Shane climbed into the truck, and once he'd executed a three-point turn, Valerie looked back at the fissure and caught sight of red ooze emerging from the crevice where they'd been standing only moments before. Within seconds, the viscous lava had spilled all the way across the road and down the driveway.

As Shane jammed the truck into gear and sped down the road, a blinding flash lit up the night sky, followed almost immediately by the *boom* of a thunderous explosion.

'What the . . .?' Valerie clapped her hands over her ears.

'Propane tank,' said Kristen. 'I saw it there next to that driveway. Good thing we got out when we did.'

TWENTY-SEVEN

As they headed back up the road to Jordan's grandparents' house, Valerie filled Kristen in on what had happened. 'Jordan pretty much admitted that she caused that explosion at BigT – to turn people against geothermal plants on the Big Island. And she had help, who I'm thinking must have been Shane. She also said that there was a woman with Daniel that night at BigT – who had to have been Amy – and that she was killed by the explosion. And it sounds like when Daniel realized she was dead, he had a heart attack. So, in a way, they killed him, too.'

The truck turned off of Leilani Avenue onto Jordan's street. 'So Jordan saw all that happen?' Kristen asked.

'I guess she and Shane must have been hiding in the bushes or something to watch the explosion they'd set up, and by the time they saw Daniel and Amy, it was too late to stop it from happening. I imagine they shoved Daniel into that lava crack after he died. Or maybe he fell in – who knows? And then they took Amy's body down to the lava in Shane's truck to get rid of it.'

Shane pulled into the driveway and climbed out of the cab. 'Jordan's got some bad burns on her legs and feet,' he said, 'and she's really out of it. I couldn't get her to talk to me at all about what happened. I'm thinking she should really get to the hospital.'

Valerie and Kristen jumped down from the truck's bed and leaned in the passenger side window to take a look. Jordan's legs and her feet – which had been clad only in shorts and slippahs – were red and swollen. Valerie could see the skin already starting to peel off in places. Jordan's eyes were closed, and she was moaning softly.

Shane's expression betrayed nothing other than worry for his friend. *So Jordan must not have said anything to him about what had happened.* She certainly didn't look like she was in any shape to do much talking.

'We can take her,' said Valerie.

He shook his head. 'No, I should do it. You barely even know her, so why should you have to go to the trouble?'

'True, but the hospital is really close to where we're staying in Hilo, so it would be far easier for us than you, since we're driving up there anyway. And I'm sure she'll have to stay over-night, given how bad these burns look. Besides, you should really go tell her grandparents what happened. So . . .'

He met Valerie's gaze, then nodded. 'Okay. I guess that makes sense. Thanks so much. But make sure you give me a call once you're there to let me know what's going on?'

Bingo.

'Absolutely.' Valerie pulled out her phone. 'What's your number? And you might as well give me your last name, too, so I can add you to my contacts.'

Two hours later, Valerie finally got to hear 'Happy Birthday' sung to her by Kristen, Isaac, and Sachiko, and then blow out the six pink candles on her chocolate ganache cake. Once everyone had been served thick slices of the decadent dessert – accompanied by snifters of a rare Cognac that Isaac had unearthed from the back of his liquor cabinet – the foursome made their way out to the lānai.

The rain had returned, and along with it the serenade of the coquí frogs piping up from their perches among the ti and pink ginger. Valerie swallowed a mouthful of the rich cake, chasing it with some of the aged brandy.

'Okay,' she said, 'I now pronounce myself ready to finish the story.'

Isaac leaned forward, his eyes eager. 'So did Shane give you his last name?'

'He did. It's Foley. And he even spelled it for me, to make sure I got it right. Not the sharpest tool in the box, that one.' With a chuckle, Valerie took another sip of Cognac. 'And I learned Jordan's full name when she was admitted to the hospital – Jordan Armstrong, if you can believe it. Great name for a pipe-fitter, right?'

'So the cops will be able to track them down, if . . .' Sachiko trailed off.

'If they decide there's enough evidence that they want to pursue the case,' Valerie finished for her. 'I called the police while we were waiting at the hospital, and they told me to come down to the station tomorrow morning to make a report.'

'But I'm betting the cops will follow up on it,' Kristen chimed in. 'Jordan rallied on the drive back up to Hilo – or maybe she simply hadn't wanted to admit to Shane what had happened. Who knows? But in any case, she spilled the whole story again, so now both of us heard it directly from her.'

'And now, thank goodness, you finally believe me about the body in the lava,' Valerie said, patting her on the knee.

Kristen responded with a sheepish nod.

'Anyway,' Valerie went on, 'Jordan told us how she and Shane freaked out after seeing what happened and took Amy's body down to the lava flow. I guess they didn't want there to be any evidence that the explosion they caused had killed anyone, but figured that since Daniel hadn't been hit by the debris, they couldn't be blamed for his death. Not sure the logic is sound, but whatever . . .'

'Not to mention the fact that they were risking other people seeing them do the deed, by taking the body out to a place known to be frequented by lava junkies,' said Isaac.

Kristen bobbed her head in agreement. 'Yeah, well, I don't think they were thinking all that straight right about then. But I think Jordan was actually glad to get it all off her chest, to tell you the truth. You could tell she feels really awful about what happened. They clearly had no intention of hurting anyone, which is probably one of the reasons they did it in the middle of the night.'

'Too bad they didn't think about the night watchman,' Valerie said with a shake of the head. 'And what horrible timing that Daniel picked that particular night to bring his girlfriend along. I guess I should email that professor to tell her what happened to Amy.' She poked at her cake with her fork, then set her plate down and turned to stare out at the curtain of rain streaming off the metal roof on to Isaac's lawn.

There was a lull in the conversation as they thought about the poor marine biologist, whose body they now knew had ended up entombed in black rock.

After a bit, Isaac cleared his throat. 'So maybe having that scare down at the fissure tonight,' he said, 'not to mention the pain she must have been in from those horrible burns, was a wake-up call for Jordan.'

'Possibly,' said Valerie. 'Or maybe once she realized I'd figured it all out, she simply decided there was no point in trying to cover it up anymore. As they were getting ready to finally wheel her off from the ER lobby to a room, Jordan told me she was going to go to the police once she was discharged and come clean about the whole thing. The nurse who was there heard her say it and asked what she meant, but by then whatever drug they'd given her earlier had kicked in and she was pretty out of it. But I did see the nurse's name tag, so if need be, she could be a witness, too.'

'How bad are Jordan's burns?' Sachiko asked.

Valerie grimaced. 'Pretty bad. Not life-threatening, it doesn't seem, but they looked even worse by the time we got to the hospital. They told us she'd definitely need to stay the night, probably longer, so I called Shane, and he's going to let her grandparents know.'

'That's good,' said Sachiko. 'I wonder if he has any idea that Jordan spilled everything.'

Valerie shook her head. 'I seriously doubt it, since he told us he couldn't even get her to talk on the drive back to Jordan's grandparents' house. And besides, if he had known, he would never have allowed us to drive Jordan to the hospital – or given us his last name and phone number.'

'Well, I gotta say, I, for one, am impressed.' Isaac reached for the Cognac bottle and poured himself another two fingers. 'You come to da island for your first time evah, and what do ya do? You solve the mystery of the body in the lava. Not bad for a *malihini*. You know, a newbie.'

Sachiko motioned for him to pass over the bottle. 'So has all this soured your opinion of our lovely Orchid Isle?' she asked, helping herself to seconds of the amber liquid. 'I mean, for goodness' sake, not only did you end up involved in a murder investigation, but to cap it off, it looks like we could now be experiencing the most destructive volcanic eruption since 1990, when the lava took Kalapana. Maybe you're not in much of a hurry to return.'

'We might not have much of a choice about it,' said Kristen. 'If there is a trial for Jordan and Shane, we'll likely have to come back as witnesses. But that wouldn't be such a bad thing, would it, hon?'

'No, not bad at all. Not that the trial stuff would be much fun, but I have to say I've grown quite fond of the Big Island – especially little Hilo Town. And I'm pretty sure Kristen agrees.'

'Indeed I do.'

Valerie sipped the last little bit of her nightcap and leaned back on the aloha-print sofa with a contented smile. 'I'm fairly confident we'll be back soon. And who can say? Maybe not just for a vacation, either.'

'Solid!' Isaac refilled her snifter, then held up his own in a toast. '*Kāmau* – cheers!' After draining his glass, a sly smile crept over his face. 'And hey, no pressure,' he said, his gold tooth catching the light, 'but dis guy I know, he happens to have one killah house for sale just a couple blocks away from here . . .'

RECIPES

VAL'S MAI TAI
(makes one cocktail)

Many Mai Tais one gets in bars these days are sickeningly sweet, as they're made with cheap dark rum and canned orange and pineapple juice, heavy on the high-fructose corn syrup. But the original recipes for the cocktail back in the 1940s were far less cloying, using quality high-proof rums from Jamaica and Martinique, fresh-squeezed lime juice and nary a can of pineapple juice in sight. (The name supposedly derives from the Tahitian phrase, *maita'i roa a'e*, which loosely translates as 'terrific!' or 'best of all!'.)

Valerie's version is inspired by the original Trader Vic's recipe for a Mai Tai, but employs amaretto liqueur instead of orgeat syrup, and includes a splash of soda water because, you know . . . *fizz*!

Ingredients

6–8 ice cubes
2 oz Myer's or similar dark rum
½ oz (1 tablespoon) orange Curaçao or triple sec
2 teaspoons amaretto liqueur
½ oz (1 tablespoon) fresh lime juice
2 teaspoons simple syrup (2:1 sugar dissolved in water)
1 oz soda water
1 lime slice, for garnish

Directions

Place the ice in a metal cocktail shaker, add the rum, Curaçao, amaretto, lime juice, and simple syrup, and shake vigorously until well chilled, then pour everything (including the ice) into an old-fashioned glass. Top with a splash of soda water and garnish with the lime slice.

POKE THREE WAYS
(serves 3 as a main dish, or 6 as an appetizer)

Poke (pronounced 'poh-kay') is thought to have been made by ancient Polynesians centuries before Western contact, who prepared it with local reef fish, seaweed, crushed *kukui* nut (candlenut), and sea salt. It wasn't until the 1960s, however, that the name 'poke' (Hawaiian for 'sliced crosswise into pieces') was given to the dish, and not until the 1990s that it became well known outside of Hawai'i. Poke's rise in popularity is due largely to the efforts of Hawaiian chef and television personality Sam Choy, who tirelessly promoted the local delicacy and even started a poke contest, an event still held each March in Kona, on the Big Island.

Modern poke recipes commonly include *shoyu* (soy sauce) and roasted sesame oil, ingredients brought to the islands by Japanese and Chinese immigrants, as well as new innovations such as avocado, kimchee, and sriracha mayonnaise.

Ogo, a seaweed commonly used in Japanese cooking, can be found at most Asian markets. If using the dried variety, be sure to reconstitute it in water before preparing your poke. Feel free to substitute *wakame*, chopped *kombu,* or some other variety of seaweed, if you wish. Furikake, a Japanese seasoning made with nori seaweed, sesame seeds, sugar, salt, and other ingredients, is available at many chain supermarkets on the Mainland.

If your tuna has a dark bloodline running through it, be sure to cut this away and discard, as it has an unpleasant flavor. You'll need about 1¾ pounds of ahi that contains a bloodline in order to end up with 1½ pounds of usable fish.

To make the three pokes below, simply mix all the listed ingredients together in three separate bowls and refrigerate, covered, for at least half an hour (or up to six hours) before it's time to eat. Serve it with crackers or chips as an appetizer, or over steamed rice for a traditional 'poke bowl.'

Traditional Hawaiian-Style Poke

Ingredients

½ pound sushi-grade ahi tuna, cut into ½-inch cubes
1 tablespoon chopped *ogo* seaweed
1 teaspoon furikake
¼ teaspoon sea salt

Sesame-*Shoyu* Poke

Ingredients

½ pound sushi-grade ahi tuna, cut into ½-inch cubes
1 teaspoon roasted sesame oil
2 teaspoons soy sauce
1 tablespoon oyster sauce
2 tablespoons green onions, coarsely chopped
2 tablespoons yellow or white onion, coarsely chopped
1 teaspoon sesame seeds

Spicy Mayo Poke

Ingredients

½ pound sushi-grade ahi tuna, cut into ½-inch cubes
1½ tablespoons mayonnaise
1 teaspoon sriracha hot sauce (less, if you're
   sensitive to spicy food)
1 teaspoon roasted sesame oil
1 tablespoon soy sauce
2 tablespoons green onions, coarsely chopped
2 tablespoons yellow or white onion, coarsely chopped
1 teaspoon sesame seeds

GRAPEFRUIT AND AVOCADO SALAD WITH PAPAYA-YOGURT DRESSING
(serves 4)

This is a flavorful and eye-pleasing salad, all of which can be prepared in advance save for the avocado slices (which turn brown quickly once cut). The tartness of the grapefruit provides a lovely contrast to the richness of the avocado, and the combination of the refreshing papaya and yogurt with the bite of the vinegar and peppery papaya seeds makes for a zesty dressing.

I like to prepare this recipe as individual, composed salads, to highlight the different colors and textures of the dish, but the downside to this is that the dressing isn't mixed in with the lettuce. So if you prefer, feel free to toss everything together in one bowl and then plate it up.

Ingredients for the Dressing
(makes about ¾ cup – more than you'll need for four people)

½ cup fresh papaya, peeled and cut into rough chunks
1 tablespoon papaya seeds
¼ cup plain full-fat yogurt
2 tablespoons apple cider vinegar
1 tablespoon lime juice
1 teaspoon honey
¼ teaspoon cumin powder
⅛ teaspoon salt
2 tablespoons olive oil
1 tablespoon water
1 tablespoon juice from the cut up grapefruit

Ingredients for the Salad

1 large pink grapefruit
1 large avocado
4 cups butter lettuce or other green leaf lettuce,
    washed and torn into bite-size pieces

Directions

Place all the dressing ingredients into a blender except for the olive oil, water, and grapefruit juice. Blend at a high speed, pushing the contents down the sides of the blender as needed, until the dressing is well blended and the papaya seeds are the size of small specks.

Add the oil to the blender and pulse a couple of times, till well blended. Then add the water, and pulse again. If it's still too thick, feel free to add more water, a teaspoon at a time. Scrape the dressing into a small pitcher and refrigerate until time for service.

Using a very sharp knife, slice the top and bottom (the 'poles') off the grapefruit, then, cutting from the north to the south pole, slice off the skin and the white pith of the fruit. Place the peeled grapefruit on a large plate (to catch the juices that run off). Turn it on its side and cut into thin slices, latitudinally, then cut these slices into bite-size pieces, removing any remaining pith or tough pieces of membrane if you desire. Place the grapefruit pieces and any accumulated juice into a bowl, and refrigerate till service. (All steps up until now may be done several hours in advance.)

Divide the lettuce among four large plates. Cut the avocado in half from top to bottom, then cut the halves in half, so you have four quarter-avocado pieces. Discard the pit, then peel the skin off the avocado pieces. Set two of the quarters together face down so they make a half, which makes it easy to slice. Then cut them into thin slices, and arrange one quarter of the avocado on each plate on top of the lettuce. Repeat with the other half of the avocado.

Scatter the grapefruit pieces on top of the lettuce and avocado, retaining the accumulated juice in the bowl.

Stir 1 tablespoon of the grapefruit juice into the dressing (more, if it needs additional thinning), then drizzle the dressing on top of the salad. (Note: You will likely have far more dressing than you need; don't overdress the salads!)

MISO-SESAME CHICKEN
(serves 4–8)

To my mind, thighs are the most flavorful part of the chicken, and with their higher fat content they remain moist even when overcooked (unlike the boneless breasts Valerie uses for this recipe, which are unforgiving and often disappointingly dry). But feel free to use any part of the bird, or buy a whole chicken and part it out yourself, then let your guests choose which piece they want. This recipe works equally well either baked in the oven or grilled on an outdoor barbecue.

Any sort of miso (white, yellow, or red) can be used for this dish, though orange (*awase* – a blend of white and red) is what I prefer. Miso is quite salty, so do *not* salt the chicken or add any soy sauce or additional salt to the marinade.

Steamed rice makes the perfect partner to this dish, as a toothsome but mild accompaniment for the flavorful chicken. Use an ice cream scoop dipped in water to make pretty rice balls on the plate next to the chicken, then scatter chopped chives and/or black sesame seeds over it all.

Ingredients

1 2-inch piece of fresh ginger, peeled and finely chopped
  or minced (about 3 tablespoons)
½ cup miso
½ cup sake
1 tablespoon roasted sesame oil
2 tablespoons brown sugar
¼ teaspoon black pepper
8 large chicken thighs
chopped chives and/or black sesame seeds, for garnish (optional)

Directions

Mix all ingredients except chicken together in a bowl until smooth.

Pat dry the chicken, then place either in a large bowl or in a resealable plastic bag. Pour the marinade over the chicken and mix, making sure each piece is covered with marinade. Let the chicken marinate in the refrigerator (covered, if in a bowl) for at least four hours, or overnight. Remove from the fridge and bring up to room temperature prior to cooking.

If baking the chicken, preheat oven to 375°F. Cover the bottom of a large roasting pan with foil (for easy clean-up – the marinade tends to burn on the bottom of the pan), shake off any excess marinade, then place the chicken pieces in the pan, skin up. (Save the excess marinade for a later step.) Roast until brown and crispy on top, and the internal temperature reaches 165°F – about 45 minutes to an hour, depending on the size of the chicken pieces. (You may want to turn the temperature up to 425°F for the last ten minutes, to ensure a crispy skin.)

If grilling, place the chicken pieces skin-side down over medium-high heat. If the grill is too hot, they will burn, so keep an eye on them. When browned, flip them over and continue cooking until the internal temperature reaches 165°F.

Once the chicken has finished roasting or grilling, remove it to a plate and cover to keep warm. Pour the excess marinade (and any liquid in the roasting pan, if that's how you prepared the chicken) into a saucepan and bring it up to a low boil over medium heat. Let the sauce cook for 2–3 minutes, then pour it into a gravy boat to be served along with the chicken and rice.

KĀLUA PORK (*KĀLUA PUA'A*)
(serves 12)

The verb *kālua* means to cook in an underground oven, and because this dish was traditionally prepared by slow-cooking the entire animal in a pit dug into the earth (an *imu*), it was historically called *kālua pua'a*, or 'Kālua Pig.' These days, however, unless they're cooking for a large *lū'au*, most folks simply slow-roast a pork shoulder in a kitchen oven and, as a result, the dish is often referred to as *kālua* pork.

Besides the smoky flavor (which this recipe replicates with a few dashes of Liquid Smoke), what gives *kālua* pork its distinctive flavor are the ti (*Cordyline terminalis*) leaves it is wrapped in while slow-cooking. Although the plant is found in abundance in Hawai'i, fresh ti leaves are not readily available on the Mainland (though they can be found online). So you might want to stow a few dozen in your luggage next time you visit the islands. (Note: this does not run afoul of the agricultural inspection regulations.) Simply remove the spines, fold them up, and freeze them in a plastic bag once you're home, then thaw before use.

If you don't have ti leaves, you can substitute banana leaves or, at a pinch, dried corn husks used for making tamales (available in Mexican markets), soaking them in water for 10 minutes before use.

This recipe employs garlic and ginger, which were not traditionally used in the dish, but they add a lovely flavor. Serve with steamed rice and papaya chutney (recipe follows this one).

Ingredients

1 pork butt, aka upper shoulder (about 8 pounds)
6 garlic cloves, cut into thin slices
1 3-inch piece of ginger, peeled and cut into thin slices
3 tablespoons Liquid Smoke
2 teaspoons salt
6 large green ti leaves

Directions

Preheat oven to 300°F.

Using a paring knife, poke 30–40 holes all over the pork roast, then insert the garlic and ginger into the holes.

Rub the Liquid Smoke over the whole roast, then sprinkle it with the salt.

Wash the ti leaves with cold water, then cut them with scissors along the stiff spines and remove the spines so that you have two long pieces from each leaf (twelve pieces total).

Lay five of the ti strips vertically across the bottom of a large roasting pan, overlapping the pieces a little. Then lay six of the pieces across horizontally on top of the others (three on the right, three on the left, meeting in the middle of the pan), also overlapping them.

Set the roast on top the leaves, fat side up. Then fold the vertical leaves over the roast, and then the horizontal leaves over them, holding them down with one hand. Secure the leaves with the last strip, by placing it on top vertically, and tucking the ends under the roast (the weight of the meat will hold it in place).

Cover the roasting pan tightly with aluminum foil (you may need to fold two pieces of foil together to make one large piece).

Roast the pork for four hours. When you remove the foil, you will see that the ti leaves have changed color, and the ti-wrapped package is now sitting in a pool of liquid (which is largely fat).

Remove the roast to another pan to cool. While it's cooling, pour all the liquid from the pan into a large Pyrex pitcher. After the fat rises to the top of the pitcher, pour it off, reserving the liquid below. (Save the fat for another use – it's great for frying vegetables or potatoes!)

When the roast is cool enough to handle, discard the ti leaves, then shred the pork with your fingers (as you would for pulled pork), discarding any large pieces of fat. Once shredded, return the pork to the roasting pan and pour the retained liquid over it all. Let it sit for at least 15 minutes, to allow the meat to reabsorb the liquid.

The pork can be made a day or two ahead of time and refrigerated, then reheated before service.

PAPAYA CHUTNEY
(makes 4-5 cups)

This simple-to-prepare chutney makes for a tasty, tart counterpart
to the richness of *kālua* pork, and is also a terrific accompaniment to an Indian curry or tikka masala. But you could also pour
it over a block of cream cheese or pâté for an easy and delicious
appetizer dip, or serve it with grilled sausages, or spread some
on your next ham or grilled cheese sandwich. The possibilities
are endless!

The recipe here employs the sweet, Hawaiian variety of papaya
which, when in season, can be purchased on the islands for as
little as six for two dollars. But feel free to substitute one of the
large Mexican variety, which are more readily available (and far
less expensive) on the Mainland – or even mangos, if fresh papayas
are not available. Choose papayas that are ripe, but still firm.

Ingredients

3 Hawaiian papayas (or 1 of the larger Mexican variety),
    about 3 pounds total
1 2-inch piece of ginger, peeled and finely chopped
    (about 3 tablespoons)
½ cup white vinegar
1 cup sugar
1 teaspoon chili powder
1 teaspoon salt
¼ cup raisins (optional)

Directions

Peel the papayas, then slice them in half and spoon out and
discard the seeds. Cut the flesh into one-inch chunks and place
in a medium sauce pan.

Add all the other ingredients to the pan and simmer, uncovered,
over medium heat, stirring occasionally, to make sure it doesn't
burn. Cook for 20–30 minutes, until it begins to thicken. (It will
thicken further once chilled.)

Let cool, then decant into glass jars. The chutney will keep,
stored in the refrigerator, for several months.

GLOSSARY OF HAWAIIAN AND PIDGIN WORDS AND PHRASES

(Hawaiian words are in italics)

aftah	afterwards
'āina	land
'aumakua	guardian spirit or family god, often manifesting as an animal
'as	that's
aunty	endearing term for an older woman
brah, bruddah	pal, friend, brother
broke da mout'	used to describe delicious food
buggah	guy, dude, annoying creature
chee	geez, wow
choke	a lot
cock-a-roach	steal
cuz	endearing term for buddy, friend
da	the
da kine	the thing, person, place, event – something you can't think of the word for
dass	that's
dere	there
dis	this
e hele kākou	let's get going

get	have
grindz	food
hālau	school, group
haole	foreigner, usually of European descent
heiau	ancient Hawaiian temple, usually made of rock
hele on	let's get moving, get out of here
hōkū	star
holoholo	go for a ride
howzit?	how's it going?
hulihuli	grilled on a spit (from *huli* – to turn, rotate)
humuhumunukunukuāpuaʻa	trigger fish, state fish of Hawaiʻi
ipu	gourd, drum made from a gourd
ʻiwa	great frigatebird
jam	get going
kahiko	ancient
kāhili	ceremonial pole decorated with feathers
kahuna	wise man, expert
kāmau	a toast meaning 'to your health'
kapu	tabu
kau kau	food
keiki	child, children
killah, killahz	killer, great
kumu hula	hula teacher

lānai	porch, veranda
latahz	see you later
lau lau	steamed pork and fish wrapped in ti leaves (from *lau* – leaf)
li' dat	like that
loco moco	white rice topped with hamburger patty, gravy, and fried egg
lolo	crazy, nuts
lomi lomi salmon	raw, marinated salmon dish (from *lomi lomi* – a kind of Hawaiian massage)
lū'au	party or feast typically including entertainment
mahalo	thank you
maika'i	good, fine
malihini	newcomer
mo' bettah	better
musubi	rice ball with vegetables or meat (often Spam), wrapped in nori seaweed
mu'umu'u	loose Hawaiian dress
no worry, beef curry	don't sweat it
oddah	other
'ōhi'a	flowering tree in the myrtle family, important in Hawaiian culture
'ono	delicious
pakalolo	marijuana, pot, grass
pali	cliff
pau	finished, done

pau hana	end of work, happy hour
pog	passion-orange-guava juice
poi	Polynesian staple food made from pounding and fermenting taro root
poke	diced, raw fish, often made with ahi tuna
pono	righteousness, balanced
pupule	crazy, demented
pu'u	cinder cone, hill
shaka	friendly hand gesture meaning 'hang loose,' 'thank you,' 'cheers'
shoyu	soy sauce
sistah	sister, female friend, pal
slippahs	flip-flops, rubber slippers
small kid time	during childhood
snap	get angry
solid	awesome, great
stay	is
stuffs	things
talk story	chat
tink	think
tūtū	grandparent
uku	a lot
ulua	Giant Trevally, kind of jack fish
'um	him, it
wen'	used to form past tense of verbs (e.g., he wen' eat – he ate)

AUTHOR'S NOTE AND ACKNOWLEDGMENTS

Note that for purposes of my story, I have taken the artistic liberty of compressing the timeline of volcanic activity that occurred on the Big Island in 2018. In actuality, the lava flow from Puʻu Oʻo down to the coastal plain at Kalapana (which Valerie, Kristen, and Isaac visit in Chapters One and Two) shut down many weeks prior to the April 30th collapse of the Puʻu Oʻo crater floor and subsequent eruption on May 3rd at the lower East Rift Zone in Leilani Estates – not the week before, as depicted in this story.

As always, numerous people generously provided me assistance in writing this book. I must first credit my intrepid beta readers: Robin McDuff, Smiley Karst, Nancy Lundblad, and Debra Goldstein (who critiqued a *very* early version of the book), as well as Māhealani Jones, who was kind enough to do a sensitivity read of the manuscript. I'm also indebted to Kris Neri, whose Sisters in Crime/Guppies class on plotting helped greatly in fleshing out the original storyline.

In addition, Lorraine Kinnamon gave me advice regarding hula; Richard and Carol Huelskamp, regarding avocados and avocado farms on the Big Island; and Bill Gilmartin, regarding sea turtles. Thanks also go out to Steve Lundblad, for allowing me to tag along with his UHH geology students as they did mapping at the PGV geothermal energy power plant; to Michael Shintaku, who advised and corrected me on my Pidgin usage; and to Judi Heher, who created the beautiful map of Hawaiʻi Island (though any remaining errors regarding any of these are entirely mine).

Finally, thanks to my fabulous agent, Erin Niumata of Folio Literary, and to everyone at Severn House Publishers, including editors Rachel Slatter and Tina Pietron, publicist Martin Brown, and cover designer Piers Tilbury.

About the author

The daughter of a law professor and a potter, **Leslie Karst** is the author of the Lefty Award-nominated Sally Solari culinary mysteries, as well as the memoir, *Justice is Served: A Tale of Scallops, the Law, and Cooking for RBG*.

Leslie waited tables and sang in a new wave rock band before deciding she was ready for a "real" job and ending up at Stanford Law School. It was during her career as a research and appellate attorney in Santa Cruz, California, that she rediscovered her youthful passion for food and cooking, at which point she once again returned to school – this time to earn a degree in culinary arts.

Now retired from the law, in addition to writing, Leslie spends her days cooking (and eating!), gardening, cycling, and observing cocktail hour promptly at five o'clock. She and her wife and their Jack Russell mix split their time between Hilo, Hawai'i and Santa Cruz, California.

www.lesliekarstauthor.com